Element of Chance

na Page first began writing as a hobby, and after
umber of her poems had been accepted by the
C and her short stories began appearing in weekly
gazines, she took to writing radio plays and crime
els. She was first published in the Crime Club,
ch later became Collins Crime.

n English graduate from Oxford, Emma Page
ht in every kind of educational establishment
n in the UK and abroad before she started writ-
full-time.

WITHDRAWN FOR

SALE

By Emma Page

Kelsey and Lambert series

Say it with Murder
Intent to Kill
Hard Evidence
Murder Comes Calling
In the Event of My Death
Mortal Remains
Deadlock
A Violent End
Final Moments
Scent of Death
Cold Light of Day
Last Walk Home
Every Second Thursday
Missing Woman

Standalone novels

A Fortnight by the Sea (also known as
Add a Pinch of Cyanide)
Element of Chance
In Loving Memory
Family and Friends

Element of Chance

Emma Page

HARPER

This novel is entirely a work of fiction.
The names, characters and incidents portrayed in it are
the work of the author's imagination. Any resemblance to
actual persons, living or dead, events or localities is
entirely coincidental.

Harper
An imprint of HarperCollins*Publishers*
1 London Bridge Street
London SE1 9GF

www.harpercollins.co.uk

This paperback edition 2016
1

First published in Great Britain in 1975 by Collins Crime

Copyright © Emma Page 1975

Emma Page asserts the moral right to
be identified as the author of this work

A catalogue record for this book is
available from the British Library

ISBN: 978-0-00-817594-8

Printed and bound in Great Britain

All rights reserved. No part of this publication may be
reproduced, stored in a retrieval system, or transmitted,
in any form or by any means, electronic, mechanical,
photocopying, recording or otherwise, without the prior
permission of the publishers.

MIX
Paper from
responsible sources
FSC C007454

FSC™ is a non-profit international organisation established to promote
the responsible management of the world's forests. Products carrying the
FSC label are independently certified to assure consumers that they come
from forests that are managed to meet the social, economic and
ecological needs of present and future generations,
and other controlled sources.

Find out more about HarperCollins and the environment at
www.harpercollins.co.uk/green

FOR GINGE
POET EXTRAORDINARY

FIFE COUNCIL LIBRARIES	
HJ457493	
Askews & Holts	12-May-2016
AF	£12.99
CRI	LV

CHAPTER I

SEVEN-FIFTEEN on a calm, palely golden Friday morning in October. Andrew Rolt – Area Manager of CeeJay Plant Hire Limited – came slowly down the stairs of his large Victorian house on the outskirts of Barbourne. He was already dressed for work in a dark business suit; the skilful cut of the jacket concealed his thickening waistline, the beginnings of a paunch. Although he was not much over forty his brown hair was liberally streaked with grey. He was still passably good-looking in a boyish way; his features retained something of a vulnerable air.

He reached the front hall and went slowly towards the rear of the house. He had slept badly again, felt little appetite at the thought of toast or coffee. He halted in the doorway of the big silent kitchen and turned his head in the direction of the dining-room with its store of bottles discreetly housed in the sideboard. He felt jittery, apprehensive. Surely the letter must come by this morning's post. It had reached his ears in the gossipy interchanges of the trade that the interviews for the Kain Engineering job were scheduled for next Monday afternoon. If his name was on the short list they must surely let him know by today.

He had expected to hear yesterday morning, had come downstairs confident that he'd find the letter in the wire cage on the inside of the front door. He'd sent off two previous applications for jobs in September, both unsuccessful; when the second application had come to nothing he realized what was holding him back. This time he had corrected the error. He hadn't put 'Living apart' in the box opposite 'Marital status'; this time he had simply written: Married.

5

But yesterday there had been no word from Kain Engineering. There is still Friday, he had told himself, rallying almost at once from the old feeling of hopelessness that rose in him at the sight of the empty letter cage; there is no need yet for despair. It was despair that threatened him nowadays, a sense of failure and isolation that confronted him in unexpected moments, leaping out from behind a word, a look. He had to break out now from the barriers closing round him. In a couple of years he would be forty-five; he must make the push without delay – and must succeed in it – if he was to escape the insidious downward slope.

He glanced at his watch. Seven twenty-two. The post was scarcely ever later than seven-thirty. He turned from the kitchen and walked hesitantly towards the dining-room. Nothing wrong with just one drink, it would make bearable the next few minutes of waiting.

In the large dining-room with its tall windows framed in long drapes of plum-coloured velvet, he stooped to open the sideboard cupboard, paused with one hand already reaching for a bottle and stood for a moment with his eyes closed. No, he would not take a drink. He straightened up, sighed deeply and closed the cupboard.

He went quickly into the hall and let himself out into the garden, kept in trim by a jobbing gardener and glowing now with the deep rich colours of autumn. Chrysanthemums, dahlias, asters; shrubs with their soaring sprays and thick clusters of berries, white, scarlet and purple.

He wandered along the neat paths, contemplated the drift of yellow leaves in the shrubbery, ran a finger over the creamy ruffles of a late rose. He had gone to a nursery five years ago when Alison had said she would marry him. He had been astounded at his good fortune, had felt a great surge of optimism, a fierce late blossoming of the romantic impulse. He had selected twenty-one rose bushes – one for

6

every year of Alison's life. He had created this pretty little rose garden with a vision of the two of them strolling beside it in warm summer evenings.

By the time the bushes had established themselves, when they had been in the ground scarcely more than two years, Alison had turned her back on the marriage, had walked out on him, had returned to secretarial work.

She hadn't mentioned divorce. She had no legal grounds for such a step and it was certainly the last thing he wanted. In the first few months after her departure he had telephoned, written, gone to see her, made a succession of appeals for her return. By degrees the appeals grew less frequent, died away. He no longer cherished any very strong hope that they would succeed and now that they had lived apart for over two years he was afraid to approach her again. His action might make her realize that sufficient time had gone by to allow a petition for divorce by consent.

Out on the road, some little distance away, he heard the sound of a vehicle. A light sweat broke out on his forehead. He began to walk back towards the house with an air of casualness. The vehicle slowed to make the turn in through the gates. It came up the drive, disclosing itself as a red mail van; it halted when Rolt stepped into view. He took the letters from the postman and flipped them apart.

'A mild morning,' the postman said. 'Could be sunny later on.' Rolt saw the postmark on the third letter. He turned over the envelope and read the seal on the back: Kain Engineering. His heart seemed to rise up in his chest, suspend its beat for a long moment and then drop back with a thud.

'They talked about rain in the forecast,' the postman said. 'They get it wrong two days out of three.' Rolt glanced up, aware that the man had said something. He smiled, nodded vaguely and plunged off across the grass, ripping

7

open the thick white paper, unable to wait till he got into the house.

He fumbled at the folded sheet. His eyes raced over the lines of typing. The words sprang out at him like whorls of fire . . . Interview . . . Monday . . . 3.30 p.m.

He raised his head and looked up at the pearly sky. The mail van went back down the drive and out into the road. A flood of joy washed over Rolt. Careful, he told himself, must keep my grip. He walked up the short flight of stone steps that led to the front door. His pace was consciously brisk, his manner controlled and competent.

I'll get Alison back, he said in his mind with total confidence. He had something to offer her now. And she'd had time to think things over, she was no longer an inexperienced girl. She'd see sense, realize where her best interests – the best interests of both of them – lay. And no doubt by now she'd had more than enough of turning out in all weathers five days a week to go to the office. She'd probably wondered why he hadn't been in touch with her lately. After all, if she actually wanted a divorce, she could have approached him as soon as the two years were up. And she had no steady boy-friend, he was pretty certain of that.

He let himself into the house and closed the door behind him with a precise click. Silence settled back over the high-ceilinged rooms, the spacious hallway, lofty staircase, wide landings. He stood looking down at the carpet with its subdued pattern of blues and greys. Things would sort themselves out, it would all come right in the end. Just to get Alison back would at once make him feel younger, more positive and hopeful, give direction and purpose to his life.

He raised his head and glanced about him. Yes, that's it, he said to himself with decision. I'll phone Alison, I'll get the whole thing settled . . . But possibly not before the Kain interview . . . Probably best not to speak to her before three-thirty next Monday afternoon . . . For if by some remote chance she put on a voice of ice, if she refused to listen to reason, how then could he possibly conduct himself with cheerful confidence during the ordeal of the interview?

No, he would get the job first and then phone Alison; he'd have something concrete to lay before her then, something more enticing than vague, optimistic proposals. He put up a hand and rubbed his chin. In actual fact, he thought, I'd offer her anything to get her back. He imagined himself phrasing the words over the phone . . . Just say what it is you want and you can have it. How could any woman resist an offer like that? Anything she wanted . . . Well, of course, it went without saying, anything within reason.

He placed his hands together, linked the fingers, rubbed the palms against each other with a sense of satisfaction and relief. He noted with pleasure his feeling of control and competence, of being in charge of himself and his existence. And now, with all that resolved, what about one little drink? Not as a prop or a crutch – certainly not. Nor as a shield or a distorting mirror. But perfectly normally and wholesomely, by way of celebration.

Five minutes later he was sitting at ease in the dining-room when he remembered the other letters the postman had handed him. He set down his glass and picked up the little pile of envelopes. Nothing of great consequence. The telephone account, a couple of receipts, and a bill for the perfume he had given Celia Brettell on her birthday last month. Her thirty-third birthday according to Miss Brettell, her thirty-eighth according to uncharitable intimates. Every year at Christmas and on her birthday – with the exception of the couple of years of his marriage – he rang the changes between chocolates, flowers, books and perfumes, being careful never to give her anything more personal. He flicked the sheet of paper against his fingers, thinking about Celia.

He had known her for years, liked her well enough. There had been a time when he had almost allowed her to steer him towards the altar, from lack of any alternative and more attractive prospect. But that of course had been in the days before Alison.

He thrust the bill back into its envelope and instantly forgot about Miss Brettell. He gathered up the rest of his mail, stood up, finished his drink and went upstairs, half smiling, thinking with pleasurable expectation about the interview on Monday.

Monday morning, ten minutes past seven. In the bedroom of her ground-floor flat in Fairview, a solid Edwardian villa set on the lower slopes of the hills that cradled Barbourne, Alison Rolt drew back the curtains and looked out at the day. A little over two miles separated Fairview from Andrew Rolt's Victorian residence on the other side of Barbourne.

Quite a pleasant day. A light veil of mist obscured the view but there was a strong hint of warmth and sunshine later in the morning.

She went swiftly along to the bathroom and turned on the taps, piled her long hair on top of her head, squeezing the springy tresses into a waterproof cap ruched and frilled with pale blue nylon.

She flung a handful of salts into the water and stepped in. There was a suggestion of the exotic about her; she was small, slender and delicately made, still three or four years away from thirty. A pale olive skin deepened by suntan, quick movements, easy grace.

The only sound came from the water running into the cistern and her own soapy splashings. But I don't in the least mind being alone in the house, she thought, leaning back in the pale green water. She wasn't nervous; she found the quiet a pleasant contrast to the daily bustle at the office.

And in any case the situation was likely to be merely temporary; the two upper flats were sure to be tenanted again before long.

She came out of her thoughts with the recollection that it was Monday morning, that she had made up her mind on Friday to start a campaign to restore the efficiency of the girls who worked under her. She was junior partner at the Kingfisher Secretarial Agency in Barbourne, she had striven for high standards in the time she had held the post – a little less than a year. She had achieved a fair degree of success, only to find some of her efforts being undone in the last month or two.

In the middle of the summer Kingfisher had finally absorbed the remnants of Tyler's, the other secretarial agency in the town. Before her move to Kingfisher Alison had worked at Tyler's for eighteen months. It was a long-established agency but it had grown increasingly complacent, opposed to inevitable change, partly because old Mr Tyler had no son or daughter to inject fresh ideas into the business. He had seen the Kingfisher start up six years ago; he had felt no concern, considering the new agency an upstart enterprise likely to remain small and unimportant or else fade out altogether.

But Kingfisher had steadily expanded, nibbling unremittingly at the edges of Tyler's business, gradually luring away staff, enticing and retaining clients. A little over a year ago Mr Tyler died. The ownership of his agency passed to his widowed sister, an elderly invalid living in a South Coast nursing home, with no interest in the business apart from the money it might bring her. One of the senior members of staff – a man of no very great competence, not far off retiring age – was promoted to manager.

The flowers had scarcely withered on Mr Tyler's grave when Alison received an approach from the rival agency of Kingfisher. Judith Padmore, the founder and sole owner of Kingfisher, had had her eye on Alison for some time, well aware that it was largely Mrs Rolt's ability and youthful energy that allowed Tyler's to struggle on at all. Miss Padmore was a shrewd, hard-working woman with long commercial experience behind her. Now in late middle age and ready to take a little more leisure, she made her proposition in a forthright manner. A junior partnership, a percentage of the healthy Kingfisher profits in return for an investment of capital and the application of Mrs Rolt's talents to the business.

It had taken Alison no time at all to say yes. She had joined Tyler's when she closed the door on her marriage. She was twenty-three years old at the time, determined to make a good career for herself; she believed she had found a suitable niche. But her ambition had increased along with her experience. She hadn't much enjoyed the final six months at Tyler's and the bleak realization that in spite of all her endeavours she was now merely part of a rapidly failing concern.

After her departure Tyler's had struggled on under its inadequate manager, finally giving up the ghost a few months ago when the manager decided to retire. Miss Padmore took over what was left of the business and goodwill, the few remaining staff, together with the furnishings and equipment, all in exchange for a lump sum paid over to the invalid lady on the South Coast.

The graphs on the walls of Miss Padmore's office already showed a marked upswing and could be expected to present an increasingly satisfactory appearance for the next year or two. But there's a fairly rigid natural limit to expansion in a town of this size, Alison thought, squeezing the sponge over her slender shoulders.

She lay back in the bath and stared up at the ceiling. She'd probably have to move on in a couple of years, seek lusher pastures. She blew out a long calculating breath.

Nothing in her thoughts so much as brushed against an image of Andrew or flicked awareness of his existence into the forefront of her mind. Her marriage – or what was legally left of it – was now totally lacking in significance for her. When some chance happening brought it to her recollection it seemed as if she was recalling with difficulty an almost-forgotten interlude. She felt more and more that exciting possibilities were opening out before her, that the real business of her life was only just beginning.

The sound of the newsboy's whistle reached her ears. It must be turned a quarter to eight. She pulled out the bath plug and stretched out a hand for a towel. She stood up and dried herself with easy, rapid movements. Along with the goods and chattels that had moved across from Tyler's in the course of the final transfer, there had also come a certain tinge of slackness that began before long to affect the Kingfisher staff. Girls started to arrive a little late in the mornings, to vanish a trifle early in the evenings, to absent themselves for an occasional afternoon without good reason.

And the time has come to root the slackness out, Alison thought, stepping out of the bath and flinging down the towel. She picked up a bottle of lotion and began to massage it into the fine smooth skin of her calves and thighs.

When she got back to her bedroom the clock showed five minutes to eight. She pulled open a drawer, looked rapidly through the filmy underthings. She certainly couldn't risk being late for work herself if she was going to get her campaign off to a good start. Some of the girls were only too quick to take advantage of any little lapse on the part of the management.

The central police station in Barbourne was a modern building, bright and airy. The reception area was almost empty at this time on a Monday morning; it had a leisurely

13

air after the busy traffic of the weekend. On a bench against the wall an old man sat alone in a patient, relaxed attitude.

Detective-Sergeant Colin Viner stood in front of the long polished counter, dealing with a couple of girls, office workers, who had come in to report an incident which had taken place – or which they said had taken place – on Friday night. Viner was not at all sure that he was disposed to believe their unsupported tale of a man springing out at one of them as she walked home alone across the hill from an evening class in the town.

There had been vague rumours for some little time of a man haunting the hills. Nothing substantiated, nothing serious. Such rumours were not uncommon; often the episode which sparked them off was nothing more than a prank, a moment's mischief.

'It's a great pity you didn't manage to get a good look at the man,' Viner said briskly. He slid a speculative glance at the taller of the two girls, the victim of the alleged assault – or more precisely, of the attempted assault, for the girl, according to her story, had taken to her heels at once with scarcely more than a finger laid upon her. She was really quite pretty in a fluid, drooping way . . . and he had always been rather partial to fluid, drooping girls . . . He flicked the thought away and returned his attention to business. He'd have liked a little more evidence than the statement of this young woman whose path – during the short time he'd been stationed in Barbourne – had crossed his own a little more frequently than he was inclined to put down to the simple workings of chance.

'If you could give me some idea of the man's age, his height – ' He ran his eye over the brief details he had jotted down about the girl: Tessa Drake, eighteen years old, shared a small flat with the other girl in Leofric Gardens, a run-down area of Barbourne. Employed as a shorthand-typist by the Kingfisher Secretarial Agency.

On her way to work now, twenty past eight by the station clock, having – so she said – spent the best part of the weekend recovering from her nasty experience of Friday night and bracing herself – with the moral support of her friend who stood now levelling at Viner a sternly challenging gaze – to walk up the steps of the police station and recount her shocking tale.

'Did the man say anything?' Viner asked without hope. 'I don't know what you expect us to do when you can tell us practically nothing.'

'Well, she was very upset.' The friend, little more than five feet in height but bristling with protective ferocity, jerked her head in indignation. 'Who wouldn't be? A man jumping out at her like that.'

Detective-Inspector Bennett came striding into the hall and swept a glance over the reception area. He closed his eyes for an instant at the sight of old James Ottaway once again on his bench, now sitting bolt upright, staring rigidly ahead. Bennett came to a halt a few yards from where Sergeant Viner was writing something down with an air of resigned boredom.

'Mandy Webb. Nineteen years old,' Viner said aloud as he wrote the words. He glanced up at the second girl. 'The same address in Leofric Gardens?' She nodded. 'And you work at the same place as your friend?'

'No. We used to work together. At Tyler's agency. When it folded up Tessa went to Kingfisher and I got a job at CeeJay Plant Hire.'

'You'd better get off to work then,' Viner said. 'Both of you. Wouldn't do to keep your bosses waiting.' He caught sight of Inspector Bennett. 'These young ladies have come across – or fancy they've come across – our phantom prowler,' he said as Bennett came over. 'Most upset,' Viner added with unsubtle irony. 'So upset they didn't notice anything about him.'

15

Bennett ran his eye over the girls, the short one like a terrier with her fringe of fawn-coloured hair, and the taller one, not bad-looking in her dreamy way. He frowned. Hadn't the tall one been into the station only a week or two back on some pretext or other? He flicked a sour-grape look at Viner's smooth tanned skin and thick dark hair; a pity the sergeant had nothing better to do than stand around encouraging silly girls to run in and out making eyes at him.

'You might explain to these young ladies,' Bennett said with threatening jocularity, 'that there's such a thing as being charged with wasting police time.' The tall girl gave him a look of faint alarm, the other lowered her eyes with an expression of contempt.

'Foolish girls,' Bennett said, gazing idly about, 'are inclined to pick up snippets of rumour.' His glance rested on James Ottaway still peering resolutely into vacancy; at least it wasn't one of the old fellow's noisily obstreperous days, something to be thankful for. 'Frivolous minds seize on a titbit,' Bennett said. They touch it up, embroider it.' He jerked his head round, frowned at the girls with a look from which jocularity had abruptly vanished. 'Then they come in here with their daft tales, trying it on, looking for a bit of importance.' He nodded over towards the door. 'Go on, scarper. Go and waste your bosses' time.' When they had taken themselves off a few yards, pink-cheeked and bridling, Bennett said loudly, 'The tall one, Miss Droopy Drawers –'

'Tessa Drake,' Viner said, unwilling to play along any further with the inspector's needling game.

'Miss Droopy Drawers,' Bennett repeated more loudly. 'She fancies you. That's what all this is in aid of.' His eyes held no amusement. 'Don't encourage her. Gives the station an untidy look.'

'I most certainly never –' Viner began with angry protest

16

but Bennett held up a hand.

'Just a joke,' he said smoothly. 'Got to be able to take a joke.' Over by the door Tessa Drake turned her head and glanced back at Viner. She gave him an amused smile.

Beneath the graceful leaves of a vast green plant set on a ledge, old Ottaway rose suddenly from his bench and said in a high clear voice, 'I come not to bring you peace but a sword.'

'He's off again,' Bennett said with weary irritation. A constable, coming up from the canteen, caught the tail end of Ottaway's utterance and quickened his pace along the corridor.

'Now Jezebel was a whore,' Ottaway said on a half-singing note. The constable reached him as he raised his right arm and cried, 'A painted whore of Babylon.'

'That's all right then,' the constable said, firmly soothing. He slipped a steely hand under the old man's elbow. 'Come along.' He began to propel his captive towards the door. 'Nobody worries about Jezebel any more.' Ottaway was well known in the station; he had long been a widower, lived alone, had grown increasingly eccentric.

A few yards from the door Ottaway halted. 'I want to register a complaint,' he said suddenly in a normal voice. 'About the posters outside the cinema. Most indecent. Not at all the thing for women and children to be faced with.'

'We'll see to it,' the constable said. 'Leave it to us. No need for you to worry.' He steered Ottaway out on to the steps, pointed him in the direction of home.

Certainly not the liveliest of mornings. Viner glanced at his watch. Might as well go and see that woman about the furnished house dispute. Probably not theft at all, simple carelessness most likely. He crossed over to the window and looked out. The mist was beginning to lift, it might turn out to be one of those softly golden October days. He wouldn't bother with a car. It was no distance, he'd enjoy the walk. He turned from the window and met Inspector Bennett's questioning frown.

'I'm just off to talk to the furnished-house woman,' Viner said.

Bennett slid him a sly, teasing look edged with malice. 'Don't go chatting her up, then. She struck me as a bit of a man-eater.'

'I can take care of myself.' Viner added a half smile to the end of his words, to neutralize the irritation showing in his tone. He'd recently got himself transferred to Barbourne after the girl he'd been engaged to had suddenly married someone else. Bennett had ferreted about till he'd uncovered the story. He'd found several opportunities to flick at Viner barbed little remarks about women in general and Viner's relationship with them – or what the inspector apparently fancied might be Viner's relationship with them – in particular.

The air was fresh and sweet when Viner came out of the station into the grey and gold morning. A few minutes later, as he walked up the High Street, he noticed for the first time a grey stone building standing between a bookshop and a bank. A fair-sized building, solid, prosperous-looking, with the name painted on a board in elegant gilt lettering: The Kingfisher Secretarial Agency.

He halted on the edge of the pavement, gazing across at the premises. Through the ground-floor windows he could see girls moving about. He felt a sharp surge of loneliness. Barbourne was barely twenty miles from his native town of Chaddesley but he had set foot in it perhaps only half-a-dozen times before his official transfer a few weeks before; the very unfamiliarity of the place was the main reason he had chosen it.

At the centre window on the first floor a girl leaned forward, lifted a hand in greeting, smiled down at him. Colin recognized her at once; Tessa Drake, eighteen years old. For several seconds he continued to look up at her with an expressionless face; she remained smiling down at him. Then he turned and walked rapidly away up the High Street.

CHAPTER II

THE INTERIOR of the Kingfisher Agency was pleasantly warm. Hazel Ratcliff pulled off her coat as she came into the first-floor office. 'That wretched bus,' she said in a voice of habitual grievance. 'It gets later every morning.' She went over to the window and stood beside Tessa Drake who was looking down into the street. 'What's so interesting out there?' she asked. Her eyes followed Tessa's gaze, lighted on a tall broad-shouldered man walking swiftly up the road. Still an eye for a well-built man, Hazel Ratcliff, in spite of the years slipping well past thirty; still hopeful in spite of precious little encouragement.

She turned from the window. 'Come on, we can't stand here all day,' she said forcefully. 'To work!' She dealt Tessa a would-be playful blow on the shoulder with twelve solid stones behind the punch. 'If we don't get started we'll have la Rolt after us.'

'You ought to find somewhere to live in Barbourne,' Tessa said idly. 'Then you wouldn't have this fuss about being late. I can't think why you want to live in the country.'

'I don't want to,' Hazel said with energy. 'Not now.' She was one of the staff who had come over in the summer from Tyler's. Her widowed mother had died shortly afterwards, leaving Hazel bereft of immediate family. 'There's nothing I'd like better than to give up the cottage and move right into town,' she said. 'But you tell me where I can get a decent flat at a reasonable rent.'

The office manager put his head round the door. 'Come along, ladies,' he said in his precise way. 'Mustn't get the week off to a bad start.' He gave Miss Ratcliff a speculative glance; he had caught the tail end of the conversation. A flat . . . just possible that he might be able to help her. A heavily built woman, Miss Ratcliff, unpleasingly wide in the hips. But a good skin, all that country air. And rather large, quite pretty eyes.

'Just coming, Mr Yoxall,' Hazel said. 'Has Miss Padmore been asking for me?'

He shook his head. 'No, but she will be, in a minute or two.' If Hazel were to lose two or three stones, package herself a good deal less dowdily, lighten the colour of her hair, she might turn out to be quite passable. He followed the two females into the corridor. He didn't turn an assessing eye on Tessa Drake, knowing that the most extravagantly drawn bounds of possibility couldn't be expected to include eighteen-year-old girls with willowy figures and pretty faces.

He went up the short flight of steps to Mrs Rolt's office and knocked at her door. 'Just one moment,' she said when he came in; she was sorting a bundle of papers. He stood silently by the desk, watching her with a calm, detached look. Without doubt a striking-looking girl, though not altogether to his taste. He didn't particularly admire the evident traces of foreign blood. He understood that her mother had been the daughter of a Greek artist, a sculptor or something of that sort. Quite an arty background really, her father had taught art here in Barbourne.

She dealt with the last of the papers, sat back and gazed at him. Then all at once she remembered his uncle's death; her face took on a look of commiseration.

'I was sorry to hear about your uncle,' she said. Old George Yoxall had died early on Saturday morning, in the local hospital where he had been taken a few weeks previously after a heart attack. He had been Mrs Rolt's landlord; he had occupied the top flat in Fairview. The middle flat had been tenanted by a pair of young men during the time Alison had rented the garden flat. Not the same pair of young men but a rather bewildering succession of young men connected to each other in a variety of ways: friends, relatives, colleagues. The last young man had gone abroad just before George Yoxall's heart attack and the matter of the tenancy had been allowed to stand over while he was in hospital.

'That's what I came to see you about,' Yoxall said. 'To ask if I might take tomorrow afternoon off to go to the funeral.'

'Yes, of course.' Highly inconvenient, but she could scarcely refuse. She would have liked to ask him what was going to happen to the flats but it seemed hardly politic to raise the question at this moment. He had a somewhat withdrawn air. Had he been deeply affected by his uncle's death? He certainly used to visit the old man regularly, she was accustomed to seeing him on the stairs at Fairview. It had been through him that she had heard about the flat in the first place, shortly after she had joined Kingfisher.

'Thank you,' he said. 'I'll be here for the morning as usual.'

She stood up. 'Oh, while I think of it –' She went over to a filing cabinet and pulled open one of the lower drawers. 'You remember the girls we interviewed the week before last for that post with the textile firm?' She knelt on the floor, leafed through papers. 'If you'd just glance at these two applications. I think we might see the girls again.' She passed him the sheets. 'One of them might be suitable for the job at the transport depot.'

She sat back on her heels and considered him for a moment as he bent his head over the pages. Might he have expectations from his uncle? Old Mr Yoxall had owned quite a bit of property. There were other relatives, she knew that, she'd glimpsed them sometimes.

She picked up a folder, glanced through it. Ah well, either Mr Yoxall or one of the executors would tell her soon enough if she'd have to move. She gave a faint sigh. She very much hoped she wouldn't have to start looking for somewhere else. Fairview would suit her very well for the remainder of the time she envisaged living in Barbourne. She liked the house; it was spacious and comfortable, the large garden so agreeably private, with a gate that gave direct access to the hill.

She stood up. 'You might take those application forms with you,' she said to Yoxall. 'Have another look at them, let me know what you think.'

At ten o'clock Alison closed the door on the rattle and clack of the large main office and walked briskly upstairs. As always on a Monday morning there were a dozen matters she must discuss with her senior partner. She came up to the landing and saw that Hazel Ratcliff was just coming out of Miss Padmore's room. The half-smiling look Hazel wore changed abruptly to one of impersonal coolness as she caught sight of Alison. She stood back against the wall to let her go by, in a posture of almost aggressive deference.

Oh Lord, Alison thought, suppressing a sigh, her attitude seems to be getting worse instead of better. She had known Hazel during the eighteen months she had worked at Tyler's and had got on reasonably well with her in spite of what Alison always felt to be Hazel's instinctive dislike for an obviously more successful and attractive female.

Hazel was the kind of woman to identify herself with her employer, particularly if the employer was a man. She had been very loyal to old Mr Tyler and when, very shortly after his death, Alison had announced her intention of

leaving Tyler's, Hazel had behaved as if she thought Alison
guilty of the grossest treachery. An opinion she saw no
reason to modify when she realized that Alison was taking
with her to Kingfisher a substantial number of Tyler clients.

Even though Hazel had now joined Kingfisher herself
there was little sign of any thaw in her manner. She seemed
to feel the ceaseless necessity to make it clear that her own
connection with Kingfisher was due solely to the lamentable
demise of Tyler's, a calamity she appeared to think Alison
had helped to precipitate by her departure.

Alison smiled now with determined friendliness at Hazel
standing back against the wall. 'Good morning, Hazel,' she
said resolutely. 'Is Miss Padmore busy just now?'

Hazel gave her an unsmiling look. 'Not that I'm aware
of, Mrs Rolt.' She went off down the stairs. Alison stood for
a moment looking after her. Hazel was supposed to divide
her time equally between both partners but already she had
unmistakably attached herself to Miss Padmore. Alison had
more or less given up summoning her, preferring to see at
the other side of her desk the cheerful face of a willing – if
less competent – junior.

She shook her head, dismissing the subject, and rapped
smartly on the door of her senior partner's office.

Judith Padmore was running a pencil down a column
of figures when Alison came in. She held up a hand for
silence till she had set down the total, then she sat back
in her chair and gazed at Alison. She was an efficient-look-
ing woman dressed with provincial smartness in a neat
tailored suit. Her hair was trimly set, carefully tinted to
mask the grey.

'We must try to do something about accommodation for
Hazel,' she said briskly. 'It's really not very sensible for her
to go on living at the back of beyond.'

23

CHAPTER III

THE BARBOURNE branch of CeeJay Plant Hire Limited was situated on a sprawling industrial estate a short distance outside the town. It occupied a large stone building with a vast yard crammed with dumpers, diggers, excavators, handling, shifting and loading equipment of every description.

In his airy office on the first floor Andrew Rolt sat at his desk, explaining the more intricate details of a contract proposal to Paul Hulme, who was standing at his side, looking down at the papers spread out before them.

'Yes, I think I've got that,' Hulme said deferentially. I'd have got it a lot quicker if Rolt had been able to keep his mind on what he was telling me, he thought. 'There is just one other point I'm not clear about.' He picked up one of the sheets, ran a finger down it.

'Leave it,' Rolt said abruptly. He pushed back his chair and stood up. 'You've got the gist of the thing. I'll fill in the gaps another time. You can put all this away now, you can get on with that other stuff for the time being.' He jerked his head at a wire basket full of documents.

Hulme began to gather up the papers from the desk. He arranged them in an orderly pile, crossed the room and put them in a drawer. He was a trimly built, neat-featured young man with an air of control and calculation. He was being trained as a hire contract negotiator and at the same time carried out a number of duties as a general assistant to Rolt.

Hulme picked up the wire basket. In the doorway he paused and looked back at Rolt. 'Is there anything I can get you? Coffee? Or tea?' No doubt about it, Rolt's manner was preoccupied, even faintly distressed.

'What's that?' Rolt turned his head. 'Oh, no thanks, nothing.' He strove to keep sharpness from his tone. 'No need to hurry too much over that stuff, take your time.' The lad had a tendency to wet-nurse him; there were times when he didn't find it amusing.

He looked down at his desk, at a sheaf of letters that must be answered. He gave a long sigh. 'Send Miss Webb in, will you?' he said to Hulme. The chore wouldn't grow any more attractive for being postponed. And he would be away pretty well all the afternoon at Kain Engineering.

Mandy Webb was in the outer office. She looked up as Rolt's door opened, picked up her notebook and came over at once on Hulme's nod. He didn't stand back for her in the doorway but remained half blocking the entrance so that she had to squeeze past. They exchanged a long, intimate, unsmiling look.

Mandy took her seat a little to one side of Rolt's desk. He shuffled the letters together, selected one at random, ran his eye over it and began to dictate. A quarter of the way through the batch, his vagrant attention suddenly abandoned the mail completely. Mandy was sitting with her legs crossed, her notebook resting on her right knee; her head was still bent, her pencil still poised. He saw her all at once not as Miss Webb, short and none too pretty, the junior secretary who had been with CeeJay a matter of weeks, but simply as a female.

He stared at her without subterfuge. What would it be like to start all over again with someone entirely new, to put the past behind him for ever? For a moment the idea seemed exhilarating as if by some magic he might find youth and innocence again along with courage. But the moment passed. I couldn't do it, he thought, clenching his fist over the scatter of letters. It would need the kind of confidence and self-esteem he had never greatly possessed even when he'd started out on life. His grip on the remnants of these essential qualities was now so insecure that he dared not risk putting it to any more exacting test than those inescapably facing him.

And the effort it would take to find the right woman, the expenditure of time, of energy. And no guarantee of any more lasting success even if he succeeded in finding and winning this mythical being.

Mandy raised her head at the lengthening silence. Her eyes, bold, confident, young, met his. He picked up the next letter and resumed dictation.

Ten minutes later he finished the pile. He sat back in his chair and watched with relief as the door closed behind her. He had barely time to draw a sweet breath of solitude when there was a brief knock and the under-manager, Arthur Ford, entered almost at the same instant.

'Come in,' Rolt said loudly when Ford was already inside the room. Ford looked surprised for a moment and then smiled as if humouring an invalid.

'Beryl's been on to me again to ask you over one evening,' he said. 'My life won't be worth living if I've got to tell her I can't persuade you.' Beneath the cheerful surface words others less cheerful rose unspoken into the air . . . All alone in that great empty house, can't be good for you . . .

Rolt closed his eyes for a second. Impossible to choke the fellow off, pushy and intrusive as he was, when all he was doing was trying to display goodwill.

'Nothing in the least formal,' Ford said. 'Just a few drinks, a bite to eat. And a hand of cards.'

Heaven preserve me from such ghastly jollity, Rolt said in his head, unable to voice a refusal until Ford committed the cardinal error of mentioning a specific date.

Ford instantly obliged by committing the error. 'What about tomorrow?' he suggested.

At once Rolt said in a friendly tone, 'I'm sorry, I can't

manage tomorrow. I've already got something fixed. But it's very kind of Beryl to think of me.' Dreadful woman, he thought, that appalling mixture of ignorance, prejudice, gentility and ruthlessness.

Ford began to marshal his guns. 'Friday then?' he said amiably.

Rolt shook his head with an air of regret. 'I'm afraid I'm busy on Friday evening as well.'

Ford let off another salvo. 'How about Saturday?'

Rolt pretended to give the notion some thought. 'Mm,' he said on a deceptively affirmative note that caused Ford's eyes to glisten in momentary satisfaction. 'Saturday ought to be – oh no, stupid of me, I've just remembered, Saturday's no good either.'

A steely determination came into Ford's expression. 'Yes, I know how it is,' he said as if abandoning the struggle. Then he fired his big guns. 'Name your own day, that'll be best. I know Beryl will be delighted to fit in with whatever's convenient to you.'

There's no help for it, Rolt said to himself with resigned amusement, all at once relaxed now that there was no way of winning. 'Wednesday,' he said magnanimously. 'The day after tomorrow. How would that suit you?'

'Wednesday would be fine.' Ford couldn't resist a smile of victory.

'But tell Beryl not to go to any trouble,' Rolt said without hope.

'I'll tell her.' Ford spread his hands. 'But it won't be any use. You know what women are.'

Rolt looked at him suddenly like a man taking part in an entirely different conversation. 'Oh yes,' he said in a voice from that other dialogue, 'I know what women are.'

A quarter to one. In the records office on the ground floor at CeeJay, Arthur Ford looked at his watch. He ought to be thinking of clearing up, popping up to the first floor to collect Robin, get off home in time for lunch. His son – in fact Robin was his only child – had left the local grammar school a year ago. He was doing three-month training stints in various departments at CeeJay, was considered a bright lad, possible executive material.

Ford glanced out of the window and saw Celia Brettell's silver-grey car pulling up on the forecourt. She stepped out on to the concrete. She wasn't carrying a briefcase, only a handbag, so this wasn't going to be a business visit but one of her personal swoops to take Andrew Rolt off to lunch.

Ford watched her approach the side entrance. Good-looking in her hard-edged way, considerably more hard-edged now than when she'd first walked into CeeJay on the look-out for good secondhand plant, ten or twelve years ago. Chestnut-brown hair, grey eyes, smooth pale skin; well groomed, carefully presented. But the whole package lacking any suggestion of mystery or romance. She had done everything she could possibly do with her appearance but there was nothing she could do about her aura, which radiated an unmistakable air of natural dominance, strong purpose, shrewdness and a highly practical approach to life and very probably also to love.

Ford neither liked nor disliked her. She was one small factor in his career situation and so he was obliged to take a certain amount of notice of her. But he couldn't help admiring her. She was successful in a pretty tough area of commercial life; she had the essential bulldog quality.

He had known her since the first time she'd walked up the steps of CeeJay, well before the day Alison Lloyd had set foot in the place as a junior secretary. Alison had married her boss in the classic tradition – and they'd all been so sure once upon a time that he'd marry Celia. When the marriage broke up after only a couple of years it wasn't very long before Celia's business visits – which had continued as usual – began to coincide once more with the approach of Andrew's lunch hour.

It occurred to Ford suddenly and with total certainty that Celia was at long last going to succeed in marrying Rolt. He stepped back from the window and went out through the door of the records office, arriving in the lobby in time to present a casual appearance of having just come down the side staircase as Celia Brettell entered the building.

'Oh – hello there!' he said with a friendly smile. 'Haven't had the pleasure of seeing you for a week or two.'

Oh yes, Celia said to herself, and precisely what is old Creepy Crawly up to this time? Aloud she said, 'That last lot of trenchers hadn't been properly maintained. You'll have to keep a sharper eye on the lads.'

His smile grew if anything a trifle more friendly. 'I'll certainly take note of it,' he said affably.

'Is Andrew about?' she asked.

He nodded. 'Yes. He's in his office. Oh, by the way,' he added, 'I've just remembered, he's looking in on us on Wednesday evening. On Beryl and myself, that is. I don't know if you'd care to join us. You'd be very welcome.' He knew that would get her; she simply wouldn't be able to say no to a chance of spending a few hours in Rolt's company, however diluted. 'Nothing very fancy, you understand, just a pleasant homely evening.'

Whatever it'll be, it won't be that, Celia thought grimly. However had Andrew allowed himself to accept such a frightful invitation? 'That's very kind of you,' she said, burnishing her expression into a smile. 'I'd love to come.' With so many lies thickening the air she couldn't resist throwing in another. 'I've always wanted to meet your wife.'

'Something else I've remembered,' Ford said with a knowing air. 'What's this gossip I hear about a merger between Sugdens and Murdoch Factors?' Sugdens was the comparatively small but highly efficient firm for which

Celia worked; Murdoch Factors was much larger, with a wider range of interests. If there was anything in the whisper – and it had reached Ford's permanently-cocked ears only recently and as the merest breath of rumour – then it seemed to him a good deal more likely that the deal would be a take-over rather than a merger.

Celia's smile vanished. 'That!' she said brusquely. 'I don't know who started that particular hare but there's nothing in it. I can assure you of that.'

'It sounded a bit of a wild tale to me,' Ford said lightly. Maybe you don't want to know about it, he said to himself, could be you'd lose your job, whether it's a merger or a take-over. Could be also, he added in his mind with a sudden sense of illumination, that it's the reason why you're closing in on Rolt. Time was going inexorably by, she wasn't getting any younger. And of course she'd always been irremediably stuck on Rolt.

'Kindly contradict the rumour if you should hear it again,' Celia said with force. She walked away towards the stairs, she went rapidly up. He stood looking after her with amused approval. That one never knows when she's beaten, he thought – and so of course she never will be beaten.

What was I about to do when I looked out of the window and saw Celia Brettell? he asked himself a moment later, staring up at the ceiling. Oh yes, he answered himself almost at once, I was going to collect Robin. He was just about to go upstairs when he heard a light patter of footsteps along the first-floor corridor and Mandy Webb came into view. He raised a hand, called out to her.

'Miss Webb – you might trot along and winkle Robin out for me. Tell him to get a move on or we'll be late for lunch.' He turned away without waiting for any acknowledgement on Mandy's part, and went off to get his coat.

It wouldn't do Mr Ford any harm to polish up his manners, Mandy said resentfully to herself as she went reluctantly off to carry out his command.

She found Robin standing by the window in an empty office. He held a sheaf of papers in his hand, he was gazing down at the car park. He was a slimly built lad of medium height; he had short brown hair with all suggestion of curl sternly suppressed.

'Your dad wants you,' Mandy said without preamble. He turned and gave her a blank look. His face was long and pale, he had large grey-blue eyes.

She felt a sudden impatient touch of sympathy for him, imagining what it must be like to be blessed with a dad like his. 'Lunch-time,' she said in a more kindly fashion. 'Your dad's all set and raring to go. You'd better get off downstairs.'

Robin made a small jerky movement of his head. 'Oh yes, thank you, I'll go right away. Very kind of you to come and tell me.'

'Don't mention it,' she said automatically. She paused on the threshold and looked back at him. She and Tessa might ask him along to one of their parties some time. He looked as if he could do with a bit of livening up. But she said nothing about it yet. She'd have to mention it to Tessa first.

It occurred to her as she went along the corridor to the cloakroom that it might also do her a bit of good with Mr Ford if she did a kindness to his one and only chick; it might sweeten old Ford's disposition towards her, make him speak up for her perhaps in due course when promotions were being handed out. She bit her lip, considering the notion. Mm, bit of a long shot, but possibly worth a try.

CHAPTER IV

AN UNEXPECTED interview with a new client meant that it was one o'clock when Alison finally managed to get off to lunch. She was very hungry, she'd had nothing for breakfast but a cup of coffee and a slice of toast. She'd treat herself to a really good lunch, take her time over it. She might try that place by the old market, it prided itself on its grills.

She paused on her way out and put her head round the door of Hazel Ratcliff's overheated little sanctum. Hazel scarcely ever went out for lunch; she brought a vast number of sandwiches and great slabs of cake from home.

'I may be a little late back,' Alison said. 'I haven't got an appointment till a quarter to three but you might take any messages that come for me.'

'Yes, of course, Mrs Rolt,' Hazel said without more than a brief upward glance. She had munched her way through the greater part of her lunch and was now engaged in crocheting a small square of tangerine-coloured wool. A little pile of completed squares in a variety of bright shades lay on a piece of white tissue paper well out of range of stray crumbs.

'What lovely colours!' Alison said. 'Are you making something for the Fair?' A Combined Charities Autumn Fair was being held in a few weeks' time with the object of raising funds which would be distributed at Christmas among various worthy causes. Alison could hardly fail to be aware of the project, for which Hazel worked assiduously; several other members of the Kingfisher staff were either busy making an assortment of saleable objects or had promised to act as stallholders and general assistants on the day.

Alison had so far done nothing to help. She intended to call in at the Fair and patronize a few stalls; she felt that was all anyone had a right to expect of her. Now it occurred to her that an offer of help might be politic.

'I'm making cushions,' Hazel said in a slightly mollified tone. She reached into a zip-topped bag on the floor beside her. 'This is one I've just finished.' She held out a cushion about twelve inches square with a brilliant design of motifs in different colours arranged in a pattern of concentric oblongs.

'That's beautiful,' Alison said without exaggeration. 'Did you design it yourself?'

Hazel shook her head. 'No, it's one of my mother's designs. She was very good at needlework.' She was silent for a moment, then she spoke in a bracing tone. 'We're using three of her crochet designs, they're all based on the same idea as this. Oblongs, squares and circles. And two gros point designs. Jacobean.'

'I'd like to see one of those,' Alison said. 'I've always been fond of gros point work.'

'I haven't got one here to show you.' Hazel pondered for a moment. 'I wonder if Mr Yoxall has.'

'Mr Yoxall?' Alison said in surprise.

'Yes.' Hazel sounded mildly irritated. 'He's very good at gros point. A lot of men do embroidery.'

'Yes, I suppose so.'

'He's making some cushions for the Fair. And he's doing a lot to help generally.' She fixed on Alison an eye full of accusation. 'Everyone's doing what they can.'

'Yes,' Alison said. 'Actually I'd like to do something to help, if it's not too late to offer. I find I've a little more free time just at present.'

'Oh well,' Hazel said, a fraction more warmly, 'that's good news. As a matter of fact we're in a bit of a jam, the woman who was going to run the *objets d'art* stall has had to go up north to look after her grandchildren. Her daughter's gone into hospital and it looks as if she's going to be there for some time. Do you think you could take on the stall? I know nothing about art, but you ought to be good at it. You have the right artistic background.' A reference to the fact that Alison's father – a well-known figure in this part of the county in his day – had been a painter, creating precise, delicate landscapes in water colours.

'Yes, I'm sure I could manage it,' Alison said. Impossible now to refuse without plunging Hazel back into hostility. She became aware of the time. 'I must go or I won't get anything to eat.'

'That's settled then,' Hazel said firmly. 'To be absolutely in order of course we should have to get the agreement of the committee.' A lively note entered her voice. 'If you're free this evening why not come along to the committee meeting? You'll need to be given all the details about the stall. The meeting's at half past seven.'

'Yes, I can manage that,' Alison said. 'Where do the meetings take place?' She knew the Fair was to be held in a church hall close to where she lived; she saw the gaily-painted posters twice a day when she passed the building.

'The members take it in turns to hold the meetings in their own houses. This week it's the chairman's house. Or I should say the chairwoman.'

'And who is the chairwoman?' Alison asked.

'Mrs Ford. Beryl Ford.' Oh Lord, Alison thought, I don't want to get mixed up with the Fords. She'd known Arthur Ford when she worked at CeeJay and during the two years her marriage had lasted; she had never greatly cared for him. 'I imagine you know where Mrs Ford lives,' Hazel added.

'Yes, I believe so,' Alison said casually. She had set foot in the house once or twice as a young junior at Ceejay.

There was really nothing she could do to wriggle out of

it now. 'Very well,' she said briskly. 'Mrs Ford's house. Half past seven. I'll be there.'

Beryl Ford was in the kitchen dishing up lunch when her husband and son reached home.

'Chicken,' Arthur Ford said as soon as the front door swung open at his key. He gave a second sniff. 'And apple pie.' Other men might go home on Mondays to an uninspiring lunch knocked up from yesterday's remains – or not even be allowed home at all but provided with a packet of sandwiches or a nod towards the works canteen – but not Arthur Ford. Oh dear no. Beryl Ford knew better than to try that one on. Or at least she knew better now after twenty years of marriage. Some things she could get away with, some areas where she could wear the trousers, but as far as grub was concerned she knew from early and deeply-etched experience precisely where the limits of tolerance lay.

'I'm not hungry,' Robin said. He followed his father into the over-furnished dining-room. Beryl came bustling in from the kitchen, carrying a tray. Her face was flushed, her brilliantly blonde hair was starting to slip from its moorings.

'Here you are at last then,' she said sharply. 'Sit down.' She began to slap food on to plates.

'I don't want very much,' Robin said mildly. His mother dug the spoon into the casserole, didn't bother to comment, piled up his plate and handed it to him. 'Eat that,' she commanded. 'Put some flesh on your bones.' He took the plate without protest and began to eat.

'You were ten minutes late coming in today,' Beryl said to her husband in a challenging tone. He made no reply but concentrated on the food. 'Don't be late again this evening,' she said on a higher note. 'I've got a committee meeting here tonight. The Charities Fair. I can't be kept

35

hanging about in the kitchen.' Neither Arthur nor Robin gave any sign that they had heard what she said. She lobbed out her own helping and plonked her thin frame down on her chair. 'I hope we find someone to take over the art stall,' she said a moment later in a somewhat less querulous tone. 'I keep asking around but I can't come up with anyone suitable.'

Arthur finished chewing a succulent morsel of chicken. He speared another on his fork. 'I hope you haven't got any committee meetings on Wednesday evening,' he said in a calm, pleasant voice. 'If you have you'd better cancel them.'

Beryl raised her head abruptly like a gun dog that had got wind of game. 'What's so special about Wednesday?' she asked, giving him a penetrating glance.

'Rolt's coming to supper,' Arthur said in a throwaway manner. Beryl flashed him an incredulous, delighted look. 'And Madame Celia is coming with him,' Arthur said, still deadpan.

Beryl flung down her fork. 'Never!' she cried. 'Not Celia Brettell! I just don't believe it!'

'Believe it or believe it not,' Arthur said with tranquil majesty, 'on Wednesday evening the pair of them will set foot in this house.' He gave a massive nod. 'For supper and cards.' He fixed Robin with a patriarchal look. 'You'll be here, naturally.'

'I was going to play squash at the youth club,' Robin said without any note in his voice other than that of flat statement.

Arthur inclined his head briefly in regret for the necessity to cancel the squash game. 'You'll be here,' he said amiably. No need to argue or raise his voice, always a trifle surprised when he heard of other men having pitched battles with their offspring.

'I suppose I'll have to lay on a banquet for his lordship,'

36

Beryl said, divided between pleasure at the thought of being licensed to splash out freely and irritation at the notion that all her efforts were going to be directed towards providing lavish hospitality for Andrew Rolt – who had as good as done Arthur out of the area manager's job at CeeJay – and that stuck-up creature Celia Brettell, with her flash car and mighty high opinion of herself. She began to consider the meal in detail. Steak? Sirloin? Chicken? Or a turkey – what about a turkey?'

'Claret,' Arthur said on a musing note. 'Or a really good hock?' Must remember to get a dryish sherry for Rolt. He held out his plate. 'I'll have a bit more of that chicken,' he said graciously. He felt a sudden keen increase in his appetite.

'I'd like some more coffee, if we've time,' Celia Brettell said. The cheese had been rather salty.

'Yes, that's all right.' Andrew signalled the waiter. Another ten minutes or so before he need take the road for his interview.

'Would you plan to move from Barbourne?' Celia asked. He appreciated the way she didn't add 'if you get the job', seeming to accept without question that he would be successful.

He raised his shoulders. 'I couldn't say at this stage. I'd have to see how it worked out.' Kain Engineering was only twenty miles away, just over the border of the next county. Near enough to let him keep his present house if he wished, but far enough removed both in actual distance and psychologically – by virtue of that county border – to provide a liberating sense of making a completely fresh start, if he did decide to move.

He steered the conversation back to impersonal topics; he had grown skilled at this in the years he had known Celia. Not that he had any particular desire to choke off her questions about this new job; it was simply that he wanted to forget the whole thing until he found himself walking in through the wide swing doors at Kain. He had been pleased when she had turned up and suggested lunch; he hadn't in the least been looking forward to a jittery meal on his own.

His nerves were agreeably steady, he noted with satisfaction as he paid the bill and saw Celia to her car. The pleasant, calm feeling lasted throughout the drive. The traffic was a good deal lighter than he had expected and he realized as he approached the main gates that he was faced with a nasty stretch of time that he hadn't bargained for.

He didn't turn in through the gates but drove a little further on to a lay-by. The feeling of serenity had drained away. He leaned back against the upholstery, closed his eyes and tried to relax. At once a host of disturbing thoughts besieged his brain. He did his best to obliterate them, but it was useless. After a couple of minutes he opened his eyes and sat up. He stepped out of the car and looked round.

A hundred yards away on the left he could see the painted sign of a pub. He bit his lip, staring at the sign. He had managed to keep off drink at lunch, he certainly wasn't going to have any now; it would be kissing goodbye to any chance of the job. He turned his head. A short distance off, on the right, stood a phone kiosk. At once his spirits lightened.

I'll ring Alison, he thought with relief, I'll tell her where I am and what I'm doing, she's bound to be interested, after all it concerns her very closely. He dug in his pocket for the coins, crossed the road and went rapidly towards the kiosk.

Alison had only a few minutes to spare before her next appointment when the phone rang on her desk. Her smooth

38

professional manner underwent an alteration as soon as she recognized Andrew's voice. Surprise, followed instantly by wariness, entered her tone.

'What prompts this call?' she asked across his opening civilities. 'I'm very busy just now.'

He gave a nervous laugh. 'I have an interview at three o'clock.' He sketched in brief details. 'I thought you might care to wish me luck.'

'Yes, of course,' she said crisply. 'If this job is what you want, then I certainly hope you get it.'

'I'm speaking from a box outside the Works.' He was desperate now to keep her on the other end of the line. 'It's a pleasant situation. Open country not far away. You'd like it.'

'Oh yes?' she said, now only half listening. With her free hand she drew towards her a file of papers. She opened it and began to scan the pages.

'And it's not much more than twenty miles from Barbourne.' His tone grew warmer. 'It wouldn't necessarily mean moving house.' She said nothing, he abandoned caution. 'It could be exactly as you pleased. We could move or not, just as you chose.'

As she turned a page his words suddenly got through to her. She withdrew her fingers abruptly from the file.

'What do you mean?' she asked sharply. 'What has your moving to do with me?'

He was at once invaded by panic that she might force him out into the open, might make him spell out his wish to mend the marriage, the terms he had in mind. And if she then rejected those proposals, leaving him to get through the next few minutes as best he could, he would face the interview in the total certainty of failure.

He gave another laugh. 'I seem to have caught you at an inconvenient moment. I'm sorry, I'll ring off.' He put down the receiver without giving her time to reply. He let out a long trembling breath, stood for a few seconds with his eyes closed, steadying himself, wiping the conversation from his mind, summoning up what remained to him of poise and assurance. ·

When the phone clicked and buzzed in Alison's ear she raised her shoulders, pulled a face of momentary irritation and then dropped the instrument back on to its hook.

She glanced at her watch. She was on the verge of dismissing Andrew from her mind when some of the implications of his call began to filter into the forefront of her brain. He seemed very anxious to get this new job; he talked as if it meant quite a bit more money. It would suit him very well if she were to return to him. And he was prepared to go to some lengths to entice her back.

'Mm,' she said aloud. She tapped her fingers on the desk. When she married Andrew he had seemed to her to represent security. She thought him well-off, successful, destined before long to become even more successful. She had overvalued his ability – and undervalued her own. But her ideas had altered. She'd learned a thing or two since she'd left him.

In the corridor outside she heard footsteps. Her client, no doubt. All thought of Andrew's call vanished from her mind.

So far the interview was going well. The four men facing Andrew across the table were sitting upright, still wearing expressions of concentrated interest. He felt alert and stimulated. He knew he had done himself justice up to this point but he daren't relax yet. The tricky bit was still to come, might raise its head at any moment.

'And your family,' the Chairman said genially, glancing down at the application form. 'I see that you're married. No children.' He looked up. 'I take it your wife is in full agreement with your application. I'm sure I needn't tell you how important that is.' He smiled. 'We like the wives to come willingly.'

Andrew gave an answering smile, indicating with a nod his general agreement with the Chairman's remarks.

'She hasn't a career of her own, or anything of that sort?' the Chairman said. 'Nothing to prevent her playing her full part here as your wife?'

Andrew hesitated, moved his head fractionally sideways, stared at the surface of the table.

'She has a job,' he said. 'But it's scarcely a career. I don't think it's all that important to her. I'm sure she'd be prepared to give it up if I was appointed.'

The Chairman gave him a long considering look. 'We like to meet the wife,' he said pleasantly, 'before we reach any firm decision.' He spread his hands. 'I take it your wife would be able to come along very soon?'

'Yes, certainly.'

'Good. Then perhaps we could fix a time now?'

Andrew shifted in his chair. 'I'm afraid I can't do that,' he said with a half-smiling, deprecating air. 'It would have to be fitted in with her job commitments. I'd have to speak to her first.'

'We've another couple of candidates to see,' the Chairman said. 'You can use the phone here.' He jerked his head in the direction of the outer office. 'Speak to your wife about it, arrange a day to suit her. Then we can have another word with you, settle it all before you go.'

Andrew said nothing, his face expressed no more than a general wish to be co-operative. 'We want to finalize this appointment as soon as possible,' the Chairman said. 'We'd like to eliminate unnecessary delays.' There was another slight pause.

'Actually,' Andrew said on a high, light note, 'my wife and I –' To his horror he found he couldn't complete the sentence, his mind was a total blank.

'Yes?' the Chairman said. 'Some difficulty there?'

Andrew's mind cleared. He nodded in relief. 'That's it,' he said. 'We're living apart. Just temporarily, of course.'

There was a slight stir round the table. 'I would prefer to speak to her in person,' Andrew said. 'It would be far better than the phone. I could call to see her this evening.'

'How long have you lived apart?' The Chairman's tone was polite and neutral, like a doctor enquiring about symptoms.

'Two and a half years.'

'A longish time,' the Chairman said. Long enough to get a divorce, his manner suggested. Or to patch things up if they were ever going to be patched up.

Andrew glanced round the table, knowing even before he did so that it was no good, they'd written him off. Men of decision were what they liked, men of regular life. His glance demolished the last vestige of hope. They were all sitting back in their chairs, relaxed, switched off, no longer bothering even to look at him, simply waiting till the next man took his place.

'Right then,' the Chairman said suddenly. He looked across at Andrew, gave him a brief impersonal smile. 'You'll be hearing from us within the next day or two.' No longer any mention of urgent phone calls to Mrs Rolt from the next room. 'Thank you for coming along.'

That is it, Andrew said to himself with fierce emphasis as he came out into the car park. Finally and irreversibly it. I have finished with Alison. My mind is irrevocably made up. I will not try to hang on to her a moment longer. I'll get a divorce and marry Celia. She'd back me up in any job, any activity. She'd resign from Sugdens if he asked her to, she'd devote herself with pleasure to being his full-time wife.

He got into his car and eased it out towards the gates. He tried to conjure up a joyful vision of domestic warmth

42

and intimacy such as he had never experienced even in his childhood. He did his best to whip up a feeling of ardour as he contemplated the idea of Celia waiting to greet him at the end of a busy day. She's had plenty of experience of the hard world of business, he told himself, she'd understand the pressures.

But the prospect remained obstinately bleak, vaguely depressing. It seemed to him that marriage to Celia would signal the end of his youth, would rush him headlong into middle age.

He drove slowly up the road, past the pub, now locked and shuttered. It would be hours yet before they opened again. And he wanted a drink very much indeed. No reason now to resist the idea. And he did after all have something to celebrate – his very decisively settled future.

He would drive on into the town, find an off-licence, have his own little private party in some secluded spot.

On the edge of the town he came to a vast supermarket with a sign that mentioned among the varied delights within a section devoted to wines and spirits. He parked the car and went inside. He bought a nice little selection of conveniently-sized bottles. On his way out again he paused and looked round the long aisles, at the female assistants, the young housewives, the adolescent girls, trying to visualize himself striking up an acquaintance with such fashionably dressed and coiffured creatures, progressing through the ritual stages of intimacy to marriage and children.

It would take months, years possibly. And he didn't have the time to wait. It would take persistence and effort, charm and gaiety, energy and ardour.

And I don't have a single damned ounce to spare of any of those highly desirable qualities, he told himself, almost with exuberance, clutching to his chest the bottles in their discreet paper sack.

It's definitely going to have to be Celia, he told himself

yet again as he crossed the car park. The idea seemed more tolerable now. He drove back towards the open country, found a pleasant spot in a lane beneath overhanging trees and opened the first of his bottles. After ten minutes the idea of marrying Celia appeared a good deal more tolerable, after twenty he became greatly pleased with it.

The whole thing would be settled by the time he was summoned to his next interview. He saw himself facing another quartet of shrewd-eyed men. He would be alert and confident. 'My wife and I reached a civilized agreement', he was saying in that pleasing vision. 'A divorce by consent. No recriminations, by far the best way. It's going through any day now. I shall be marrying again very soon, a sensible, competent woman – '

He frowned, took another swig at his bottle and rephrased that. 'A most charming woman, highly suitable in every way. And a successful businesswoman into the bargain. A great asset. Yes, certainly she would come along to be introduced.' She most certainly would, he thought, she'd leap at the chance. 'And she'd resign her post at Sugdens, no question about that.' No question at all, he echoed, she'd be penning her resignation before he got the marriage proposal out of his mouth.

The bottle was now empty. I'll phone Alison before I start on another, he thought. I'll tell her what I've decided. He would go along to see his solicitor in the morning of course – and he'd get round to mentioning the whole thing to Celia at some time or other, no immediate rush about that – but just at this moment he felt a strong impulse to say it all to Alison. Burn his boats, get it over and done with. As he set the car in motion and drove along looking for a phone kiosk he felt light-headed, almost happy.

Alison was drinking a cup of tea when he rang. She had

managed to snatch a few minutes' peace, was sitting at her desk cradling the cup in her hands.

'I've made up my mind,' Andrew said in a quick voice, high and accusatory. 'I want a divorce. On the two-year-by-agreement principle. I take it you've no objection. I expect you're bloody pleased.'

He'd been drinking, Alison noted. 'How did the interview go?' she asked. 'Am I to congratulate you?'

'No bloody good,' he said. 'It was the marriage set-up that did for me. They didn't like it, they didn't like it one little bit. They like things to be one way or the other. And come to that,' he added almost in a shout, 'so do I. I've had enough of this neither-fish-nor-flesh nonsense. They wanted me to produce a wife, a one hundred per cent wife, dinner parties, functions, business trips, the lot.'

He'd want a pretty quick divorce, she thought. Tie the whole thing up at the solicitors' right away, file the petition pronto, not much delay in that sort of case these days. He'd want to be able to marry Celia with the speed of light, produce her like a rabbit from a hat the next time he was asked.

'I'm sorry about the job,' she said.

'Ah well.' His tone was faintly mollified. 'Better luck next time. I'll get along to my solicitor tomorrow morning, get him cracking with the divorce. No point in hanging about.'

'Divorce,' she echoed on a reflective note. 'I'm not so sure I really want one.'

He was brought up short, she heard him gasp.

'You mean – you're considering – you mean – you might come back to me?' By God, he wished she'd told him that when he'd phoned her earlier. He felt a wild leap of his heart, he could have sung out with joy. What did the lousy interview matter now? Plenty of better jobs. He grinned at his image in the little mirror on the kiosk wall.

'We'll meet,' he said with persuasive force. 'We'll talk things over. Get it all settled. I'll come over to Fairview this evening.'

'Don't get the wrong idea,' Alison said. 'I'm not committing myself to anything at this stage. You must understand that.'

'Yes, yes,' he said impatiently. 'Of course I understand. Very natural.' She couldn't be expected to climb down from her high horse all in an instant, she'd have her pride to consider.

'All I'm saying just now,' she added, 'is that I'm not sure I want a divorce. I'd need to think about it very carefully.'

'We could make a fresh start,' he said with joyful energy. There are great jobs going, terrific salaries. I could tackle anything if you came back. I'd give you anything you want.' Maybe he hadn't been the most generous husband in the world but he'd learned his lesson, he'd shower her with luxuries. 'We must meet,' he said again. 'I can tell you anything you want to know, listen to anything you've got to say.'

'Not just yet,' she said. 'I mustn't be rushed. Be fair, you have rather sprung this on me.' Marriage hadn't taken long to turn him from a moderately open-handed lover into a tight-fisted husband – probably, she judged now, his natural attitude. The idea of reunion seemed likely to release his purse strings once more.

'Yes, I suppose so,' he said grudgingly. 'Of course you must take what time you need.'

She glanced at her watch. 'I must ring off. I have an appointment.'

'Oh – yes – certainly,' he said at once. He felt great, marvellous, as he put down the receiver. He left the kiosk, went back to the car, shoved the bottles aside in a rush of disgust. He didn't need any booze now, he was on top of the world, reborn.

He set the car in motion, headed towards home. His brain was full of plans, moves, applications, interviews, in a fierce resurgence of hope.

CHAPTER V

SHORTLY AFTER half past five Alison put on her coat. The sky had grown leaden, it promised to be a chilly evening. As she opened her office door she saw Hazel Ratcliff going briskly by with a handful of papers. Hazel paused and gave her a sharp look.

'You won't forget about the meeting, Mrs Rolt?'

'Of course not,' Alison said. 'Half past seven, I'll be there.'

Hazel's features relaxed slightly. 'I hope it doesn't rain,' she said in a more affable tone. 'But it seems as if it's going to.'

'You'll have your work cut out to get home and back again for half past seven,' Alison said.

'I shan't even try,' Hazel said with energy. 'It would be impossible with the buses as they are now.' She jerked her head in the direction of her own room. 'I've brought extra sandwiches. I'll stay on here and catch up with a bit of work till it's time for the meeting.'

I do believe I detected a faint increase in warmth in her manner, Alison thought with satisfaction as she went off down the stairs. She paused for a moment. Perhaps she ought to ask Hazel to join her for a meal, it might be a good move.

But she wasn't going to eat at home herself. There was

hardly any food in the flat and she didn't in the least feel like battling round the streets in a last-minute effort to shop. She was going to call in at the Mayflower café for a snack and a chance to sit back and draw her breath before the rigours of the evening.

No, she would eat alone. She set off again down the stairs. It really would be altogether too much to ask that she should take Hazel along to the Mayflower and sit opposite her while she chomped her way through a mountain of baked beans.

Large drops of rain were starting to fall as Colin Viner pushed his way out of the supermarket. Still undecided how to deal with the flatness of the evening opening out before him, he took a firmer grip of his shopping bag and began to mooch along the pavement.

A flurry of rain drove him into a doorway; he turned and glanced at the shop window and saw that it was in fact a café. His spirits rose fractionally. He could go inside and have a cup of tea, give himself time to consider how to kill the next few hours.

The place was almost full but there was a table for two over against the wall with one empty chair. The young woman occupying the other chair leaned forward to pick something up and Viner saw her more clearly. A good-looking girl, long dark hair gleaming under the light. She sat back in her chair again and looked idly out at the street. A slightly olive skin, large dark eyes.

He felt a stir in some quarter of his brain, a teasing half-recollection. Oddly combined with a strong flavour of distaste. He frowned. Had he seen her before? Here, in Barbourne? No, surely not, for that would mean he had come across her in the last week or two and he couldn't have forgotten her so soon.

He pushed open the café door. Half-a-dozen people came

48

towards him from the direction of the cash desk, anxious for buses and home. An elderly woman, hurrying a little too fast, caught the heel of her shoe against a chair leg and almost fell to the floor, saving herself at the last moment by clutching at the trim waist of a very tall upright old man in front of her.

'God bless my soul!' the old man said in loud clear tones, feeling himself encircled for the first time in twenty-five years in a powerful feminine embrace. Tins and packets cascaded from the woman's holdall, rattling and bouncing between the agitated feet of customers pressing towards the exit.

'I'm ever so sorry,' the woman said in a deeply humiliated voice. Viner bent down to pick up the groceries. A small cardboard drum had rolled under one of the tables so that he had to kneel and fish it out, murmuring apologies to the occupants of the table, who continued to consult their menus without paying the slightest attention to either himself or what they clearly considered an ill-bred little uproar.

I suppose I'd better be going, Alison thought, roused from her reverie by some minor commotion at the other side of the tearoom. She looked about, gathered up her things. Rain no longer blew against the window, the sky was beginning to clear. She wouldn't bother taking a bus, she had time to walk.

As she came away from the cash desk she became aware of a tall young man getting up from his knees a couple of yards away, giving her a rueful grin. He was helping some old duck with her gear. He shepherded her to the door and then turned back into the café, looking over at Alison, almost as if he knew her.

She was faintly puzzled. Was he someone she ought to recognize? Some client from the agency – or from her days at Tyler's perhaps? Then all at once she knew him. Good heavens! Colin Viner! After how many years?

She swung round to face him, laughing. 'Colin!' she said. 'It is Colin Viner, isn't it?' It must be twelve or thirteen years since she'd last seen him. He'd been a couple of forms above her at Chaddesley Grammar School; she'd had to leave, had been transferred to the Barbourne school when her father had taken a post as art lecturer at the Barbourne College of Art. It was just herself and her father by then; her mother had died during an influenza epidemic three years before.

He was beside her now, smiling down at her, striving to recall her name. Just when he thought he'd have to confess he couldn't remember it, his brain flung up the long-ago syllables.

'Alison!' he said in triumph. 'Alison Lloyd!' It came to him in the same moment that he hadn't known her all that well, she was a couple of years younger than he was. And it came to him also that he hadn't much liked her. But the reason for his dislike – that eluded him.

'I'm not Alison Lloyd any more,' she said. 'I'm Alison Rolt. I got married a few years ago.' She pulled a face. 'Not a very good idea, it came unstuck.'

People began to push past them. 'We'd better move,' he said. He walked beside her to the door, came out and stood on the windy pavement.

'What are you doing in Barbourne?' she asked. 'Do you live here now?'

'I was transferred here a few weeks ago. I'm in the police. A detective-sergeant, to be precise.'

She made a little grimace of affected awe. 'Fancy!' She scrutinized his face with a candour left over from the shared days of childhood. 'You haven't really changed all that much.'

'Come and have a drink this evening,' he suggested. Infinitely better than sitting alone in his lodgings. 'Or dinner,' he said. 'We could have a good old gossip.'

She shook her head. 'This evening's no good. I have a committee meeting.' She laughed. 'It's not really my style. I've been roped in to help with the Charities Fair. But I could make it another evening. Tomorrow – or Wednesday.'

'Wednesday then,' he said. 'The Montrose Hotel? Seven-thirty?'

William Yoxall was the first member of the Charities Fair Committee to arrive at the Fords' house. Robin Ford answered his ring at the door and ushered him into the dining-room, where his parents were engaged in some last-minute rearrangement of the furniture.

'It's no good,' Beryl Ford was saying sharply as Yoxall came in. 'That trolley will have to go out, otherwise some-one is going to have to sit on top of the sideboard.' She gave Yoxall a distracted glance. 'You here already? It's not gone seven, surely?'

'No,' he said soothingly. 'You've plenty of time. I'm on the early side.'

'You can give me a hand with this then,' Arthur Ford said. He jerked his head at the side table, laden now with china, cutlery, silverware. Plates of fancy biscuits, little cakes elaborately iced.

'Certainly.' Yoxall took one end of the table and heaved it back under Arthur's directions into a more convenient position.

'Always the same,' Arthur said with philosophic joviality. 'Beryl can never settle down to enjoy a social evening unless she's made one hell of a domestic upset first.'

'Another couple of chairs from the sitting-room,' Beryl said to Robin. 'Those two straight chairs by the window.' She darted an anxious glance into the mirror above the hearth, raised both hands and stabbed at her carefully constructed hairdo. She was wearing a tight-fitting dress of electric blue crepe festooned with pleated whorls and frills that did nothing for her bony figure.

'That's it then,' Arthur said forcefully a few minutes later. 'If you're not satisfied now you never will be. Come on, Robin, we'll make ourselves scarce before your mother has time to think up a fresh move.'

'Come into the kitchen,' Beryl said to Yoxall. 'You can talk to me while I get on with one or two jobs. Oh – I was nearly forgetting,' she added on a higher note. 'You'll never guess who Hazel Ratcliff has got to take over the Art stall.' She flung William a look full of challenge. 'Go on! See if you can tell me!'

'I've no idea,' William said mildly.

'Mrs Rolt! There,' she added as she saw his eyes blink open. 'I knew you'd be surprised. She's coming along this evening.' She led the way into the kitchen. 'We must have everything just so for her ladyship.' She reached into a cupboard and took out a coffee percolator with important movements. 'I'm not having her go away and say she found anything to criticize.'

'No, indeed.'

'I expect you think her very good-looking,' Beryl said, almost accusatory.

'She certainly has a striking appearance.' His tone lacked enthusiasm. 'I can't say I greatly admire that type.'

'My own opinion exactly,' Beryl said with energy. 'Altogether too exotic for my taste.' She pulled down the corners of her mouth. 'Her mother was a foreigner, I understand. A Greek, I believe.'

William nodded with a reflective air. Then he looked about him. 'Is there anything I can do to help?'

She sent a harassed glance round the room. 'No, not really.' She banged things down on to a tray. 'That wretched creature Yardley phoned again to ask if he could serve on the committee,' she said suddenly. 'He's got a nerve! After the way I choked him off last time, I really couldn't credit that he'd ask again. He sounded as if he'd had more than enough to drink and that was at five o'clock in the afternoon.'

'I hope you weren't too hard on him,' William said. At forty-two Yoxall was too young to have served in the war, but he had some kind of notion of what things had been like for Brian Yardley.

Now turned fifty, gaunt and greying, Yardley had been a local hero in 1940 when William was a child at primary school. A Battle of Britain pilot, shot down in the final days of that epic struggle, appallingly burned, put together again afterwards over a long period punctuated with bouts of despair and bitterness, Yardley had eventually forced himself to surface once more into the life of Barbourne, take his grotesque face – that had been so pleasing to look at when he had climbed into his plane that August day – and his disfigured body about the streets and thoroughfares. A course, William had often thought, requiring very nearly as much courage as anything Yardley had done in the war.

'I've no patience with him,' Beryl said. No, you haven't, Yoxall thought. She would never trouble to look below the surface disorder of the personality that now served Yardley in some sort of fashion as his last remaining shield against the terrors of existence; she couldn't be bothered to show mercy to the disturbed, distressed soul underneath.

'He's still trading on his war service,' she said, 'even if he doesn't mention it. We're all supposed to overlook the fact that he's half drunk half the time.'

Yardley had tried his hand at a number of jobs in the painful time of his attempts at readjustment. He had succeeded at none of them. For the last few years he had run a small antique business; he seemed to be making a living out of it. At all events he hadn't yet gone bankrupt.

'It wouldn't have done any harm to let him help with

53

the Fair,' Yoxall said.

Beryl made a sound of distaste. 'He simply wants to be noticed. Anything to get attention. He's prepared to force himself on people – ' She was interrupted by a ring at the front door. 'I'll go and answer that.' She glanced at Yoxall. 'You'd better go on into the dining-room.'

'Why, Mrs Rolt!' he heard her exclaim a few moments later in a voice like syrup dripping from the blade of a knife. 'How very nice to see you! Do come in. I was delighted when Hazel rang to tell me . . .'

I'd forgotten the atmosphere of this house, Alison thought as she suffered the attentions of Mrs Ford. She remembered all at once how it had seemed to her when she was a junior at CeeJay, sent to the house with some query when Arthur Ford was absent from the office because of a passing indisposition. Cramped and crowded as if some manic interior decorator had attempted to fill every inch of space.

And covers on everything that could conceivably be covered : the telephone, radio magazines, the backs of chairs, tops of furniture, even the seat in the lavatory. And what wasn't hidden away was caged or confined, barricaded behind the doors of built-in fitments, thrust into decorated containers and canisters, enclosed in glass, fenced in behind metal grilles.

It hadn't changed much since she had last stepped over the threshold. New carpets, a more violent shade of paint, wallpaper of a different but equally restless pattern; the essentials remained the same.

The doorbell rang again. Cars drew up outside. Beryl's face took on a glow of pleasurable concentration as she darted about, admitting, ushering, chattering.

'Seven o'clock!' she cried as the clock on the mantelshelf chimed, just when she was closing the door of the dining-room behind the last arrival. 'All ready to start on time!'

An hour and a half later when the arguing, feuding and

54

jostling for position had reached a temporary lull, Arthur put his head round the door. 'I hope I'm not disturbing the cogitations,' he said jovially. He nodded greetings round the table. 'I'm just off,' he said to his wife. He jerked his head in the direction of the outside world. 'I shan't be very late.' He smiled expansively at the circle of faces. 'Enjoy yourselves.' His face vanished from the aperture.

'We might as well take a break now,' Beryl said as the front door closed behind him. Concentration had been effectively broken, refreshments would allow the combatants to restore themselves for the second half of the fray. She sprang to her feet and went out into the passage.

'Robin!' She sent a piercing shout into the upper regions. 'Come down and give me a hand!'

He came down almost at once, made himself useful, handed cups and plates, talked politely to the committee members.

Alison accepted a canapé from the dish he held out. She gave him an unthinking, automatic smile. A faint flush rose in his cheeks. He lingered beside her, still holding out the dish.

'Wake up there!' Beryl called out sharply to him a few moments later. Alison caught her eye, briefly registered the quality of its gaze – controlling, possessive, more than a little tinged with suspicion and hostility. She looked up at Robin, flashed him another smile but this time fully switched on, brilliant.

'I'll have another of those,' she said. 'They're delicious.' She began to chat to him with animation, asked him about his interests, if he ever went to the theatre.

'We let him have plenty of friends,' Beryl said loudly. She was busy with the coffee a couple of yards away. 'We must know who his friends are, of course, it's only sensible.' She directed a jet of coffee into cups. 'He gets out a good deal.' She jerked at Robin a compelling glance. 'You'll be going down to the youth club later on this evening, I dare say.'

'Very probably,' he said mildly.

'It's the youth club run by the church,' Beryl said. 'They cater for a nice type of youngster. Not like some of these clubs, nothing but breeding grounds for hooligans.'

'Would you like any more of these?' Robin asked Alison, again proffering his dish. She smiled and shook her head. 'One of these then,' he suggested, picking up a platter laden with minute pastry tarts.

'Thank you.' She took one. 'They look very good.'

'Pass them round to everyone,' Beryl said loudly from her station at the coffee.

'You can bring me some coffee on your way back,' Alison said mischievously as he moved away to obey his mother's commands. 'And some of those tempting little eclairs.'

'Will the meeting last much longer?' a hesitant female voice enquired from the end of the table. 'I only ask because it gets dark earlier now and I don't altogether care for walking home alone over the hill. One hears such alarming tales.'

'We won't be all that much longer,' Beryl assured her, adding in a robust tone, 'But you needn't worry, surely. It's only girls and young women these beastly men go for, isn't it?'

CHAPTER VI

ANDREW PASSED a restless night, uneasy spells of dozing from which he was jerked awake by agitating dreams. It was a relief at last to find that his bedside clock showed ten minutes to seven, that he might now consider the night over and the new day begun. He flung back the covers. Energy welled up in him. He snatched at his dressing-gown and went rapidly out of the room and along the corridor.

In the bathroom he frowned at his mirrored face as he shaved. His mind darted about, searching for some outlet. There was absolutely nothing he could do until Alison made up her mind about coming back to him. He couldn't fill in any new application forms. It would be a waste of time even to study the Situations Vacant columns; it would merely rouse him to fresh irritation if he came on some tempting opening he couldn't explore until he knew what he was going to write in that insignificant-looking little box opposite the words: MARITAL STATUS.

Ah – an idea occurred to him, positive and reassuring. He could go along after all and see his solicitor, discuss the whole thing with him, see what the situation would be if by some remote and horrid chance Alison should finally decide not to return. Gosling handled a good many divorce cases, he would understand the tricky convolutions of matrimonial disagreements; just to talk matters over with him at this stage would be useful.

He stooped to put the plug in the bath, smiled as he ran the taps. Action, that was always the thing, nothing was more lowering to the spirits than idle brooding.

The sound of a raised voice, blurred but angry-seeming, reached Alison's ears as she came out into the corridor from the main office at Kingfisher on Tuesday afternoon. A man's voice, rather thick and incoherent, coming from the open doorway of Hazel Ratcliff's room.

A brief pause, Hazel's indistinct reply, and then the man's voice again, louder, more argumentative. I'd better go and see what's wrong, Alison thought. It had been a long and weary morning and now with Mr Yoxall gone to his uncle's funeral, it promised to be an even longer and

57

more wearisome afternoon.

Hazel was standing just inside her door, talking earnestly to the man beside her. 'Is anything wrong?' Alison asked as she approached. They both turned and looked at her. She saw that the man was Brian Yardley; tall, thin almost to the point of emaciation, dark hair turning grey. And that face – that disturbing reminder to the comfortable citizens of Barbourne in the piping days of peace that there had been other times and other men.

'It's all right, thank you, Mrs Rolt,' Hazel said stiffly. 'I can cope.' She was standing a couple of feet away from Yardley; she looked ill at ease.

'It seems perhaps that you cannot,' Alison said. 'Now, Mr Yardley, what is it?' She had often seen him about the town, had bought one or two pieces from his antique shop, but it was the first time she had encountered him on the premises of Kingfisher.

'You're Mrs Rolt,' he said as if placing her with difficulty. He gave off an odour of spirits; he seemed more than a little drunk. 'Alison Rolt.' He smiled suddenly. 'Alison Lloyd. I knew your father.' He turned and stabbed a finger at Hazel's ample chest. 'A fine artist, her father.' But the sight of Hazel roused him again. 'Hundreds of pounds worth of business you've lost me,' he said belligerently. 'Possibly thousands.'

'What are you talking about?' Alison demanded.

He glanced back at her. 'I'm talking about my book lists. She lost a couple of pages. Sent the lists off with half of them missing. Lost me hundreds and hundreds of pounds.'

'I wasn't aware that Kingfisher had done any work for you,' Alison said with a frown.

'Well, yes, we have,' Hazel said unhappily. 'That is, I did some work for Mr Yardley. That is –' She seemed about to burst into tears.

'I'm going to have compensation,' Yardley said. 'I'm

58

not going to take this lying down.' He swayed, put out a hand and steadied himself against the wall.

'Would you kindly explain?' Alison said to Hazel. 'And we'd better all go into your office.'

Hazel led the way inside, pulled forward a couple of chairs, closed the door. She began a rather muddled account of how Mr Yardley had been a client of Tyler's for a few months, during the closing stages of that agency's existence. He had his monthly lists of old and rare books duplicated and sent out to dealers and private customers all over the British Isles and to several foreign countries as well. Then, six or seven months ago, there had been some kind of row between Yardley and the manager of Tyler's. Hazel wasn't too sure of the details but afterwards the manager had refused to handle any more of Yardley's work.

'So I did it for him,' Hazel said, avoiding looking at Alison. 'On a private basis, that is.' Yardley sat with his eyes closed, he seemed to have gone to sleep.

'I see.' Alison frowned. 'Then why is this argument taking place here? If Mr Yardley is a private client of yours, you must handle his business outside these premises.'

Yardley's eyes jerked open, he sat up. 'I demand compensation,' he said. 'I know my rights.'

'He isn't a private client of mine any more,' Hazel said. 'He's a client of Kingfisher now. When I took him on I was still at Tyler's of course, but that arrangement ended a couple of months later, when I came to Kingfisher. I spoke to Mr Yoxall about it just after I came here and he said it was all right to take Mr Yardley on to the Kingfisher books in the ordinary way.'

'Then it's a pity Mr Yoxall isn't here at the moment,' Alison said with displeasure. 'You ought to have consulted me about it, not Mr Yoxall.' You consulted me about as little as possible, she thought, and a nice mess you seem to have made of it. If Yardley really had lost money through

59

some carelessness on the part of Hazel, and if he really was a client of Kingfisher – she drew her brows together. There might be a question of compensation after all. She stood up.

'I must ask you to leave now,' she said firmly to Yardley. 'I'll go into all this with Mr Yoxall as soon as I can.' And that's not going to be very soon, she thought; her desk was piled with papers demanding her attention. With any luck Yardley would go off the boil in a day or two, would forget his grievance.

She had got him out through the door, skilfully over-riding his protests with exhortations and reassurances, when she felt Hazel briefly touch her arm.

'If we offered him something now,' Hazel said, 'I think he might take it, the matter might go no further.'

'What do you mean, offer him something?' Alison asked sharply. A notion sprang full-blown into her mind. She glanced from one to the other. Were they in some kind of collusion? Had the little scene been staged for her benefit? The argument in the doorway timed to occur just as she emerged from the main office?

'A hundred pounds,' Hazel said. 'I'm sure he'd take that to go no further. Otherwise it might turn out to be a lot more.'

'Is this what happened at Tyler's?' Alison asked. 'Did he try it on there? Did he get some money out of the manager?'

Hazel bit her lip. 'I told you, I don't really know what happened there. I just thought it might save Kingfisher a lot of trouble.'

'I most certainly will not agree to anything of the kind,' Alison said. 'All this will be thoroughly gone into.' And without bringing Miss Padmore into it, she added to her-self; she had immense contempt for the kind of executive who could settle nothing without running to higher authority. 'In the meantime say nothing about this. And if there are mislaid papers, do your best to find them.'

She marched across to where Yardley was leaning against the wall. She took him by the arm and shepherded him resolutely out of the building, remaining at the door until he had disappeared from sight, weaving his way among the afternoon shoppers.

William Yoxall glanced about the chapel with satisfaction. The funeral had certainly been arranged with taste and discretion. A very fair-sized gathering of relatives, friends and business associates had come along to see Uncle George off in decent style.

There was a subdued rustle as the mourners rose to their feet in readiness for the next hymn. On William's left stood young Paul Hulme from CeeJay; as a schoolboy Hulme had done holiday jobs for Uncle George. Hulme had always liked the old boy, had taken an hour off work to see him gathered to his fathers.

There was a brief commotion at the back of the church, the sound of uncertain footsteps coming up the aisle. William moved his head fractionally and saw Brian Yardley edging towards him along the pew. He's off again, William thought, recognizing the none too subtle indications, he's had more than a couple of jars already.

Yardley caught his eye and gave him a pleased nod, then settled himself into position at William's side. As the first notes of the organ stole into the air William held out his hymn book so that Yardley could share it, at the same time giving him an encouraging, friendly smile.

'The Lord's my shepherd, I'll not want.' William opened his mouth and sent the words soaring triumphantly upwards. On his right Yardley began to sing in a deep ragged roar; in the pew in front Uncle George's elderly solicitor emitted a thin pipe. It came to William that the solicitor had spoken to him a little earlier, had asked if he intended

61

staying behind for the reading of the will. It occurred to him suddenly and with joyful force that Uncle George might have remembered him, that it was possible the words of the hymn meant exactly what they said.

The phone rang on Hazel Ratcliff's desk just after half past three. 'Stephen Maynard here,' said the voice at the other end. Hazel gave a smile of pleasure. 'I have a couple of manuscripts,' he said. 'One is rather urgent. I'm afraid it's lengthy.'

'That's all right,' she said at once. 'I'll manage it, however long it is. Would you like me to call round for it?'

'There's no need to put yourself out. I've got to go into town immediately after school. I'll look in at the Kingfisher about half past four. The script's a bit difficult to follow in places, I'll have to explain things here and there.'

'That will be all right,' she said warmly. 'I'll make sure I'm free when you call.' When he had rung off she sat looking down at the receiver with a faint smile. Maynard was a client she had brought over with her from Tyler's, a straightforward agency client, in no way a private customer of her own although she had always done his work herself. He was in charge of history teaching at the local grammar school, had taught there for six or seven years. A quiet, studious man, devoting his free time to writing and research in his own subject.

She had first met him five or six years ago when he had called in at Tyler's to ask about their rates and terms of work. She had typed a few manuscripts for him and then there had been a long gap when apparently he wrote nothing or at least nothing that came her way. She saw him about the town occasionally during this time and always with a glow of pleasure. About twelve months ago he had contacted her again; he had begun to submit papers to learned journals, had had a number accepted. It was some time now since she had heard from him. I'm glad he's writing again, she thought. She smiled, stood up and walked over to a cabinet; she began to hum a gay, lilting tune.

Rolt had managed to persuade his solicitor to spare him twenty minutes. 'If you can get along at four o'clock,' Gosling said, 'I'll fit you in between clients.' At a quarter to four Andrew left his office at CeeJay and drove into Barbourne. He felt stimulated, almost light-hearted as he sat in the outer office waiting to be summoned into Gosling's sanctum.

At one minute past the hour he was ushered in. Gosling was a man of fifty or so with a placid manner. Andrew had rushed round to see him the day after Alison marched out two and a half years ago. He had listened impatiently to Gosling's exposition of the legal situation, had shaken his head furiously at the mention of divorce. All he had wanted then was for Gosling to tell him how to get Alison back. And of course Gosling hadn't been able to tell him, even if he had considered such advice any part of his job.

He listened now to what Rolt had to say, cupping his chin in his hand and looking down at the desk, from time to time sliding a glance at his client.

'I'm pretty certain,' Andrew said as he came to the end of his tale, 'that she'll come back to me.' Mm, Gosling said to himself, it's on the cards, I suppose. Best thing all round if she does. Rolt had always struck him as a man who – apart from any yearning he might have for love and affection – felt a powerful need for a conventionally regulated background.

'She'll keep me dangling for a while, naturally,' Rolt said with a faint smile. 'She couldn't be expected to come running back. But I expect she'll give me her decision in a few weeks.' He spoke the words casually but from the intolerable stretch of time they conjured up in his mind he might just as well have said a hundred years. He smiled again. 'If by any chance she should decide not to come back –' He shrugged his shoulders. 'What I'd like to know is what the legal position would be if she tells me she wants a divorce.' He spread his hands. 'I'm sure the whole thing could be arranged perfectly amicably if that did prove to be the case.'

'Glad to hear it,' Gosling said. 'I wish everyone was as sensible. Now – you've been apart over two years. You can get a divorce by agreement. No difficulty there. Wouldn't take very long either. The Court would have to approve the financial settlement of course –'

'Financial settlement?' Andrew said on a high note. 'What financial settlement? Alison has a good job, good prospects, she's young, she lived with me less than two years, she chose to walk out without any legal grounds for complaint. I've never paid her anything by way of maintenance since she left. She's never asked me for a penny in the time we've been apart. Never so much as mentioned it. Why on earth should I have to give her anything now?'

'When I use the words financial settlement,' Gosling said equably, 'that doesn't necessarily mean that either of you will be called on to pay over anything to the other. It simply means that the Court will have to know how matters stand between you financially, and that the state of affairs – whatever it is – must appear reasonable to the Court in the light of all the circumstances.'

'Ye – es, I see that,' Rolt said.

'It may very well be,' Gosling added, 'that you will not be required to pay any maintenance at all. If your wife is anxious for a divorce, and if she is clearly capable of maintaining herself, then you need only agree to her request for a divorce on the clearly spelled out understanding that she doesn't ask you for any money.'

There was a brief pause. Andrew shifted in his chair. 'But she may not actually want a divorce. She may refuse to come back to me and yet not ask for a divorce. She may prefer matters to stay exactly as they are now.'

'I should scarcely think so,' Gosling said mildly. 'She's a young woman. She would surely wish to be free to remarry.' He gazed blandly at Rolt. 'Any boy-friends – as far as you know?'

Rolt shook his head at once, with energy. 'Nothing serious. I'm pretty certain of that. I've seen her about the town over the last couple of years,' he added with an air of confident authority. 'She certainly doesn't lack escorts. But that's just what they appear to be, good-looking respectable escorts, a matter of convenience really.' Not that he had seen very much of her. Their tastes and natures differed, they didn't make the same kind of friend or frequent the same kind of place. When he had seen her it had been as often as not no more than a glimpse in the distance. On the rare occasions when they had met face to face they had both behaved with formal politeness. 'She seems to be concentrating on her career,' he said.

'In that case,' Gosling said, 'if, as you suggest, she has no real wish for a divorce, then she may very well ask you for money in return for her agreement to a petition.' He held up his hand for a moment as Rolt opened his mouth to argue. 'Probably not by way of maintenance, though she may very well demand that as well – '

'Demand?' Rolt interjected. 'Alison's not the type to go demanding – '

'She would most probably,' Gosling went on as if Rolt hadn't spoken, 'ask for a lump sum. Half the value of the matrimonial home would be the usual thing – ' Rolt made an incredulous sound which Gosling ignored. 'And very likely a bit more besides,' Gosling added. Separated wives, in his experience, rarely parted with any legal right at less than its full market value, often for considerably more.

'You'd need her consent,' he explained with a kindly air. 'And her consent is a saleable commodity. She is in no way obliged to give it. She can charge you for it whatever she judges the traffic will bear. All perfectly legal, I assure you. It's quite usual in such cases.' He tapped his fingers on the desk. The wife could often get a great deal more by way of marketing her consent to a divorce than she could ever get by replacing the gold ring on her finger. And without any of the tedious little chores and demands that not infrequently accompanied the replacing of that ring.

Rolt sat in silence, biting his lips, digesting the information.

'You can of course simply let the situation remain as it is now,' Gosling said. 'Take no further steps in the matter. In another three years or so you can divorce her with or without her consent.' He raised his shoulders. 'The Court would still have to approve the financial settlement but they'd simply look at all the facts. I very much doubt that in three years' time you'd have to pay her a penny piece.'

'Three years!' Rolt echoed in tones of protest. 'I can't wait that long.'

Mm, Gosling thought, and your wife will probably by now be well aware that you can't wait another three years. Most unwise of Rolt to speak to her before coming to see him, to let her perceive the value of the cards she held.

Gosling put the tips of his fingers together. 'If you go ahead with the divorce now, it is conceivable that it would mean selling your house and giving your wife half the proceeds. You could then buy something rather smaller for yourself with what was left.'

'I couldn't do that,' Rolt said at once. 'I need the house.' What kind of showing would he make in a new, important job if he was living in some miserable little box? And how would Celia like to start married life in that sort of style?

He stared at the further grim possibility of having to shell out some sizeable alimony by way of an additional sweetener.

'I definitely couldn't afford all that,' he said with emphasis. 'No question of it.'

Gosling glanced at his watch. 'It would certainly seem better all round if you and your wife came together again,' he said in a pleasant, detached tone.

'Yes, of course.' Andrew's voice at once took on a brisk and cheerful tone. He pushed back his chair and stood up. 'And there's every likelihood of that happening.' He smiled, braced his shoulders. 'I just hope she doesn't keep me hanging about for too long, waiting for her answer.'

And I hope so too, Gosling thought, your nerves don't look as though they'd stand too much of that. He held out his hand. 'I hope things turn out the way you want them.' Within thirty seconds of the door closing Gosling had forgotten Rolt and was devoting his concentrated attention to a file concerning a particularly interesting case of industrial compensation.

The script proved to be every bit as long and involved as Stephen Maynard had said it would be. For the best part of fifteen minutes Hazel sat beside him in agreeable proximity while he took her through the difficult passages. Their hands touched occasionally as they leaned over the desk, turning the pages, running a finger along a tricky line.

'I think that's about it,' he said at last. He straightened the script and pushed back his chair. There was a tap on the office door.

'Oh, Hazel – ' Mrs Rolt entered at the same moment as Hazel called out, 'Come in.' She halted at the sight of the tall fair-haired man glancing up at her with a startled look. 'I'm sorry,' she said. 'I didn't know you had a client with you.' She smiled. 'I came to see if there was any tea going.

I'm dying of thirst.'

'Yes, of course, I'll see about it right away.' As Hazel got to her feet she slid a glance at Maynard and saw him sitting there glued to his chair, unable to take his eyes off Madam Rolt.

'And I'm sure Mr – ' Alison said easily.

He became suddenly aware that he was still seated. He got to his feet. 'Maynard,' he said. 'Stephen Maynard.'

Alison smiled again. 'I'm glad to know you.' She flicked a look at Hazel. 'I'm sure Mr Maynard would like a cup of tea.'

'Yes, thank you, I would,' he said at once. 'I came here straight from school. I teach at the grammar school,' he added, seeing her eyes striving to place him.

'I'll bring another cup,' Hazel said. She moved to the door. 'And some biscuits,' she added extravagantly. Neither of them seemed to hear her, she had a brief sensation of having abruptly vanished from the scene.

When she came up again to the landing with the tray of tea she heard the sound of their voices and Mrs Rolt's laughter, gay and confident. She halted for an instant, drew a long breath, sighed and bit her lip. Then she shrugged, and moved on towards the office. As she set her fingers on the doorknob she heard them settling when and where they were to meet for a drink later in the evening.

Five minutes to eight. There was no sign of Stephen Maynard in the lounge bar of the Unicorn. Alison glanced at her watch. Actually she was a trifle early. She went into the bar and sat down on an upholstered bench behind a corner table.

She had hardly settled herself comfortably when someone pushed open the door, stood peering about for a few seconds and then said triumphantly, 'Mrs Rolt!' She looked over and let out a long exasperated breath. Brian Yardley!

68

He came weaving towards her. 'Alison Rolt!' he said with warm affection. 'Dear little Alison Lloyd!' He dropped to a half-kneeling position on the bench opposite her, leaned over the table, smiling fondly. 'I knew your dear father,' he said sentimentally. 'A man you could trust.' He frowned. 'Unlike some.'

He dipped a hand into a pocket, brought out a small green figure, smoothly rounded, delicately carved, and set it down plonk! on the table. 'Look at that!' he said fiercely. 'I bought that yesterday at an auction not twenty miles from here. Sold to me as jade. I took it for jade. You'd take it for jade. Anyone would take it for jade – '

'Would you please go away,' she said coldly.

'I'm not going to take it lying down,' he said, giving her a look of great cunning. 'Cheating, that's what it is. Everyone cheats now. Even you. Little Alison Lloyd.' He shook his head, overwhelmed by sadness. 'Even me.' He stared at her, he seemed about to burst into terrible sobs.

'I asked you to go,' she said in tones of ice. 'I don't wish to make a scene.'

'Who's making a scene?' he said loudly. 'Are you making a scene? I'm not making a scene.' He glared round the bar. 'If anyone's making a scene, let me know, I'll sort them out.'

A young man came up to the table with a minimum of fuss. 'Come along, Brian,' he said in a soothing tone. He gave Alison a brief glance. 'I'll see to him,' he murmured.

'You won't see to me,' Yardley said with echoing clarity. 'You're not getting rid of me.'

'I wasn't trying to get rid of you, Brian old man, I was just offering you a drink. I thought you might like to join me over there.' I know him, Alison thought suddenly, he's one of the young men who used to rent the middle flat at Fairview, surely. The one who worked at CeeJay, she rather thought – not that he'd been at CeeJay in her day, he'd be too young for that.

'Oh well, that's different,' Yardley said, mollified. 'That's another matter altogether.' He allowed the young man to take his arm.

'I'll see he doesn't bother you any further, Mrs Rolt,' the young man said. So I was right, she thought, it is one of those young men, he knows my name. The pair had just about reached the bar when the door opened and Stephen Maynard came in. He looked pleased and relieved when he saw her.

'I'm sorry,' he said as he came up to her table. 'The father of one of my sixth-formers dropped in just as I was about to leave. I was afraid you'd give me up for lost and go home.'

She smiled up at him. 'I certainly haven't been bored.' Over at the bar Yardley put up a hand and pushed the young man aside. 'Do stop interfering,' he said irritably. He evaded a restraining hand and made his inexorable way back to Alison's table.

'Is this your friend?' he said belligerently to Alison. He jerked a finger at Maynard. 'Is that your boy-friend? Take my tip, don't have anything to do with him, he's a wrong un.' He leaned forward, spoke confidentially. 'I owe it to your dear father to warn you.' He nodded emphatically. 'You'd have done better to stick to Rolt. A much sounder proposition.'

Maynard was still on his feet. He looked at Yardley with amused tolerance edged with the possibility of a rapid switch to anger. 'You're drunk,' he said in a detached manner as if offering Yardley a piece of vital information.

'Hulme'll tell you this chap's a wrong un.' Yardley jerked his head over at the young man watching resignedly from the bar. 'He knows.'

'We've had a little difficulty with this man at the agency,' Alison said to Maynard in an undertone. 'I'm afraid he's seen fit to attempt to pursue it here.'

'We'd better go,' Maynard said. 'No point in trying to make a drunk see reason.'

Hulme came discreetly up to them again. 'I'll take him right off somewhere else,' he said. 'You needn't trouble yourselves about leaving.' He put an arm under Yardley's elbow, looked at Maynard and said with an ironic inflection, 'Good evening. Mr Maynard. Sir.'

'Hulme,' Maynard said.

Hulme gave a little smile. 'Yes. Hulme.'

Maynard glanced from Yardley to Hulme, back again to Yardley.

'I really will see he doesn't keep doing his Banquo's ghost act,' Hulme said with a grin. Yardley seemed to have sunk into a somnolent state, he let himself be led firmly out through the door.

'Hulme,' Alison said reflectively when they were finally relaxing over drinks. 'I remember now, he is the young man who works at CeeJay.' She explained briefly about the middle flat, the succession of assorted tenants. 'You seemed to know each other,' she added after a moment's silence.

'Yes,' Stephen said. 'I hadn't seen Hulme for quite a while till this evening. I used to teach him at the grammar school here. Not a lad I greatly cared for.'

'I rather got the impression he didn't greatly care for you either,' Alison said.

He shrugged. 'We got across each other when he was just a lad, fifteen or sixteen. He's the type to wear a chip on his shoulder ever afterwards.' He appeared disinclined to pursue the subject.

'And Yardley?' she said. 'Do you also know him?'

'I imagine everyone in Barbourne knows Yardley.' Maynard gave a little shake of his head. 'He seems to be slipping downhill pretty rapidly.' His eyes considered some invisible image. 'A man like that, with his war record.' He sighed, shook his head again. 'It's all a very great pity. In the end people get tired of making allowances.'

He smiled suddenly, leaned forward and touched her hand. 'Let's forget this silly business. What would you like to drink?'

Some little time later when he had suggested going on somewhere for dinner and they were discussing the merits of various eating-places, she happened to turn her head and saw that Hulme was sitting alone at a table set in an alcove quite close to her own table. For some reason she couldn't altogether define, the realization gave her a curious lingering sense of unease.

It was after midnight when Alison let herself into Fairview. The door of the sitting-room was ajar. She opened it wide, reached up and found the light switch, clicked it on.

'Hello, Alison,' said a voice from the other side of the room. She turned, startled. Andrew was sitting in an easy chair, leaning back, looking at her.

'I thought I'd have heard from you by now,' he said in a slurred voice. 'About coming back to me.'

CHAPTER VII

THE DINING-ROOM of the Montrose Hotel was spacious, elegantly furnished. Viner and Alison sat a table near the window; a waiter bent over the table, serving the sweet. As soon as he had moved away Viner resumed the conversation.

'What I'd like to know,' he said with energy, 'is how your husband got into your flat. You surely don't leave windows open or doors unlocked when you go out?'

'I always see that the front door is properly secured,' Alison said defensively. She smiled. 'When I remember, that is.' The front door to Fairview had rarely been locked during the time that the young men inhabited the middle flat; they and their friends came in and out at all hours. Now that she was alone in the house she had tried to correct the habit but had fallen into another – equally reprehensible no doubt in the eyes of a detective-sergeant – of not bothering to secure the windows or lock the inner door leading to her own flat.

'It wasn't very difficult to persuade Andrew to leave.' She looked about the room with an animated glance. 'He wanted to know if I'd made up my mind about the divorce. I told him I couldn't decide an important matter like that in five minutes. A few weeks would be more reasonable.'

'I have the impression all the same,' Colin said idly, 'that your mind is made up. You've decided to agree to a divorce.'

She smiled. 'Yes, I have. I'll let him have his divorce, of course I will. I've no wish to block his path. It's just that I've got to look at all the angles, it's only sensible.' She picked up her spoon. 'He'll probably marry Celia Brettell and they'll be very happy. They're old enough at all events to know what they're doing.' She flicked a glance at Viner, wryly amused. 'I was so green when I married Andrew.' She laughed aloud.

I remember that laugh, Viner thought suddenly, that mocking note. Memory began to stir. Something to do with her laughter, the reason he hadn't liked her.

'I was so naïve,' she said. You were never that, Viner thought. Not even at school. Not even at thirteen.

'I was twenty-one when I got married,' she added. 'So very young.' Not all that young, he thought. Not too young to know what you were about.

'Mm,' he said aloud, non-committally. 'We all learn a bit as time goes by.' There was a pause which lengthened. 'Where is your father now?' he asked into the silence. It occurred to him that she had made little mention of her father and then only in the past tense.

She stopped eating. 'I imagined you knew.' She looked across at him. 'He died four years after we moved to Barbourne. He never really got over losing Mother.'

So she had been only seventeen when she was left alone in the world. 'Had you any other relatives?' he asked.

'Not really. A distant cousin or two in Scotland. Plenty of relations of my mother's in Greece of course, but I've never met any of them.' She picked up her spoon again. 'I left the grammar school right away and took a secretarial course. There wasn't a lot of money.' There had never been a lot of money and long acquaintance with that state of affairs had prompted her to put what little her father left her into the bank, from which in due course it emerged to pass into Judith Padmore's account when Alison became her junior partner.

She ate the last of her peach flan. 'I was eighteen when I finished the secretarial course. CeeJay was my first job.' She was silent for a moment or two. Then she turned her head and looked at Viner but her glance didn't meet his, she was looking into some thought of her own. 'I met someone yesterday,' she said. 'An interesting man. He teaches at the local grammar school.' Her face had a relaxed, almost sleepy expression.

The waiter appeared, gathered up plates, set down a bowl of fruit. 'Anyway, I shan't be alone at Fairview much longer,' Alison said lightly. 'It seems old George Yoxall left the house to his nephew. That's William Yoxall, the office manager at Kingfisher. The rest of the property went to other relatives.'

'And is Yoxall going to let the two empty flats right away?' Viner asked.

'He's going to let the middle one. He said he has someone in mind for it. He's moving into the top flat himself very shortly. He's a bachelor, he lives in digs. He's delighted at the thought of a place of his own. It's a very pleasant flat, the top one, good big rooms, a fine view.' She drew the bowl of fruit towards her. 'You don't have to worry about me.' She took a little bunch of grapes, bloom-skinned, rosy purple. 'It's pleasant to talk to you.' She gave him a teasing smile. 'There's no sense of inhibition. Comes of having been children together, I suppose.'

Supper at the Fords' house ended with an impressive array of cheeses and fruits.

'If everyone has had an elegant sufficiency,' Arthur Ford said at last with ponderous affability, 'then I vote we adjourn to the lounge for coffee.' He gave his wife an un-subtle nod. 'I'm sure Miss Brettell would like to go upstairs and make herself even more beautiful.' He bowed towards Celia with heavy gallantry. 'If that is possible.' His gaze took in Andrew Rolt and Robin. 'We males will see about setting up a table for cards.'

Oh . . . oh . . . Lord . . . Celia said in her mind with a long despairing groan. I simply cannot face it. 'That will be delightful,' she said gaily. She picked up her evening bag and followed Beryl into the passage and up the stairs.

In the sitting-room Andrew settled himself uneasily into an armchair and watched Robin dealing with the card table. A pleasant enough lad, studious-looking, a bit on the quiet side perhaps, but time would probably take care of that.

'And now for a little treat,' Arthur Ford said. He switched on the television set, fiddled with the controls. A line of girls sprang into view, beautiful, willowy, in minimal costumes.

'Ah,' Arthur said with satisfaction. 'Can't beat a good beauty contest. I thought we might just manage to catch the end of it.' He glanced at Rolt. 'Which of them do you fancy?' He stabbed a finger at the screen. 'I like that one – oh, they've moved – there she is now, second from – oh, they've moved again.'

Rolt nodded vaguely, scarcely seeing the brilliant colours, the shifting pattern of curving forms. Arthur sat down in a chair close to Rolt, looked over at Robin who had finished his task and was now levelling an expressionless glance at the smiling beauties. 'How would you like to find one of those in your Christmas stocking?' Arthur said to Robin with forceful matiness. Robin drew a long weary breath. 'I'd have been glued to the set at your age,' Arthur added rousingly. 'Blasé, all you youngsters these days, that's what it is, thoroughly spoilt, the lot of you.' Robin closed his eyes for an instant; he remained standing by the card table.

Upstairs in the front bedroom Beryl sat at the dressing-table, fluffing powder over her face. Celia Brettell was perched on one of the twin beds, watching her. Beryl picked up a comb and made a series of little dabs at her coiffure; still brightly blonde, she intended to give it another five years before she changed over to pale ash.

'I do like your ear-rings,' she said. 'Jade, aren't they?' Celia nodded. 'A present, I expect?' Beryl said. Celia made no reply. 'Sor – ry,' Beryl said loudly. 'Shouldn't have asked.' She sprang to her feet. 'If you're ready, we'll go down. I must say,' she added as she threw open the door, 'I envy you your job. Travelling about, meeting lots of different people.' They reached the hall, and she flung open the door of the sitting-room. 'And that car you drive, I like that very much.' They went into the room.'

'I like your car, too,' Robin said from his station by the card table. 'But your offside wing mirror has had a knock. I noticed it yesterday afternoon.' There was a brief silence. 'In Grange Road,' Robin added, a note of hesitation creeping into his voice. He had been about to add, 'Outside the

Unicorn' but decided against it for some reason he couldn't clearly define.

'And pray, what took you to Grange Road yesterday afternoon?' Arthur demanded of his son.

'I was sent out from CeeJay,' Robin said in a flat tone. 'On a business errand.'

Rolt turned his head and looked at Celia. 'I didn't know you were in Barbourne yesterday,' he said in a low voice. 'I understood you were going up to Leeds.'

Celia smiled, glanced at Robin with an easy, tolerant expression. 'So I did. I was in Leeds all day. Must have been some other car Robin saw.'

Again there was a little silence. It was her car, Robin said in his mind. And she was sitting at the wheel, with her head stuck out of the side window, saying goodbye. That had been a man's figure, partly obscured from Robin's view, bending down to speak to her. A man's shoulder and arm, glimpsed at that angle. Robin said nothing; he merely looked back at Celia with a level regard.

Arthur gave his son a reflective stare. 'Do we actually require your presence here any longer?' he asked. 'We don't need five for cards. Didn't you say you were going to play squash at the youth club? You can cut along, I'm sure Mr Rolt won't mind. And while you're at it,' he added, 'take some of that fruit from the bowl in the dining-room, shove it in a bag and call into Gran's with it.' Arthur's mother, old, ailing and crotchety, lived near the youth club. 'It won't take you half a mo to pop in and and see how she is. Give her my love, tell her I'll look in tomorrow evening.'

CHAPTER VIII

OCTOBER MOVED forward in a succession of sweet mild days. Drifts of leaves in the Barbourne parks, on the slopes of the hills. In the well-mannered squares the trees turned colour, copper, russet and bronze. Morning mists; spiders' webs in the garden hedges, gleaming steely silver when the sun at last broke through. Noontides brilliantly gold, declining into softly hazy afternoons.

The citizens of Barbourne settled themselves into the comfortable routines of autumn. Preparations for the Charities Fair went briskly forward. And Hazel Ratcliff moved house.

On the morning after Uncle George dropped six feet into his final resting-place, William Yoxall marched boldly up to Hazel's sanctum at the Kingfisher and offered her the tenancy of the middle flat at Fairview. She accepted at once, joyfully. I'll move in on Saturday week, she decided after a few moments' consideration; that would give her time to dispose of superfluous furniture, have a good sortout.

On the Thursday evening before she was due to leave the cottage she went through the rooms listing items that were to go to the local saleroom. In the sitting-room she stood for some minutes looking down at the large Chesterfield where her mother had spent so much time during her last illness. She would dearly have loved to keep the sofa but it was far too big for the flat.

She sighed, seeing her mother lying there, still working sometimes at her embroidery, smiling, talking cheerfully to visitors who called in, neighbours, friends, girls from the office. On a couple of red-letter occasions Stephen Maynard had sat over there in the big chair by the hearth, chatting pleasantly to the invalid.

She walked over to the chair and dropped into it, leaning back with her eyes closed, feeling the cushioned embrace warm about her. In the depths of her mind, below the level of conscious thought, memory began to wake.

That old story Paul Hulme had got hold of – or concocted or distorted or somehow dredged up – what precisely was it he had said that far-off day, perched on the edge of her desk in Tyler's agency? Paul was still at school then, working at Tyler's during the holidays, acting as general dogsbody in that happy time when the agency still knew what it was to experience a rush period. It was shortly after Stephen Maynard had first called in at Tyler's. She had been sitting at her desk, checking her copies against his manuscript, and Paul had leaned over as he chatted to her, had glanced down and seen the name on the title sheet. 'Maynard,' he'd said with a significant inflection, 'I could tell you something about Stephen Maynard.'

A ridiculous story, she had thought at the time, a tale manufactured from gossip, rumour, spite or malice; certainly nothing any sensible person would take seriously. She had said so forcibly to Paul and he had lapsed in the end into sulky adolescent silence. Now she strove to resurrect the details, perhaps after all not entirely invented, perhaps with some slender basis in reality.

It seemed that Hulme had a cousin who was a journalist on the *Gazette*, a regional newspaper of some standing, and the cousin had told Hulme that a year or two before Stephen Maynard came to Barbourne, there had been a certain amount of talk and speculation about the death of Maynard's wife. At the time Maynard had been teaching in Eldersleigh, a town at the other side of the county. Hazel couldn't remember the exact details but the salient facts as Paul had related them concerned Maynard's young,

79

pretty and flirtatious wife, a noisy quarrel, an inquisitive neighbour and an electric hairdryer.

She frowned. Mrs Rolt was going about with Stephen Maynard; it might do no harm to drop a hint, just the merest suggestion that perhaps one might exercise caution in new relationships. Hazel pursed her lips and nodded to herself. It was possibly always best if people knew what was said, then they could never turn round afterwards and blame one for keeping silent.

She glanced round the room. Yes, she was pleased to be leaving. It would in many ways be very convenient to move into Fairview.

Alison finished reading her post. She sat down at the kitchen table, poured herself another cup of coffee and sent an embracing glance over the day ahead. From the flat upstairs came the sudden sound of a door banged shut. She looked up at the ceiling with a frown.

At lunch-time on Saturday she had come home from the office to find a removal van drawn up outside Fairview, men traipsing in and out carrying furniture, and Mrs Lingard – who cleaned in each of the three flats – standing in the hall grumbling about mud, dust and scratches on the paintwork.

'Not a word mentioned to me about anyone moving into the middle flat,' Mrs Lingard had complained to Alison. 'Mr Yoxall really could have said.' Yes, and Hazel really could have said too, Alison had thought. Hazel had worked at the agency as usual throughout Saturday morning, had uttered not one syllable to Alison about the fact that her goods and chattels were being carted in through the front door of Fairview. And ten minutes after Alison had halted in astonishment at the gate, Hazel had marched coolly up the steps, had given Alison – still standing in the hall exchanging observations with Mrs Lingard – no more than a civil word and a look, had introduced herself to Mrs Lingard and then gone calmly upstairs to her new abode.

But after all, Alison said to herself now as she took her breakfast things into the scullery, I suppose there is no real reason why Hazel should inform me of her plans, I'm certainly no crony of hers. She raised her shoulders, dismissing the subject.

But it wasn't quite so easy to shrug away the recollection of the malicious insinuations Hazel had introduced into what had started out as a perfectly normal business conversation in the course of the morning's work at Kingfisher last Friday. Alison made a face of distaste, remembering the nature of those unsubtle, unpleasant hints. Stephen Maynard's wife had died some years ago; there had been an inquest and a verdict of Accidental Death. He had told her the bald facts at a very early stage in their friendship. He had related them calmly and flatly, with an air of profound detachment that seemed to result from the conscious and habitual exercise of discipline, controlling old and savage pain, rather than from indifference or callousness.

I suppose there will always be those who will whisper and gossip whenever chance offers them an excuse to peer through the slats at other people's lives, she thought with repugnance; such persons certainly didn't merit the dignity of serious attention.

She moved briskly about the flat, tidying, straightening. In the sitting-room she halted, looking down with a frown at a little pile of papers she had left on top of her davenport a couple of days ago. Surely she had never arranged the papers with such neat precision, the edges so trimly squared. She was seized again by the disquieting notion that someone was going through her things. The feeling had begun to visit her only in the last few days; she had done her best to brush it away, believing it was simply an irrational reaction to Hazel Ratcliff's presence in the house.

She picked up the papers, personal documents of various kinds, and put them away in a drawer. She was unable to lock the drawer, there were no keys to the davenport. Perhaps Mrs Lingard had marshalled the papers into order yesterday morning, on her routine cleaning visit. Yes, that was probably it. She glanced round the room, pleasant, well-proportioned, some of her father's paintings on the walls, a bowl of scarlet dahlias on a low table. There seemed no other sign of disturbance.

I must guard against getting paranoid, she told herself with a wry grimace. People who lived on their own often began to develop odd little fancies.

I know, she thought suddenly, I'll phone Colin Viner later on this morning. I'll ask him if he can meet me for lunch. I'll speak to him about it, see what he thinks. He would probably tell her not to be so silly.

She went into the bedroom, feeling better, more braced, ready for the day. She opened the wardrobe to take out her coat and paused again with her hand on the rail. On the shelf above the rail she kept her handbags. One bag, made of soft blue suède, she always laid flat on its side; if she stood it up it tended to sag out of shape. Now the bag was propped up against her brown leather satchel. She would never have left it like that. Or could she have done so, absentmindedly, for once? She sighed, put up a hand to her head, then with an angry movement snatched her coat and shrugged it on.

Half past twelve. Viner shuffled together the papers on his desk, stood up, yawned and stretched. Another twenty minutes before he could get off for lunch. He went out into the corridor and strolled along to the main hall; he paused and glanced idly at the sparse scattering of people.

Complainers mostly. You could always tell by the stance, the tone of voice. Over by the door old James Ottaway had waylaid Inspector Bennett, was holding forth about confetti littering the streets in the vicinity of churches.

'Sweep it up if you don't like it, old chap,' Bennett said brusquely.

A stoutish middle-aged woman wearing the uniform of a district nurse came hurrying into the reception area. She had a fresh healthy colour, her grey hair was drawn back into a knot.

'Oh – Inspector – ' she said as soon as she caught sight of Bennett. He turned and gave her a wary look.

'Yes, Mrs Cope?'

'It's the dark nights coming on again,' she said rapidly. 'And I have to be out in all weathers, as you very well know.'

'And your specific request this time?' Bennett asked, briefly closing his eyes.

'The lighting,' she said forcefully. Bennett raised his shoulders, let them drop again. 'They ought to continue the lighting over the hills.' She stabbed a finger at him. 'And don't go telling me it's impossible. Men can get to the moon, the council can light the path over the hills.'

'I'll bear it all in mind,' Bennett said with weary resignation. On the desk a phone rang. 'If you'll excuse me,' he said, abandoning her with alacrity. Viner watched as Mrs Cope took her disgruntled departure. Bennett raised a hand and signalled to him. 'It's for you.'

'Hello there,' Alison's voice said when Viner picked up the receiver. 'Any chance of your meeting me for lunch?'

By twenty past one the restaurant was almost full. Alison finished her soup, crumbled the remains of her bread roll. 'Hulme strikes me as a rather odd young man,' she said on a musing note. 'There's something about his manner, an impression of hostility just below the surface.'

'It might be nothing personal as far as you're concerned,'

Viner said mildly. 'It might simply be that he doesn't like women.'

'That had occurred to me.' She frowned suddenly. 'But I saw him a couple of days ago with Mandy Webb, they seemed on very friendly terms.' Again she had that vague feeling of ripples, interweavings. 'Though I never remember seeing Mandy Webb at Fairview when Hulme lived there.'

The filing system in Viner's mind flung up a scatter of details. 'Nineteen years old,' he said. 'Works at CeeJay as a shorthand-typist.' He caught Alison's questioning glance. 'Mandy Webb,' he said. 'A fringe of hair like a Yorkshire terrier.'

She laughed. 'Yes, that's the one. I knew her when I worked at Tyler's. She was just a raw junior then. Don't tell me she's been in trouble with the police?'

He shook his head. 'No. I just ran across her a week or two ago. A very commonplace sort of girl.'

'Yes, she is.' Alison felt all at once reassured. 'Rather a silly creature.' But surely no sillier than herself, making mountains out of molehills. Of course she'd simply been imagining things; no one was going through her belongings.

Viner watched the waitress clear away the soup, bring the roast pork. Difficult to realize that Alison, so poised, so sure of herself, had been a junior herself not all that long ago. Easy enough to see how she had come to marry Andrew Rolt. He cast his mind back to Rolt as he had seen him a week or so ago during a visit he had paid to CeeJay in the course of a not very important enquiry into the activities of a bunch of young hooligans who had got into the vehicle yard at night. Rolt had paused on his way out, had spoken to Viner as he stood talking to Arthur Ford. Viner had scrutinized his face, his bearing, with discreetly masked curiosity. A courteous, urbane man – and those restless, oddly boyish eyes looking out from the pleasant façade.

The waitress removed the serving dishes. Viner picked up his knife and fork and began to eat.

Stephen Maynard glanced out of the car window at the late-night streets, almost deserted at this time on a Wednesday. 'It'll be half term on the thirteenth and fourteenth,' he said to Alison sitting beside him. 'That's next Monday and Tuesday.'

He halted his car at the traffic lights, watched idly as a boy edged his way between the vehicles. The lad turned his head, paused for a moment and then smiled, raised a hand in greeting. 'Robin Ford,' Maynard said. 'Left the grammar school last year. Wanted to go into catering but his parents wouldn't hear of it. Not sufficiently classy for them. They were very keen for him to go to a university but he didn't have that kind of ability.'

'I know him slightly,' Alison said. 'His father works at CeeJay, with Andrew.'

'Oh yes, of course,' Stephen said. 'Surely Robin works there too? Yes, I remember now, in the end the parents did put him into business. I shouldn't have thought he was all that well suited to it. Not ruthless enough.'

The lights changed, he slid the car into motion. 'What about half term?' he said. 'Is there any chance of your getting some time off on one or both of those days?' His manner was relaxed, expansive, after a good dinner and an agreeable evening. 'We might take a trip somewhere interesting.'

'I'll try to arrange something,' Alison said. 'I'll speak to Judith Padmore tomorrow.' She pondered the matter briefly. 'She's going off on Friday afternoon herself, to stay with her married brother. She does that from time to time. I'll be holding the fort on Saturday morning, so I don't think she'll object if I take Monday off. I really don't think

I can ask for two days, though; this is quite a busy time of year.'

They reached Stephen's cottage. 'I hope the mild weather lasts over your holiday,' she said as she stepped from the car. 'I'd enjoy a break.'

The cottage was mid-Victorian, architecturally undistinguished but sufficiently roomy, comfortable, and with a large garden. Stephen went into the kitchen to make coffee. Alison wandered round the sitting-room, idly examining its furnishings.

On either side of the chimney breast, shelves laden with books ran from floor to ceiling. She picked out a volume here and there, glanced at it, returned it to its place. At the end of one shelf a number of books lay on their sides in a small pile. She took up the pile and saw underneath a photograph frame, face down.

Casual curiosity made her turn the frame over. She glanced down and for a moment imagined with a thrust of surprise that she was looking at a photograph of herself. But in the next instant she saw the message written in a lively hand across the dress: To my darling Stephen, With all my love, Ann.

She drew a sharp breath. Ann Maynard, Stephen's wife. From the kitchen she heard the rattle of crockery. For a moment she hesitated, then with a decisive gesture she put the frame on the shelf. She had just replaced the books when Stephen came back into the room.

The canteen at CeeJay was almost empty at eleven-fifteen on Thursday morning. 'You're on the late side,' one of the assistants said to Mandy Webb as she came up to the counter.

'Yes.' Mandy gave a sigh that changed into a long yawn. 'There was a bit of a panic on, some papers that got mislaid, you know how it is – don't anybody dare go for coffee till we find the precious papers.' She stretched, grinned. 'Any doughnuts left? I'm starving.'

At a table over by the window she saw Robin Ford looking out at the steely sky. She hesitated, then shrugged and steered a course towards the vacant seat opposite him. Might as well ask him to the birthday party. He probably wouldn't turn out to be the life and soul of the festivity but he'd come in useful with the chores. And he might just conceivably loosen up and enjoy himself. She gave his profile a critical glance as she approached. Mm, he wouldn't be at all bad-looking if only he had a little more bounce.

'Mind if I sit here?' she said, slapping down her tray and drawing back the chair without waiting for his response. 'Wake up!' she said in a friendly fashion as he continued to gaze up at the sky.

'Oh – I'm sorry.' His head came round, he gave her a faintly startled look. 'I wasn't aware – '

'That's all right,' she said cheerfully. She took a huge bite from a doughnut. 'Saturday evening,' she said, still chewing. 'Tessa and me, we're having a party. It's Tessa's birthday. Come along, it ought to be quite lively.'

He gave her a thoughtful glance. 'Saturday,' he said. 'I'm afraid I can't manage that. Mr Rolt's coming to supper.' Saturday was the twentieth anniversary of his parents' wedding. His father had announced the fact to Rolt well in advance; his manner had strongly suggested that he would interpret as a mortal insult any attempt on Rolt's part to wriggle out of the festive evening.

'Rolt?' Mandy said on a high, interested note.

'Yes,' Robin said flatly. 'And Miss Brettell.'

Mandy inclined her head in a movement that said, Well now, fancy that, didn't realize you were on terms with the mighty.

'I can't very well go out,' Robin said.

'Yes, I can see that.' She took another vast bite. 'But the

87

party won't begin till say nine or ten, it won't get warmed up for at least another hour or two. Rolt and his lady-love won't stay at your place all that late, will they?'

'No, I shouldn't think so. I expect they'll be gone by eleven.'

'Well then, come to our place after they've gone home. Simple enough.'

He smiled suddenly. Oh yes, a distinct improvement when he smiles, she thought. 'Yes, I could do that,' he said. 'I don't see why not.'

'Good,' she said briskly. 'We'll expect you then. Leofric Gardens, number twenty-nine. No need to tell you which flat, you won't be able to avoid recognizing it, there'll be a bit of a din going on.' She grinned. 'We always ask the neighbours, it avoids trouble. Most of them are young, they come along. Those that don't want to come have fair warning, they clear off somewhere peaceful for the evening. It works quite well.'

Alison was undressing for bed on Thursday night when the phone rang in the sitting-room. She yawned, went to answer it, gave her number as she always did. No reply. 'Barbourne 7583,' she repeated, more loudly. Still no answer.

'Hello!' she said sharply. 'Is there anyone there?' The sound of someone breathing. 'Hello!' she said again.

At the other end the little clatter of the receiver being restored to its stand.

On Friday morning Inspector Bennett dropped Sergeant Viner outside a fishmonger's in the High Street. There had been a clumsy break-in a couple of days before, nothing much taken, amateurs most likely.

'Shouldn't take you too long to deal with that little lot,' Bennett said. 'Then there's that business over on the housing estate. See you about eleven or twelve.' He pulled away from the kerb.

As Viner turned towards the shop entrance he saw Tessa Drake coming towards him. In the few moments before she caught sight of him he thought how young she seemed. And really very pretty. Then their eyes met and her face broke into a delighted smile. She quickened her pace, almost ran up to him.

'I'm so glad I've seen you,' she said a little breathlessly. 'I was hoping I would. It's my birthday tomorrow. We're having a bit of a party, Mandy and me, at our place. Will you come? I wish you would.'

'That's very kind of you,' he said in a formal tone. The lines of her face immediately drooped. Like a child, he thought, no subterfuge. 'But I'm afraid I must say no. I'm going off for the weekend – till Sunday morning at least.' He fancied a breath of country air, intended to do some walking.

She sent an intent look over his features. 'If you get back earlier than you expect – or if you change your mind and don't go away after all, just come. I'd be very pleased.' She gave him a sudden mischievous grin. 'I believe you've got a note of our address.'

The phone rang shortly after Alison got home from King-fisher. Her mind was still full of the day's work as she went to answer it and it was several seconds before she realized that the caller was declaring neither an identity nor a purpose.

'Who is that?' she demanded loudly, urgently. 'Who's there?' She felt threatened, invaded. 'What do you want?'

And then once again, the distinct sound of the receiver being replaced at the other end.

CHAPTER IX

As soon as Hazel Ratcliff opened her eyes on Saturday morning she knew she was going to have one of her heads. She pressed her fingers against her temples, trying to diminish the dull, ominous ache, forced herself out of bed, went over to the window and drew back the curtains. A clear bright morning. At least it was going to be a fine day for the Fair.

She looked back at the bed with longing, then resolutely put temptation from her.

A couple of hours later she was sitting at her desk at Kingfisher with her head cradled in her hands when she heard someone come into the room. She sat up, did her best to appear briskly professional, but without success.

'You look terrible.' Alison stood at the other side of the desk, eyeing her. 'I thought you didn't seem well earlier on. What's the matter? Have you got 'flu?'

Hazel shook her head. 'No, it's one of my migraines. I'll be all right. I've taken some tablets.'

'You're going straight home,' Alison said firmly. 'I'll call a taxi.'

'No, really,' Hazel said with protest. 'I can't leave. I have to go out to the Wheatsheaf at eleven. It's for Mr Wickham. I can't let him down.'

'Don't worry about Mr Wickham,' Alison said. 'I'll send someone else.'

'There isn't anyone else free,' Hazel said. 'Or at least not anyone we could send to Mr Wickham.' He was one of her VIP clients. He had come over with her from Tyler's, certainly could not be entrusted to some feather-brained girl.

'I'll find someone,' Alison said. She could go herself if necessary. Quite some time since she'd actually been out on a secretarial job, she'd rather enjoy it.

In the first-floor room at the Wheatsheaf Alison drew the final page from her typewriter and checked it carefully. Easy to make a mistake in this kind of work – complicated export forms and customs declarations. When she had finished she stood up and wandered about the room; it was one that Mr Wickham retained permanently at the hotel. The Wheatsheaf was close to the airport, was situated centrally in the wide area in which Wickham conducted the dealings necessary to maintain a steady flow of antiques, *objets d'art*, paintings, prints and books towards various outlets in Europe and the United States.

At this moment he was down in the bar playing host to some friends in the trade who were just off to attend an auction in the neighbourhood. He's taking his time about it, Alison thought with growing irritation after she had spent five minutes wandering about and staring out of the window. She couldn't take herself off; she wasn't certain that Wickham had no further work for her. And it would be grossly unprofessional for her to go down to the bar and remind him of her existence.

She knelt down by a packing case filled, according to the declaration, with English porcelain. The top had not been fastened down but it was impossible to catch a glimpse of the padded and wrapped contents. Beside the case a number of stout cardboard tubes lay on a table; one tube had not yet been sealed. She picked it up and gently drew the contents part way out of the container. Coloured prints of Impressionist paintings. Ah – some modern examples too. She began to finger them carefully apart, looking down at them with critical interest.

There was a sound from the doorway and she glanced

up. Wickham was standing on the threshold, looking at her with surprise.

'Oh – I'm sorry,' she said, immediately beginning to ease the contents back into the tube. 'I'm afraid I got rather bored, I'd finished the typing.'

'Let me do that,' he said with a friendly air, taking the tube from her and looking down at the prints. 'I ought not to have kept you waiting so long.' He restored the cylinder to its place on the table. 'Now, I'll just cast an eye over the work you've done and then I think that will be all.' He picked up the sheaf of papers and scrutinized them. She watched him for a few minutes; he was a rather tall, heavily built man of about sixty. A tanned skin, short grey hair. A strong intelligent face.

She turned her head and looked out of the window at the hotel forecourt, cars drawn up, a busy to and fro of clients, staff carrying luggage. A man stepped out of a car and came towards the entrance. She knew him at once: Brian Yardley. He was carrying a briefcase and a brown-paper parcel. He paused, looked up at the hotel and caught sight of her. His face broke into a grin; he raised a hand and waved. She made no acknowledgement. She turned from the window and saw that Wickham was shuffling the papers together.

'This seems perfectly satisfactory,' he said pleasantly. 'I don't think I need keep you any longer.'

The remainder of the morning at Kingfisher was more than usually irritating. Loose ends of the week's work that stubbornly refused to be neatly tied; clients ringing up at the last moment to demand extra staff on Monday for a rush period they might have foreseen days ago.

At twelve-thirty Alison sprang to her feet and snatched her coat from its hook. 'I'm going home,' she said aloud. 'I've had enough for today.' And the pleasures of the

92

Charities Fair still to come, the entire afternoon and probably the best part of the evening stretching ahead in strenuous boredom. She gave a long despairing sigh and went at a rush towards the stairs.

Out in the sunshine she felt momentarily restored to better spirits. And then a voice called her name, a man's voice, gratingly familiar. She halted and turned her head. A few yards away Brian Yardley was closing the door of his car.

'Hang on,' he said. He came towards her with haste. In one hand he clutched his briefcase. He suddenly put out the other hand and she was seized with a sharp fear that he was going to strike her.

'Oh, leave me alone!' she said in a low vehement tone, jerking herself back out of his reach. The heel of her shoe caught on the edge of the lowest step leading down from the Kingfisher; her foot was wrenched agonizingly sideways. She screwed up her face in pain, tears sprang to her eyes. She stumbled, almost fell to the pavement, put out a hand and managed to regain her balance but inadvertently put her weight again on the injured ankle. She let out a sobbing breath, unable to speak.

'Here – let me –' Yardley slipped a hand under her elbow, his face full of concern.

'Take your hands off me,' she managed to say. 'Get out of my way.'

Yoxall, who had been looking out of a second-floor window, came running down into the street. 'Let me help you,' he said urgently. 'Here, lean on me.'

'If you could just call me a taxi. I'll be all right.'

'I'm afraid you won't be all right for a little while. You won't be able to put much weight on that foot.'

She made a sound of anger. 'Now I'll have to find someone to take over my job at the Fair this afternoon.'

'I'm going to take you to the doctor,' Yoxall said. 'And

then I'm going to take you back to your flat. No, it's no trouble, I won't hear of your going alone.'

'Kindly don't beat about the bush,' Celia Brettell said, her voice sharply accusing at the other end of the line. 'I simply want to know what game you think you're playing.'

'I'm not playing any game,' Alison said wearily. She was lying back in an easy chair in her sitting-room, her feet resting on a low stool. A stout walking-stick with a curved handle – lent to her by Mr Yoxall – was propped against the arm of her chair. 'If you could see me at this moment,' she added with a faint smile, 'you wouldn't think me capable of much in the way of games. I've wrenched my ankle, I'm out of action for the time being.'

'I'm sorry to hear that,' Celia said a trifle grudgingly. 'But I'm not going to let you evade the issue. Why on earth are you keeping Andrew dangling? You don't want him, let him go.'

'I'm certainly not holding on to him,' Alison said with energy. 'Far from it. For your information we are currently in the process of arranging a divorce.' She heard the sharp intake of Celia's breath.

'Oh,' Celia said. 'I didn't know – '

A thought flashed into Alison's mind. 'While we're talking about games,' she said in a clear, incisive voice, 'have you by any chance taken to playing an unpleasant little game yourself?'

'Unpleasant little game?' Celia echoed.

'Yes. Ringing this number, to be precise. Uttering not a solitary syllable, and then ringing off.'

'Why on earth would I play a stupid trick like that?'

'I'm sure I don't know,' Alison said crisply. 'That's why I'm asking you.'

'I can't imagine why you should think it was me,' Celia said. 'I do most positively assure you it was not. It's prob-

94

ably just one of those heavy breathers – you know – everyone's pestered by them at some time or other. They're quite harmless.'

'I suppose it's possible,' Alison said abruptly.

'By the way,' Celia said on a placatory note, 'please don't tell Andrew I phoned you – ' she gave a little laugh – 'about your hanging on to him.'

Alison suppressed a sigh. 'No, I won't tell him. And now I must ring off. I've got several calls to make. This wretched ankle means I've got to scout round and find someone to replace me at the Fair this afternoon.'

She had made some calls and was about to dial yet another number when the phone rang. She picked up the receiver, impatient at the delay, and gave her number.

Silence. Oh Lord, she said to herself, profoundly irritated, not the old non-speaking nutter again. But just in case it wasn't she repeated clearly, 'Barbourne 7583.'

No reply. 'Are you insane?' she asked in a bright, cutting tone although some part of her brain sent out a warning signal: Don't communicate with a distorted personality, sever the connection instantly. 'What purpose is served by this behaviour?' she added, in spite of the signal buzzing louder in her brain. 'What sane purpose, that is?'

At the other end of the line she heard the little clatter of the receiver being set down without haste.

CHAPTER X

IT HAD TURNED very cold in the night. White frost still glittered the tufts of grass in the hollows of the hill. But the sun shone brilliantly, there was no wind, the leaves lay crisp and coppery underfoot.

Viner reached the top of the slope and stood looking

down at Barbourne, and beyond, at the beautiful prospect of woods and fields. He had enjoyed himself immensely, had slept at pubs, walked all day in clear sparkling weather.

Not a morning for standing still. He began to whistle as he set off down the path.

'Hey – mister!' a boy's voice, shrill, urgent. He turned.

'Yes?' Two lads, very young, nine or ten years old, came racing towards him. 'Do you want me?' he asked.

The foremost lad halted suddenly, his expression changed to one of lively alarm. 'You're a copper, aren't you?' he said accusingly. 'I've seen you.'

Viner raised his shoulders. 'We all have our grisly secrets,' he said, grinning. 'What did you want? To know the time?'

'No,' the second lad said, defiantly uncaring. 'We thought you might know about the murder.'

'Murder?' Viner frowned. 'What murder? Where?'

'She said, here in Barbourne,' the first lad supplied. 'I don't know whereabouts.'

'Who said?' Viner asked, his tone losing its sharp edge. Some idle rumour, no doubt.

'A woman in the newspaper shop. We went in for some sweets. She was talking to the man behind the counter. She said something about a woman from one of the agencies.'

'Not a woman,' the other boy said. 'She said a girl from one of the agencies.'

'Agency?' Viner said sharply. 'What kind of agency? Do you mean a secretarial agency?'

'I don't know,' the lad said with protest. 'I didn't understand what she meant when she said it. I tried to ask her but she told me to clear off. She said it wasn't the kind of thing we ought to be listening to.'

'One of the agencies,' Viner repeated. The words seemed to have an authentic ring, not the kind of thing a boy would conjure up from nowhere. 'Are you sure she said murder?' he asked.

The boy nodded impatiently. 'Yes, I keep telling you, that's what she said. I don't know whether she meant it was a woman who was murdered or a woman who did the murder.'

'You don't know nothing about it, do you?' the second lad said to Viner with sudden scorn. He jerked his head at his mate. 'Come on, I'll race you.' And they were gone, swooping down the other side of the hill.

Agencies, Viner said to himself. Was the woman even talking about Barbourne? Had she even been referring to fact? Might it not have been some play, film, television or radio programme she was talking about? Had she even existed outside the boys' imagination?

But the unease remained. He became aware that he was growing chilled, that he was still halted where the boys had stopped him. Hot coffee – that was what he needed. It struck him that he was fairly close to Fairview. He could call in on Alison, ask her if she'd heard anything. He plunged off again down the slope, quickening his pace.

Probably nothing more than an idle tale. And even if there was something in it, it was probably nothing at all to do with the Kingfisher. He began to construct a couple of sentences he could say to Alison in case the whole thing was moonshine, in case – it suddenly occurred to him – he was disturbing her from a Sunday morning late lie-in. He paused at the thought, half minded to turn round. But a moment later his feet carried him on again.

Some distance farther on he came to a sharp turn in the path and here it was possible by craning the neck to look down into Highfield Road. He stopped, leaned out over the path at a perilous angle, motivated by some impulse he could scarcely define.

Below him he saw a crowd rigid on the pavement, the gleaming tops of a row of official cars.

'Christ!' he said aloud. His heart began to beat in wild,

massive thuds. He drew back from the edge, put a hand up to his face. Then all at once he remembered Hazel Ratcliff; she lived at Fairview, worked at Kingfisher.

He began to run down the rest of the slope, flying over the stony ground. Now he was very near to where the path dropped to the road. A gate barred the way. He was forced to stop, open it, close it behind him from old training. A sound rose suddenly up from the waiting crowd, a long sobbing sigh. He looked down and saw that the men were bringing out the plastic shell, the temporary resting-place.

And saw also, following the men, alone and unsteady, her face distorted and stricken, the plump ungainly figure of Hazel Ratcliff.

CHAPTER XI

'ALISON EURYDICE ROLT,' the constable said into the phone. 'Twenty-six years old. Married, living apart from her husband.' He spelled out the tricky middle name, went on to ladle out such sparse items of information as he was allowed to feed to the Press: the cleaning woman, Mrs Lingard, calling at Fairview this morning to offer friendly assistance to Mrs Rolt in view of her accident; the lack of any response to her repeated rings at the doorbell; the summoning of the landlord, William Yoxall, from the top flat; the use of his pass key; the discovery of Mrs Rolt lying back in an easy chair in her sitting-room, clearly dead for many hours. A walking stick lying on the carpet to the right of her chair; an overturned footstool nearby.

'The post mortem is in progress now,' the constable said. 'We'll probably have the pathologist's report tomorrow.' He made no reference to other facts, not yet definitely established, on which Authority had for the time being clamped an iron hand: the cushion, still resting on the dead woman's face when Yoxall threw open the door, a powerful indication of death by suffocation; the preparations for a light meal under way in the kitchen, the eggs whisked in a basin, two slices of bread ready to toast, a little pile of grated cheese on a plate with the grater standing beside it, the omelette pan placed on the electric cooker with a knob of butter inside it, the butter still unmelted; water and coffee measured into the electric percolator but the appliance not yet plugged in; the cooker control in the OFF position.

'If you ring again tomorrow,' the constable said, 'we should be in a position to let you have more detailed information.'

The next curve in the road disclosed the busy spaces of the airport. 'Take it easy,' Inspector Bennett said to the driver. 'Wickham's plane isn't due out for another half-hour.' Some little time had elapsed before routine questioning had uncovered the fact that Mrs Rolt had gone out to Wickham's hotel on Saturday morning to carry out secretarial duties. Hazel Ratcliff hadn't mentioned the visit, which had come to light when Yoxall spoke of it in the course of his statement.

No particular significance would have been attached to Mrs Rolt's trip to the Wheatsheaf had it not been for a sudden flash of recollection on the part of Mrs Lingard. The cleaning woman had finished relating her story to the police and was sitting in Hazel Ratcliff's flat where she had been instructed to wait in case further questioning was needed, when she suddenly clapped her hand to her mouth, sprang to her feet and rushed downstairs to snatch at the sleeve of a sergeant.

'I've just remembered,' she said. 'Mrs Rolt had a phone call yesterday lunch-time. From a Mr Wickham.' It seemed

99

that shortly after one o'clock, while Mrs Lingard was standing by a window at Fairview watching out for Mrs Rolt who normally paid her wages on Saturdays, the phone had rung and she'd taken a message.

'Mr Wickham wanted to know if Mrs Rolt had got back to the flat,' she told the sergeant. 'I said she hadn't, not knowing of course that she'd hurt her leg and that Mr Yoxall had taken her to the doctor's. Mr Wickham said he'd either phone again later or he'd call in at Fairview during the afternoon or evening. I fully intended to write down the message as I always do but he'd just about rung off when poor dear Mrs Rolt turned up, looking really quite done up after her fall. What with Mr Yoxall fussing about and me getting her settled and then staying on to make her something to eat, well, as you can imagine, the phone call went clean out of my head.'

So here they were now with orders to snatch Wickham from his plane and bring him in for questioning. 'A waste of time if you ask me,' Inspector Bennett said sourly as he stepped out of the car. 'Rolt killed her, I'm damned sure of it. Always the husband in a case like this.'

Fifteen minutes later, with Wickham standing beside them, resigned and equable, they were busy retrieving his baggage. 'Heavy stuff you've got there,' Bennett said, watching a couple of men lifting a packing case.

Wickham raised his shoulders. 'There's porcelain in that one.' He glanced idly about at the restless activity, the knots of passengers. His hands were thrust into his pockets; he looked detached, at ease.

'That lot over there,' Bennett said, nodding towards some long cylindrical packages. 'What's in those?'

'Prints,' Wickham said. 'Old Masters mainly, some modern stuff. There's a big demand for British-made prints in Europe, we do them rather well over here.' He glanced at his watch. 'I very much hope,' he said with a pleasant comradely air, 'that at some stage in this particular game someone is going to take note of the old English custom of eating lunch at one o'clock on Sunday.'

Andrew Rolt's voice had taken on a note of deep weariness. 'Miss Brettell and I left the Fords' house at about ten past or a quarter past ten yesterday evening,' he said. 'I remember looking at my watch at a minute or two after ten and thinking that we might be able to get away in another few minutes.' He gave the faintest shadow of a smile. 'An evening at the Fords is not the sort of occasion one would care to prolong.'

Across the desk Detective Chief Inspector Naylor made no reply to this hint of pleasantry. 'You drove Miss Brettell back to her flat,' he said, as if repeating some statement of Rolt's.

Andrew shook his head, drew a long breath. 'No, I did not. I explained that to you earlier. We both went to the Fords' house in our own cars and so we left in our own cars.' He spoke slowly and carefully now, but with the slightest suggestion of slurring at the ends of words as if his tongue had begun to feel thick in his mouth. 'Celia said she was tired and wanted to go straight home to bed. I'd had a pretty long day myself, I thought I'd get an early night too.'

'So you did what?' Naylor pressed him.

Andrew looked at him with his head tilted back, his jaw drooping open, his eyes half closed. 'I've already told you all this. I drove home, put my car in the garage, let myself into the house and went upstairs to bed.'

Naylor stood up. 'You can go home,' he said abruptly. Rolt jerked his eyes open in surprise. 'If we need you we'll send for you,' Naylor added. He watched the door close behind Rolt. A few moments later a constable knocked at the door.

'I'm sorry to bother you, sir,' he said, 'but Mr Wickham's getting rather impatient. He's very anxious to have a word with you.'

Naylor flexed his shoulders. 'And I'm anxious to have a word with Master Wickham,' he said briskly. 'Wheel him in.' The constable was just about to go when Naylor said, 'Hang on a moment. Get Inspector Bennett to come along first. I think I'll have him here while I talk to Wickham.'

'I can't see why there's all this delay in talking to me,' Wickham said as he came into the room a minute or two later. I'm a businessman, my time's valuable, I can't afford to – '

'Yes, yes, I understand all that,' Naylor said blandly. He nodded towards a chair. 'Now why don't you sit down and we can have our little chat right away. We'll let you off century English fairings might be wholly or partly full of that.' He spread his hands. 'Just a simple matter of a little co-operation.'

Wickham gave him a sharp glance, turned his head and slanted a look at Bennett, who gazed back at him with an expressionless face. 'Of course I'm anxious to co-operate,' Wickham said in a milder tone. 'In every way that I possibly can.'

'Glad to hear it,' Naylor said amiably. 'Makes the job much easier.' He nodded again at the chair. Wickham lowered himself on to the edge of the seat as if he fancied it had been wired to produce electric shocks in the occupant.

'Now.' Naylor dropped into his own chair, fixed Wickham with a no-nonsense eye. 'We might as well get started.

Five minutes later he leaned back in his chair and gave a little grunt of cautious satisfaction. Wickham remained bolt upright in his seat, continued to watch Naylor with an unwavering glance. He hadn't been very forthcoming about the fact that he had called on Mrs Rolt on Saturday afternoon, had indeed for some time not exactly lied about the visit but danced energetically all round the fact, doing his best to allow them to assume that he hadn't gone in person to Fairview but had merely spoken to Mrs Lingard on the phone at lunch-time and had then taken no further steps to contact Mrs Rolt.

But they'd finally got him to admit that he had called at the flat – not from any positive knowledge on the part of the police but merely from a hunch and by dint of jumping on his story from every conceivable angle. He hadn't been in the least put out, had grinned and said, 'Can't blame me for trying. No one likes to get mixed up in a murder, old boy. And it's damned inconvenient to have to kick my heels in the hotel for another day or two.'

Yes, he had spoken to Mrs Rolt. Had she personally admitted him to the flat? He hedged again at that, still uncertain what they actually knew. Eventually he shrugged and said, 'It so happens it was Miss Ratcliff who let me in. She was just leaving the house when I arrived.' Shortly before two-thirty; on her way to the Fair, no doubt. And Miss Ratcliff hadn't seen fit to mention Wickham's visit to the police, Naylor pondered. Had she simply forgotten it? 'I know Miss Ratcliff of course,' Wickham said. 'She's the one who usually does my paperwork. I didn't see any point in ringing Mrs Rolt's bell and bringing her out to the front door, so I just went in. Miss Ratcliff mentioned that she'd hurt her foot.'

Yes, he had phoned Fairview a second time, had spoken to Mrs Rolt. She had agreed that he might call round. But had he in fact phoned twice? Naylor asked himself. Or had he merely appeared at Fairview without advising Mrs Rolt of his intention? In that case how had he intended to gain admittance to the flat? Was it by mere chance that Hazel Ratcliff had been on the doorstep when he turned up? Hazel Ratcliff . . . who had known Wickham for some considerable time . . .

'And the reason for your visit?' Naylor asked.

'Oh, purely a matter of business.' Wickham waved a hand. 'I was struck by Mrs Rolt's competence. I've felt more than once in recent months that it might be a good idea to take a personal assistant with me on some of my trips abroad. The longer, more important trips. It occurred to me on Saturday that Mrs Rolt might be an ideal person for such a post. She might welcome the occasional change from her desk in the agency, she would probably enjoy the work; she seemed more than usually knowledgeable about artistic matters. I thought it ought to be possible to arrange it without overmuch interference with her job at King-fisher.'

'And how did Mrs Rolt receive your proposition?'

'With marked interest. She promised to think it over, discuss it with me at a later date.' He had stayed no more than fifteen minutes at Fairview, had taken himself off to other business in a nearby town, could supply names and times if necessary.

Naylor stood up. 'All right,' he said. 'That'll be all for the moment.'

'For the moment?' Wickham said with protest. 'How much longer – '

Naylor held up a hand. 'We've already been into that. We're not trying to keep you away from your business out of spite or mischief.' They'd have to get an expert to examine every item in Wickham's baggage. He had a man on the job at that moment, phoning round. Not the easiest thing on a fine Sunday afternoon, laying hands on an art expert.

Wickham blew out a long resigned breath, nodded curtly, said with an attempt at cordiality, 'Ah well, nothing for it but to make the best of it, I suppose.'

'What do you make of him?' Naylor asked Bennett when the sound of Wickham's departure had ceased. 'Do you think he might have gone back to Fairview at around nine or nine-thirty in the evening? He might have fixed that with Mrs Rolt on his afternoon call. He might have said, 'Think it over, I'll call round this evening when you've had time to reflect on it.' She would have been very likely to sit down, lean back comfortably in her chair and chat with him if he had in fact called again in the evening.'

Bennett frowned. 'Are you implying that the man's some kind of nut? To attack her suddenly and without reason?'

'I didn't suggest it might be without reason,' Naylor said. 'She was up at the Wheatsheaf working for him that very morning. Who knows what piece of information she might have stumbled across that he didn't want broadcasting to the world?'

'Mm,' Bennett said. 'Sounds a bit far-fetched.'

'I'm not so sure,' Naylor said. 'Anyway, with luck we'll have someone to examine the baggage tomorrow.' Just in case Wickham had been up to any fraudulent tricks. Not all that difficult or uncommon in the art export business. The contents of cases didn't always coincide with the details given in the accompanying documents, and many consignments went through the Customs without any real check.

A box that had been declared as holding nineteenth-century English fairings might be wholly or partly full of priceless Chinese ceramics. Small, immensely valuable items could be secreted inside large and relatively valueless pieces. Containers might be constructed with false sides and bottoms. Hidden away in a consignment of fifth-rate oil paintings might be a Reynolds or a Rubens which had been reversed in its frame and then painted to show an uninspired still life to the enquiring eye.

Hollowed-out books could act as hiding-places for a

wide variety of costly objects or highly-priced contraband – including drugs. The risk of detection was minimal, the profits frequently enormous.

Naylor got to his feet, stretched his cramped muscles. 'At all events we can get cracking on the cushion and the chrysanthemum,' he said with a return of energy. According to Mrs Lingard the embroidered cushion that had been used to smother Mrs Rolt had not been part of the normal furnishings of the flat. She had never seen it before, and it had certainly not been there when she had left the flat at around two o'clock on Saturday. And the single large chrysanthemum head lying on the carpet a couple of feet away from where Mrs Rolt lay back in her chair – Mrs Lingard knew nothing of that either. There were no other chrysanthemums in the flat. And according to Mrs Lingard there had been no chrysanthemums in the flat in recent weeks. She was quite positive about it.

The flower head was fresh, broken off with an inch or so of stem still attached. A very fine, well-shaped bloom, an unusual shade, deeper than salmon-pink, not as vivid as flame, the deeply curved petals tipped with sulphur yellow.

'I've got men working on both matters now,' Bennett said. Naylor gave him a brief nod. The cushion was one of the type made for and sold at the Charities Fair. It could have arrived in Mrs Rolt's flat from one of several different sources. And the chrysanthemum could have been part of a bunch brought by some friend, lover or well-wisher, the rest of the bunch removed again, one bloom snapping off, falling unnoticed to the ground. Why remove the bunch? Because it had been presented to Mrs Rolt by the murderer and would point a finger unerringly in his direction? That certainly seemed a possible explanation.

Naylor moved to the door. 'Plenty to get on with,' he said briskly. 'No shortage of lines to work on.'

CHAPTER XII

THE POST MORTEM was still in progress. Naylor came down
the steps of the hospital mortuary and walked towards his
car. Time to fit in a couple of interviews before he need
return. First Celia Brettell, then the Fords. He gave Miss
Brettell's address to the driver and settled back against the
upholstery.

He didn't expect to get a great deal out of her. If she
was Andrew Rolt's girl-friend then she could probably be
relied on to back up his statement that he had spent the
major part of Saturday evening in her company at the
Fords' house. Rolt had stated frankly and immediately that
he had called to see his wife at Fairview at about seven-
fifteen yesterday evening. It seemed that they were still on
terms of communication, that a divorce by consent was
being set in process. It was abundantly clear that Mrs Rolt
was alive and well after he left a few minutes later.
Scarcely conceivable in any event that Rolt would attempt
to lie about the main outlines of the evening, with four
witnesses to his presence – or absence – from the supper
and game of cards.

And the Fords, the husband a subordinate of Rolt's at
CeeJay, the lad a very junior employee of the same company, neither of them likely to go out of their way to land
Rolt in the cart. Mrs Ford – presumably she'd simply say
what happened. Or if she was in any kind of doubt –
about a precise detail of time, for instance – then she'd
probably go along with her husband's recollection of the
matter. They'd have had time, all four of them, to cast an
eye back at the events of yesterday evening, to run over in
their minds what they were going to say. But that was the

case with witnesses as often as not, couldn't really be avoided.

They reached the modern block where Miss Brettell rented a flat. She was waiting for Naylor in the sitting-room which was carefully and expensively furnished, bright colours, clean lines.

'Let me get you some coffee,' she offered as soon as he had sat down. But he shook his head.

'No, thanks. I haven't much time to spare right now.' The immediate impression she made on him was of calm and self-possession. Not bad-looking in her way but no glamour, nothing to stir the blood. She didn't burst forth into a gushy utterance about how shocked, astounded, appalled and so on and so forth she had been at the news of Mrs Rolt's death. In fact after the polite preliminaries she said nothing whatever, sat opposite him with a look of courteous alertness, waiting for him to speak. A cool customer, Naylor said to himself, a pretty hard nut to crack.

When he left the flat ten minutes later he didn't go directly to the Fords' house but called in at the police station and spent some little time assessing the latest gobbets of information and hypothesis. On his way out again he picked up Sergeant Viner. 'I'm off to Ford's place,' Naylor told him. 'Checking on Rolt's movements yesterday evening.' He flicked a sharp glance at Viner, noted his air of restless energy. It hadn't taken Viner long to abandon the rest of his day off, get back to duty. The dead woman had apparently been at school with him, they had recently met again. Good-looking girl, Naylor thought, just as well the relationship hadn't been any closer.

'I didn't get a lot of change out of Miss Brettell,' Naylor said casually. 'But then I didn't expect to.' He paused, waited till Viner had edged the car into the main road. 'She's obviously not prepared to sell Rolt down any kind

of river,' he went on. 'She agrees that they left the Fords'
not long after ten o'clock. By half past ten she was tucked
up alone in her bed with a couple of aspirins and a glass
of milk.'

'That's Robin Ford,' Viner said suddenly a few minutes
later. 'Over there.' He'd encountered the lad on his visit
to CeeJay a couple of weeks back when there was that
business of the break-in at the yard. Not that young Ford
had been in any way involved in that episode, which was
clearly a piece of casual vandalism.

Robin was walking quickly, his fawn duffel coat buttoned
up against the wind, his hands in his pockets. 'Probably on
his way home,' Naylor said. 'We'll give him a lift.'

Arthur Ford left his house as soon as the interview with
the police was over, and went off to call round to his
mother's. It seemed the old lady was unwell, had been
ailing for some time. Arthur Ford had in fact spent part of
Saturday evening with her, had felt obliged to offer his
apologies to his supper guests at about nine o'clock and go
round to see her.

He had looked in on her earlier on Saturday, had felt
concerned about her but not concerned enough to cancel
his supper party, thought his guests would understand,
intended to be away only twenty minutes or half an hour
but had lingered on, not noticing the time, and hadn't
actually returned home by the time Rolt and Miss Brettell
left. He thought that by then it must have been getting on
for eleven. He stayed up for a while, chatting to his wife,
went to bed around midnight.

Robin Ford stayed in the sitting-room when the two
policemen stood up to leave. He had given his account of
Saturday evening in a straightforward and courteous
manner. After Rolt and Miss Brettell had left – at about

twenty past ten, he thought – he had walked down to Leofric Gardens, had spent the time until one-thirty on Sunday morning at Tessa Drake's birthday party. When he left the girls' flat he had returned home and gone straight to bed.

Beryl Ford accompanied the two men into the hall. She had been helpful enough, had agreed to do her best to provide as speedily as possible a list of the persons who had bought the cushions at the Fair; it seemed that all the cushions had been sold. She held out little hope of being able to compile an accurate list; it struck her as an almost impossible task. But she was willing to try.

'I can't say I was ever particularly fond of Mrs Rolt,' Beryl said in a high voice tinged with defiance. She gave Naylor a bright challenging look that stopped just short of hostility. At least it makes a change, Naylor said to himself, usually they insist on singing the praises of the deceased. Damned shame, Arthur Ford had said loudly and emphatically a few minutes ago, Mrs Rolt was a fine-looking girl.

Beryl turned and glanced at her reflection in the mirror of the hall stand. 'She thought a very great deal of herself,' she said, still with the same air of unswerving adherence to the truth. She put up a hand and made a few passes at her hair. 'I don't deny she was clever.' Naylor watched her expression in the glass, consciously virtuous, self-congratulatory. 'But a modest violet she most certainly was not.' She dealt her hairstyle a blow which very nearly proved mortal, dislodging a couple of pins and causing a large tress to fall over one eye.

Nor did Mrs Ford seem very smitten by either Rolt or Miss Brettell, judging from the pursed-lip way she'd spoken about them earlier. 'I never could stand folk who make a song and dance about trifles,' she said. 'Celia Brettell can make an awful fuss about things when she has a mind to. She thought she'd dropped her brooch. She had us looking for it and it was in her handbag all the time. But it never occurred to her to apologize to us for making us crawl round the floor. You'd think she'd done us a favour, allowing us to join in the hunt.'

But Mrs Ford had – although grudgingly – confirmed the time at which Rolt and Miss Brettell had left the house. 'It was definitely before half past ten,' she'd said. 'I know that because I was clearing up in the kitchen after they'd gone. I had the radio on and I heard the time check at half past ten. They hadn't been gone many minutes, so it must have been twenty-five past or perhaps twenty past when they left.'

'Could it have been before ten?' Naylor had pressed her but she shook her head.

'Oh no, that I do know. I distinctly remember looking at the clock and thinking, it's gone ten and Arthur not back yet. I didn't know whether to try to keep Mr Rolt and Celia Brettell here till he got back, or not.'

I suppose the corroboration of someone who is envious and disapproving towards you is worth half a dozen friends nodding their heads in time with your story, Naylor said sourly to himself, studying Mrs Ford's bony features in the glass.

'Celia Brettell will marry Rolt now,' Beryl said, slanting at Naylor's mirrored face a deeply significant glance. 'She's been after him for years. Since long before Miss Alison Lloyd appeared on the scene.' She turned and swept the two men before her to the front door.

'Any further information I can give you,' she said as they went out into the bitter, swooping wind, 'don't hesitate to ask.'

The pathologist rubbed a hand across his face. 'That's the gist of it,' he said. 'I'll let you have the full report tomorrow.' He shook his head to clear it. 'I could do with some coffee.'

Naylor made his way out to the car. Quite definitely death due to asphyxia. She'd put up precious little struggle, just an agitated flailing about of the arms and legs in a desperate fight for breath. That seemed to indicate that she knew her attacker, felt relaxed in his – or her – presence, had felt able to lean back, at ease.

The stomach was empty. That squared with the evidence of a meal being prepared in the kitchen. She must have been disturbed as she was about to switch on the cooker. And, thanks to what Stephen Maynard had told them about his phone call to Mrs Rolt on Saturday evening, they had a pretty clear notion of what time that must have been.

Always supposing, of course, that Maynard was telling the truth.

'Maynard,' Naylor said aloud, drawing his brows together in a frown. Apparently he hadn't been her boy-friend many weeks. You ought to let Mr Maynard know about Mrs Rolt's death, Hazel Ratcliff had said at a very early stage in the proceedings. He'd want to know, she had said with an intense, faintly disturbing look, he was a friend of Mrs Rolt's.

They'd followed up the lead at once. There was no real suggestion that the association had deepened into love – or indeed into any kind of powerful feeling. Maynard's manner, talking about the dead woman, had been quiet and disciplined. And yet . . . Naylor wasn't totally satisfied about Maynard. He believed he had detected signs of strong emotion held rigidly in check. Emotion a good deal stronger than one would expect if he had only recently embarked on a pleasant friendship – or mild flirtation – with the girl.

CHAPTER XIII

NAYLOR LEANED back in his chair and closed his eyes. 'At around seven-fifteen yesterday evening,' he said in precisely articulated tones, 'Andrew Rolt called at Fairview on his way to supper with the Fords. He rang the bell and was admitted by Mrs Rolt after some slight delay because of her injured foot. It had reached Rolt's ears that she had hurt herself in a fall and he wished to enquire after her state of health and offer any help of which she might stand in need.

'He found her in reasonably good spirits, she declared herself perfectly well able to manage with such other assistance as she could command, they had a pleasant, friendly chat, he took his leave at seven-thirty and drove to the Fords' place.' He jerked his eyes open. 'Or so he says. Now. Any flaws in that little tale?'

'No one saw him enter or leave,' Inspector Bennett said at once. 'But then neither Hazel Ratcliff nor William Yoxall were in the house at the time.' He raised both hands and pressed his fingers against his cheeks. 'I can't see that it matters. There's pretty conclusive evidence that she was alive well after seven-thirty. Hazel Ratcliff called on her at about eight-fifteen, and Stephen Maynard talked to her on the phone at about eight-thirty.'

'And you accept all that as totally conclusive evidence that she was alive when Rolt left her flat at seven-thirty?' Naylor said.

'Yes, I do.' Bennett made an emphatic movement of his head. 'Hazel Ratcliff called on Mrs Rolt immediately on returning to the house from the Charities Fair. Asked her how she was, told her about the Fair, offered to cook her some supper, was told politely that Mrs Rolt could manage on her own, that she was going to make herself an omelette and get an early night.'

'I don't know that we can be absolutely sure that Miss Ratcliff did call on her,' Naylor said. 'It's evident that she wasn't an ardent admirer of Alison Rolt, but I don't imagine she would like it to be thought now that she wasn't neighbourly enough to call and see if she needed anything when she'd injured her leg.'

'Mrs Rolt was more or less her employer,' Bennett said on a protesting note. 'Surely she would call on her in the circumstances, however she felt about her personally.'

'I'm not saying she didn't call on her,' Naylor said. 'She may or may not have called. But in either case she would very probably say now that she did call. Therefore I believe her statement is valueless as far as we are concerned.'

'But if she didn't call,' Bennett said stubbornly, 'how do you account for the fact that she knew Mrs Rolt was going to cook an omelette?'

'That's easy to account for,' Naylor said. 'Mrs Rolt repeated her intention of cooking an omelette when she spoke to William Yoxall. Miss Ratcliff had supper with Yoxall later that evening, she could have heard about the omelette from him.'

'And Miss Ratcliff was one of the first on the scene in the morning,' Sergeant Viner put in. 'The evidence of an omelette being prepared was quite plain to be seen in the kitchen. Miss Ratcliff could have picked up that item of information then and inserted it into her statement to give it a more plausible air, if she was bent on appearing more neighbourly than she in fact was.'

'All right then,' Bennett said. 'I'll forget about Miss Ratcliff. But there's Yoxall's statement. He spoke to Mrs Rolt at about a quarter past eight.'

'He didn't actually see her,' Naylor said. 'He merely

spoke to her through the door.'

Bennett raised his shoulders. 'I can't see that that makes any difference. If he was lying about the fact of his visit then he'd have gone the whole hog and said he saw her face to face, that she opened the door and spoke to him.'

'Mm,' Naylor said. 'You may be right.'

'So,' Bennett said with conviction. 'Yoxall knocked at her door, called out to her not to disturb herself, knowing her difficulty in moving about. He asked her if she'd like a cup of tea, was told No, thank you, she was shortly going to cook herself an omelette. He then continued on his way upstairs.

'Hazel Ratcliff heard him and came out on to her landing. They exchanged a few words about Mrs Rolt and went on to discuss the success of the Charities Fair. Yoxall suggested that Miss Ratcliff might like to come up to his flat and have a cup of coffee with him. They could continue the conversation there. He was expecting a cousin of his – an elderly widow – to call in. Miss Ratcliff accepted and went up.

'The elderly cousin arrived a few minutes later. All three of them stayed in Yoxall's flat for the rest of the evening. They had supper together, they watched television. Miss Ratcliff went back to her own flat at about eleven o'clock. She didn't call on Mrs Rolt again as there was no sound from the ground floor and she had every reason to believe Mrs Rolt was in bed asleep.'

Bennett leaned forward. 'Yoxall confirms this account of the evening. And so does his widowed cousin. Now I'm prepared to believe that one or other of them might be bending the truth a little in order to appear in a more neighbourly light to the rest of the world, but I'm not prepared to believe all three of them are bending the truth. Unless you think they were all in cahoots, that they planned together to murder Mrs Rolt.' He looked at Naylor with a challenging eye. 'And that's about as daft a notion as it's possible to harbour.'

He raised a hand suddenly. 'Ah!' he said with triumph. 'I was forgetting – there's Maynard's phone call as well. Maynard spoke to Mrs Rolt at about half past eight. You're scarcely suggesting that all four of them were lying, Yoxall, Miss Ratcliff, the widowed cousin and Maynard, the whole bunch of them in a plot to do away with Mrs Rolt.'

'No, I'm not suggesting that.' Naylor threw a glance at Viner who was sitting motionless, his gaze abstracted. 'What about you? Do you accept Stephen Maynard's story that he talked to Mrs Rolt at some time after seven-thirty, that is, after Andrew Rolt left her flat?'

'Yes,' Viner said after a slight pause. 'I think I do, sir. Maynard rang to ask if she would like him to come round. She refused, said she was going to make herself some supper as soon as she rang off. She even told him exactly what kind of omelette she was going to make. He told us that she said a cheese omelette, and it was a cheese omelette she began to prepare. So it does very much look as if he learned that fact from her in the course of a phone call.'

He paused, closed his eyes for an instant. 'Maynard says he phoned her at about eight-thirty. Assuming that she then did what she said she was going to do – go straight into the kitchen and begin to prepare the meal – it was probably about a quarter to nine when she abandoned her preparations, presumably because she was interrupted. Taken together with the statements of the other two, I would call that pretty conclusive evidence that she was alive after Andrew Rolt left the flat at seven-thirty.'

'You say she was probably interrupted,' Naylor said. 'By what, do you imagine?'

Viner hesitated. 'I was going to say by a ring at the door. And the admission of the person who killed her.' He contrived to keep his tone steady. 'But I see now that it might just as well have been the ring of the telephone that called her out of the kitchen. She could, for instance, have received a phone call, could have completed it, replaced the receiver, sat down in the easy chair for a minute or two to think over the telephone conversation, closed her eyes and perhaps slipped into a half doze – we do know she'd taken a sedative earlier.

'The murderer might have entered the flat just about that time, letting himself in with a key he'd got hold of one way or another. She might never have opened her eyes, might never have known there was anyone in the room, might have been killed in her sleep.' His voice fell away into silence.

'It could have happened like that,' Naylor said. 'Quite conceivable, even if not the most obvious theory.' Such little struggle as she had put up might have been no more than the reflex action of the limbs under threat of imminent death. 'But I rather think it was the doorbell and not the phone that called her from the kitchen.'

'Yes, sir, so do I,' Viner said.

'It certainly accounts more naturally,' Inspector Bennett put in, 'for her going to sit down in an easy chair. She must have known the caller well enough to invite him – or her, of course – into the sitting-room. Well enough to relax in his company, lean back in her chair. It was Andrew Rolt,' he added flatly. 'Wherever he says he was at a quarter to ten.'

Naylor fixed Bennett with a cold eye. 'Beware the fixed idea,' he said in a tone devoid of friendliness. 'It performs no possible kind of service for anyone.'

Bennett said nothing, merely inclined his head slightly by way of acknowledgement, he sat with his face carefully wiped clear of resentment.

'One can't rule out the possibility,' Viner said, 'that it was Stephen Maynard who rang her doorbell while she was preparing supper.' Naylor gave him a penetrating look, jerked his head at him to continue. 'Suppose he never made the phone call he says he made,' Viner went on. 'Suppose he just called round to see her, having heard at the Fair that she was incapacitated. Or he might have phoned her as he said, but a little earlier. She might not have said anything to him over the phone about being on the point of preparing supper. She might have mentioned that fact to him as she let him into the flat.'

'Ye . . . es,' Naylor said. 'Or he might have made the phone call exactly as he says, might have immediately got out his car and driven over to Fairview, knowing that she was in the flat and intending to stay there. It wouldn't have seemed all that strange to her when she answered his ring at the door. He could have said, 'As soon as I put the phone down I realized I had to see you this evening, that I wouldn't be able to sleep properly unless I did.'

'Of course she could have asked him to supper over the phone,' Viner said. 'And then started preparing it, gone to answer the door when he arrived.'

'I don't think so,' Naylor said. 'She'd hardly have sat down to talk to him in that case. They'd surely both have gone straight into the kitchen and she'd have carried on preparing the supper. And there was only one cup and saucer, one plate put out in the kitchen. And the amount of food was just enough for one person. Everything points to the fact that she expected to eat her supper alone.'

'He could still have walked in on her uninvited,' Viner said. 'And if she wasn't expecting him for supper, then it would be quite natural for her to sit down and talk to him. The cooker hadn't been switched on, nothing was going to burn if she decided to talk to him for a few minutes.'

'What it comes down to,' Naylor said, 'is that you maintain that we can't unquestioningly accept Maynard's statement about either the fact or the timing of his phone call.'

'Yes, I suppose that's it,' Viner said.

'And I have already explained why I can't accept Miss Ratcliff's statement about calling on Mrs Rolt,' Naylor went on.

Bennett set his jaw. 'But it still leaves us with Yoxall's statement,' he said, 'that he spoke to Mrs Rolt through her door at about eight-fifteen.'

'Yes,' Naylor said in a tone of sudden decision. 'I believe it does. So, for the time being then, we'll take eight-fifteen as the early boundary to the period during which she must have died.'

There was a tap at the door and a sergeant came in. 'Miss Padmore is at the desk, sir,' he said to Naylor. 'She's rather upset.'

'I'll see her.' Naylor got to his feet. 'I don't imagine I'll be very long,' he said to Bennett. As he came out into the corridor he nodded towards one of the interview rooms. 'I'll see her in there.'

Miss Padmore came in a couple of minutes later. 'It was a dreadful shock,' she said to Naylor in a low voice. 'I heard the news a little while ago.' She sat down in the chair facing the chief inspector.

'I've been out of Barbourne. I drove over to Stockborough on Friday afternoon. I left Kingfisher a little early.' Stockborough was a small town about thirty miles from Barbourne. 'My brother and his family live a few miles out of Stockborough, I often go over there for a weekend. I didn't know anything about what had happened till I got back to Barbourne.' Her face trembled slightly. 'I'd left a note of my brother's address with Hazel Ratcliff. I usually leave a note of where I'm to be found if I'm away. Apparently one of your men tried to contact me two or three times today but none of us were in the house. We'd all gone over to some friends of my brother's for the day.'

Her voice steadied. 'When I got back to Barbourne a little while ago, the woman in the next flat knocked at my door as soon as she heard me come in.' She drew a long breath. 'Rather a theatrical sort of woman, she quite seemed to enjoy the drama of what she had to tell me.' She was silent for a moment. 'And it wasn't as if Mrs Rolt was someone she'd never clapped eyes on. She'd seen her more than once, even spoken to her on occasions, when she came to my place.' She dismissed the memory of her insensitive neighbour with a sharp movement of her shoulders.

'As soon as I felt able to, I drove over to Fairview. I spoke to the policeman there, and to Hazel, and William Yoxall.' She gave Naylor a calm look. 'Then I thought I'd better come along here.'

'You did quite right,' Naylor said.

'It's been a great shock to me.'

Naylor nodded. 'Yes, I can imagine.'

'She was a good businesswoman.' She put up a hand and touched her cheek. 'Competent and reliable. I could leave her in charge with an easy mind.' She closed her eyes briefly. 'A young woman like that. At the beginning of her life. Who could have done such a terrible thing?'

CHAPTER XIV

INSPECTOR BENNETT was sorting through a sheaf of notes when Naylor came back into the room. He glanced up with an air of enquiry.

'Nothing of great consequence,' Naylor said. 'Miss Padmore seems to have got on all right with the dead woman. And there's no doubt she'll be considerably inconvenienced by her death.' He dropped into his chair.

'I've been thinking about the question of access to Fair-view.' Bennett shuffled the notes together. 'It seems clear there was some habitual carelessness in the locking of the first and second doors that led into Mrs Rolt's flat.'

'Mm,' Naylor said. The three flats at Fairview shared a common entrance. In order to enter Mrs Rolt's flat, one had to go in through the front door, cross a hallway and go in through a second door. The staircase ran up to a first-floor and second-floor landing, with a single door giving entrance to the flat on each level.

'The front door to Fairview might easily have been left unsecured on Saturday evening,' Bennett said. 'The murderer could simply have walked in through the front door and then let himself into Mrs Rolt's flat with a key. When he encountered her, assuming it was someone she knew, he could just have smiled and said, 'Your door was open, I walked in. I hope you don't mind. I know you've hurt your foot. I didn't want to bring you out to the front door unnecessarily.' And supposing he was carrying a present for her, holding it out to her as he spoke, then her initial irritation – if she was irritated, we don't know, she might have been quite pleased to see the caller – her irritation might be forgotten, she might have asked him to sit down, possibly out of no more than common courtesy. Difficult to be snubbing to someone who has just brought you a gift and enquired after your health.'

'Ye . . . es,' Naylor said. 'And if she was careless about locks, she might not have known whether in fact she had secured the second door, the one to her own flat. If she was in the kitchen, clattering about, and the caller came right into the kitchen holding out the gift, smiling, talking about open doors, she might have assumed she'd left both doors unlocked, might not have realized the caller had access to one of her keys.' He pulled down the corners of his mouth. 'All supposition of course.' Then he said on a more cheerful note, 'At least the cleaning woman, Mrs Lingard, seems to be a truthful witness. I see no reason to doubt her story.'

'No,' Bennett said. 'I can't see why she should want to lie.'

'She offered to phone Mrs Rolt at a quarter to ten on Saturday night,' Naylor went on. 'To ask if she was all right, and if she should call round in the morning.' There was no phone at Mrs Lingard's house but she always spent Saturday evening with her sister and it was from her sister's house that she proposed to ring.

According to her account, Mrs Rolt had welcomed the idea but had suggested that she should phone Mrs Lingard, instead of the other way round. The reason she had given was that it would be more convenient for her, because of her wrenched foot, to choose her own time in getting to the phone, rather than have to attempt to reach it in a hurry, from another room perhaps. 'Though another possible reason, in Naylor's opinion, was that she might have expected to be entertaining a boy-friend and so might wish to be free of avoidable interruptions.

'Mrs Lingard received no call at her sister's,' he said. 'And at a quarter to ten, as she was beginning to think about going home herself, she decided to phone Mrs Rolt.' Growing a little worried that Mrs Rolt might perhaps be feeling ill, might be unable to reach the phone. 'She made the call, let the phone ring for quite some time without getting any reply, rang off, dialled again just to make sure she'd got the right number, again let it ring for a couple of minutes, again with no reply.' She had debated with her sister whether or not to call round there and then but her sister had been of the opinion that Mrs Rolt had forgotten her promise to phone, had gone up to one of the other flats, or was simply having a bath; or had even been taken out for a meal by Stephen Maynard.

So Mrs Lingard had been persuaded to dismiss her concern – at all events for the time being. It had returned to her with renewed force next morning as soon as she woke. As she had no phone she went round to Fairview immediately after breakfast, and found that instinct had after all been right.

'It seems highly probable,' Bennett said, 'that Mrs Rolt was already dead when Mrs Lingard first phoned at a quarter to ten.'

'Either that,' Naylor said, 'or she was actually in the process of being murdered.' He had a swift clear vision of the murderer pressing the cushion down on her face, the sharp ring of the phone almost under his hand, the frenzied increase in pressure, the unceasing nerve-racking ring, the arms and legs uselessly beating the air, beginning to slacken, the phone finally dying into silence. And then abruptly beginning again like the insuppressible voice of accusation. The desperate renewal of force, extinguishing the last traces of life. The shrill peal going on and on, as if someone were there in the room, standing watching, calling out. The sound ceasing at last. Then the long moments of waiting, more than half expecting the phone to break out again into its urgent summons, the terror that a door might open in one of the other flats, someone might come down to see if Mrs Rolt was all right, having registered those long-continued rings. And finally, the realization that no one was coming, the phone wasn't going to ring again, it was all right, the path was clear for escape.

'She was dead or dying at a quarter to ten,' Naylor said in an unemotional tone. 'I believe she was already dead before nine-thirty.' Miss Padmore, Miss Ratcliff, everyone seemed to agree that if Alison Rolt said she'd make a phone call at nine-thirty, then she would undoubtedly make it at nine-thirty. A pretty meticulous businesswoman by all accounts. 'Either dead or dying by nine-thirty,' he repeated. That squared with the pathologist's opinion, the state of the body.

'We can now set the time limits as lying between eight-fifteen and nine-thirty.' Naylor turned and gave Bennett a level look. 'And that would appear pretty positively to let Andrew Rolt out, as during that entire period he was very clearly in the Fords' house in the presence of four other people.'

'In the presence of four other people until nine o'clock,' Bennett said. 'Arthur Ford went round to his mother's at that time. There were only three other people after that.'

I ought to say something about Paul Hulme, Colin thought. He was beginning to feel a sense of unreality, as if they were all taking part in a theatrical performance. He ought to tell them Hulme once lived in the flat above Alison's. And he ought to mention also that Alison fancied someone had been going through her things. A kind of numbness was spreading through his limbs, seemed to be infecting his brain, his tongue, his willpower. With an effort he turned his head and regarded Naylor.

'I don't know if you're aware,' he said. He paused, passed a hand across his face and began again. Naylor saw the soft unfocused look in his eyes.

'Take it easy,' he said. 'No need to get it all out in one breath.' Delayed shock, he thought, only to be expected.

'I think I ought to mention – ' Colin said. But now he couldn't for the life of him remember whether he had already raised the points or not. His thoughts seemed to come from a distance, strained through cotton wool.

'That's all right,' Naylor said in a soothing tone. 'I dare say there's a lot of stuff that'll come to you that'll be of use to us.' He pushed back his chair. 'But just for now, get off down to the canteen, take half an hour, get something inside you.'

It was past ten o'clock. William Yoxall sat facing Naylor across the desk. The chief inspector's attention wandered for a moment from the sound of Yoxall's voice. At this time on a more normal Sunday evening he'd be dozing at home in front of the television set. He shook his head, sat up, and fixed Yoxall with a resolute gaze.

'Certainly,' Yoxall was saying. 'I do indeed amuse myself with embroidery. I am in fact very good at it. I invariably work in gros point, I am unable to crochet. I would add furthermore,' he added with a note of aggression creeping into his tone, 'that I do not consider skill in embroidery an unnatural talent in a male.'

'Did you make this particular cushion?' Naylor asked, indicating the labelled exhibit, a square cushion, a formal Jacobean design, ripped open now along three sides by official fingers.

'Oh yes,' Yoxall said at once. 'I made that one.'

Inspector Bennett, sitting to one side of Naylor's desk, jerked his head round in surprise. He had taken it for granted that Yoxall would deny having made the cushion; neither of the other two embroiderers had appeared anxious to claim credit for it. Beryl Ford had declared it was none of her handiwork and had unhesitatingly attributed it to William Yoxall. She had maintained that she had worked no gros point cushions for the Fair, believing her standard not good enough; she had made only crochet cushions. 'And in any case,' she had added, 'none of my cushions were square, all mine were round.'

Hazel Ratcliff was prepared to countenance the notion that the cushion might be one of hers, but felt that it could equally well have been one made by her mother in the last few weeks before her death. There had been six or seven of those; Hazel had put them in with the others to be sold at the Fair.

And when asked if Mrs Ford had worked only crochet cushions for the stall, Hazel had looked doubtful, had said she couldn't be sure, she had rather been under the impression that Mrs Ford had made one – if not two – in gros point. 'Her gros point is really quite good,' she'd said. 'I don't know why she says it isn't.'

'How are you able to be so positive that this embroidery is your work?' Naylor asked Yoxall.

'One can surely recognize the appearance of one's own handiwork,' said Yoxall with a certain loftiness. 'But there's a way to be quite certain.' He leaned over and fingered back the top of the cushion. 'There, take a look at that.' He stabbed a finger at the underside of the embroidery. 'The way the new threads are introduced into the pattern, the way the old ones are finished off. People vary in the methods they use. And that's the way I do mine.'

He sat back in his chair again. 'I really can't see any point in your bothering to find out who made the cushion,' he said suddenly in a shrewd, matter-of-fact tone. 'Presumably the murderer bought the cushion at the stall and took it to Mrs Rolt's flat as a gift for her. Doesn't seem to matter two hoots who embroidered it.'

He fixed Naylor with a sharp glance. 'Or the murderer may have been given the cushion by someone else, someone who had purchased it at the Fair. And furthermore,' he added triumphantly, 'it may not have been the murderer who brought the cushion to Mrs Rolt's flat. It may have been brought quite innocently by someone else. Then when the murderer wanted to smother her, he simply looked round and picked up a cushion. Any cushion. It seems to me you're wasting your time bothering with the thing at all.'

'That's how you see it, is it?' Naylor said in a tone of

detached enquiry. 'The murderer standing over her, looking round for the cushion?'

'Yes, more or less.' Yoxall frowned, turned his head, looked over at the wall. 'It must have been someone she knew and trusted. He'd see her settle into her chair; he'd say, let me make you a little more comfortable. He'd walk across, pick up a cushion and say, have this behind your head. She'd look up at him, smiling. She'd raise her shoulders, tilt her head back a bit, her hands would be on the arms of the chair. He'd bend over her, talking, laughing, put one hand lightly on her shoulder and then suddenly, bring down the cushion, smack! on her face. Bring the other hand round, press down, hard. He'd have his full weight bearing down on her, she wouldn't be able to resist. And with her feet on the stool she'd be in an awkward position to start with. It wouldn't take very long.' He stopped, blinked, glanced at Naylor.

'No, I don't imagine it would take very long,' Naylor said. 'She wasn't any very great size.'

Yoxall pursed his lips, widened his eyes in a reflective stare. 'Capable of mischief, you know, Mrs Rolt.'

'Oh?' Naylor's tone was encouraging.

'Shouldn't speak ill of the dead and all that,' Yoxall said. 'But I suppose the police don't count.'

'I dare say not,' Naylor said with an inflexion of irony.

'I was at a committee meeting,' Yoxall said. 'To do with the Fair. Mrs Rolt was there too. Mrs Ford – Beryl Ford – is by way of being rather a dominating mother, I don't know if you're aware of that.' Naylor said nothing, inclined his head by the merest trifle. 'Mrs Rolt led Robin Ford on, just to amuse herself, it seemed to me – and because it made Mrs Ford mad. Robin's only a lad after all, I shouldn't think he's more than eighteen or nineteen, not really fair game.'

'Mm,' Naylor said non-committally.

'Mrs Rolt had quite a nasty temper when she chose to show it,' Yoxall said on a confidential note. 'Foreign blood, you see. Comes out like that sometimes. Sudden wild temper.'

'Indeed?' Naylor said.

'And she could say very cutting things when she had a mind to. Cruel things.' He stroked his thin neck. 'Just thought I'd mention it.'

CHAPTER XV

MONDAY MORNING was wet and cheerless. It had rained since dawn, a steady downpour that promised to continue all day. At ten minutes before noon Sergeant Viner halted his car outside the last flower shop on his list. A bright modern façade, the window display brilliant with dahlias, asters, carnations . . . and chrysanthemums. Colin scrutinized the showy heads – white, apricot, gold, bronze. Nowhere in the vases could he spot the twin – or even the distant cousin – of the bloom that had been dropped on the carpet at Fairview.

He sighed and walked towards the entrance. The same story over again. Nothing remotely approaching the quality of the Fairview bloom. But he would have to ask his questions just the same. It was possible that there might have been a delivery of unusually fine chrysanthemums for last weekend.

The assistant came forward, smiling. Her smile flickered out a minute or so after Viner opened his mouth.

'No,' she said firmly when he came to the end of his spiel. 'I'm afraid I can't help you. The kind of flower you describe is very probably an exhibition bloom.' She gestured at the containers. 'We wouldn't normally sell anything like that.'

He pressed her further. Could she make any suggestion as to where blooms of that quality might have come from locally? She frowned in thought, striving to be helpful.

'You certainly couldn't expect to find flowers like that at a cottage gate or on a street barrow. And they'd be far too good for a market stall. And in any case there isn't a flower stall now in Barbourne.' He knew that already; Inspector Bennett had been quite definite about it. The council had frowned on all classes of street trading in recent years to such an extent that barely half-a-dozen stalls survived now in a little cobbled square near the centre of town. It was pretty certain that in a year or two these relics of a rural past would also be frowned out of existence. The old woman who had kept the last flower stall had died a few weeks back. No one would be permitted to replace her; no one had even suggested doing so.

'There isn't even a vegetable or produce stall in Barbourne now,' Viner said, echoing Bennett's information. Crockery, furnishing materials, haberdashery, shoes, nylon tights, shirts, dresses, raincoats: that was about the limit of what could be bought in the market these days.

'Of course all the local councils aren't as down on street traders as Barbourne,' the girl said. She mentioned the names of nearby towns, and sizeable semi-rural hamlets. 'You'd still find flower stalls there, I'm fairly sure.'

Viner nodded. Bennett already had men working on those lines. The area in which enquiries were being carried out was very wide; it included places where Gerald Wickham might conceivably have shopped on Saturday afternoon. If nothing came up pretty soon the area would be steadily enlarged, the enquiries would press relentlessly on.

'Personally,' the girl said, 'I would imagine that the

flowers came from a private grower.' She pulled a little face. 'Could be almost anybody.' Viner closed his eyes for an instant at the vision that had already presented itself to him : all those legions of gardeners, amateur and professional, greenhouse specialists, backyard enthusiasts. And somewhere among them, just possibly, one dedicated plant breeder stooping lovingly over a superb chrysanthemum, rosy orange tipped with sulphur yellow. 'There are the local horticultural societies,' the girl said. 'The secretaries of the various flower shows. And other shows of course; there are often flower classes at those as well.'

'Yes,' Viner said flatly. Bennett had men working on those lines too. 'You can't suggest any other source?'

She shook her head. 'If I do think of anything I'll let you know.' He thanked her and went out of the shop, hurrying through the rain to his car. He sat for a few moments checking over his list. Next call – the retired grocer who had run the flower and produce stall at the Fair and had general oversight of the floral decorations in the hall. Not that he had any expectations of coming up with anything there, he had already spoken to the man over the phone.

He had also spoken to several people who had attended the Fair in various capacities : Miss Ratcliff, Yoxall, one or two constables from the uniformed branch, women from the police canteen. They had all shaken their heads at the suggestion that anything resembling the Fairview chrysanthemum had graced the display in the hall. But one never knew. You pressed on and on. Someone somewhere might remember something, might be blessed with a sudden flash of imagination, might open his mouth and utter the words that would unlock the puzzle.

He slipped the list back into his pocket, sat hunched over the steering-wheel looking at the day ahead. At three o'clock the inquest would be held, or at any rate opened.

He passed a hand over his face, sat up and switched on the ignition.

'The fingerprints are all cleared up now,' Inspector Bennett said with satisfaction. 'All but for one group,' he added. 'That group is all from the same hand, on the frame of the sitting-room door.'

Naylor looked up sharply. 'Don't give me the all-but-one-small-group routine,' he said. 'I want the lot cleared up.'

'Just a little longer,' Bennett said soothingly. 'We'll have all the prints accounted for by tomorrow, I shouldn't wonder.' Could be days before that's true, he added to himself more realistically. Chasing up everybody who might conceivably have set foot in Mrs Rolt's flat in recent times wasn't a job that could be finished in five minutes.

Naylor grunted. 'Go on,' he said. 'Who've we got already?'

Bennett looked down at the list. 'The cleaning woman, Mrs Lingard. Of course she gave the flat a good dusting and polishing on Saturday morning, so she pretty well eliminated whatever prints were there already.' And just as well, otherwise they might have been at it till the year dot, trying to identify all kinds of smudgy relics from way back. 'A lot of Hazel Ratcliff's, only to be expected.' He cleared his throat. 'Andrew Rolt.' He glanced at Naylor, who merely nodded. 'Stray prints of Stephen Maynard. A lot of William Yoxall's.'

'That figures,' Naylor said. 'Yoxall took her home after her accident, probably fussed about like an old hen.'

'And a couple from Wickham. That's the lot, except for the group we haven't identified. The middle fingers of the left hand, the thumb and the palm.'

'Not Celia Brettell's by any chance?' Naylor asked suddenly. 'You didn't forget her?'

Bennett shook his head. 'No. We remembered Miss

Brettell. They're not hers. None of hers there at all.' He moved his shoulders. 'Proves nothing of course. Cold day, anyone might have been wearing gloves, male or female. The murderer need only have been in the flat a few minutes, probably killed her in the course of the first little social interchange, settling Mrs Rolt back with a cushion, in preparation for a chat, need never have got as far as being expected to remove gloves.'

The inquest was nearly over. Naylor had stationed himself near the exit so that when the court-room began to clear he would be in a position to have a word with anyone leaving.

William Yoxall was there, observing everything with keen interest. Just before the hearing opened, Beryl Ford had slipped into a vacant place at the back of the hall. Andrew Rolt was positioned well to the fore, looking as if he hadn't had much sleep. Young Paul Hulme sat beside him, glancing frequently at Rolt with a watchful air. And close by – Brian Yardley.

The sight of Yardley had given the chief inspector food for thought. We rather forgot Yardley, he said to himself, studying that tormented face. Not a man one might at first think of as easy to overlook, but a character like that, well known in Barbourne, on nodding terms with practically every police officer, tolerated, excused, pitied – precisely perhaps the person one would in reality forget, the outlines of his personality being permanently etched into the general consciousness and so obscured by a glaze of familiarity.

It was Yardley who had been to some extent responsible for the stumble which had prevented Mrs Rolt from attending the Fair. She came out of the Kingfisher, Yardley had said, I spoke to her, she chanced at that moment to miss her footing. No one, it seemed, had pressed Yardley as to what it was he had spoken to Mrs Rolt about, whether what he had said had taken her by surprise or in any way disturbed her.

I simply concluded Yardley had given her the time of day or asked about some work being done for him by the agency, Naylor recalled now with irritation. It never did to draw obvious conclusions about even the most apparently simple happenings.

It occurred to him that Yardley, having caused the stumble, might have decided to call to see how she was, take her some flowers. A very natural thing to do.

He glanced round. His eyes came to rest again on young Hulme. He remembered with a frown that as the court-room had filled up before the start of the proceedings, he had observed a friendly-looking interchange between Yardley and Paul Hulme. He rubbed his chin thoughtfully. Sergeant Viner had mentioned to him an evening that Mrs Rolt had spent with Stephen Maynard, Yardley making a drunken nuisance of himself, being shepherded away at last – by none other than Paul Hulme. That young man seems to stir a finger in more than one little pie, Naylor said to himself.

'Just one moment,' he said a few minutes later when the hearing was over and the inquest adjourned as expected. Naylor leaned forward and laid a hand on Hulme's sleeve. Hulme turned his head and glanced at Naylor with no indication of surprise. His eyes carried a look of lightly veiled amusement. 'I'd like a word with you,' Naylor said. 'If you wouldn't mind stepping over here.' A few feet away Yardley saw the encounter, gave Hulme a single tiny nod and pressed on through the exit. No matter, Naylor said to himself, I'll deal with Yardley later. Better not leave it too late though, if he wanted to catch Yardley sober.

Hulme looked across to where Rolt stood talking with an air of great weariness to a reporter from the local news-paper, then he followed Naylor to a quiet corner. Naylor had just opened his mouth to question him about his tenancy of the middle flat at Fairview when Hulme said, 'I see Maynard decided to skip the inquest.'

'Maynard?' Naylor frowned. 'How could he get away to attend the inquest? He's at school, surely, teaching.'

Hulme grinned. 'Oh no, he's not. It's half term at the grammar school. He's got today and tomorrow off. You ought to pay more attention to detail, Chief Inspector. I fancy the reason Maynard's not here is that he's rather lost his taste for inquests.'

'What do you mean by that?' Naylor asked sharply.

'Do you mean to say you don't know?' Hulme looked as if he was about to break into laughter. 'You hear things about police incompetence but I would never have believed you carried it to such lengths.'

'Perhaps you'd answer my question,' Naylor said.

'Oh, most certainly, most certainly, no objection at all. Only too pleased as an upright citizen to help the constabulary fish their chestnuts out of the fire.' He paused, his eyes lost their teasing look. 'I like to see justice done, Chief Inspector. I do rather particularly have a taste for that.' At that moment a constable came up to Naylor with a message from Bennett.

'All right,' Naylor said. 'I won't be more than a couple of minutes.' He turned again to Hulme. 'You were saying?'

Hulme's face wore now an expression of fierce intensity. 'Maynard killed his wife. He got away with that. Are you going to let him get away with this one too?'

Naylor's watch showed six minutes to five as the car turned in through the gates at CeeJay. I should just about catch Hulme, he thought, looking out at the driving rain, I should like a good long chat with that young man.

But Hulme had gone out on a job, according to Robin Ford who was standing just inside the main door, buttoning himself into his duffel coat. 'He won't come back in here again this afternoon,' Robin added with certainty. Yes, he said in response to a further question, Mr Rolt was still in the building, he'd very probably be in his office on the first floor.

And Rolt was there, sitting at his desk with a pile of papers in front of him, clearly a long way from thoughts of home.

'Just one small matter,' Naylor said pleasantly when he had sat down facing Rolt. 'I gather you paid a visit to Mrs Rolt's flat late at night about four weeks ago.' Rolt became very still. Naylor saw in his eyes, the angle of his head, the instant question: How had the police scooped up that little crumb of information? Both the other flats had been unoccupied at that time, no listening ears or curious eyes to record, remember. 'On Tuesday, October the seventeenth,' Naylor added in a matter-of-fact tone.

Rolt sat back in his chair with a relaxed movement. Scarcely likely he would know Sergeant Viner was a friend of the dead woman, Naylor thought, he's probably totally unaware that she discussed the breakdown of her marriage with a member of the Barbourne CID. For an instant he felt a distasteful sense of double-dealing.

'What I would like to know,' Naylor said, 'is how you got into Mrs Rolt's flat that night. You were already inside when she reached home.' Rolt's face took on a frown, he moved his head as if trying to recall the incident. 'You have a key,' Naylor said. 'You used that to let yourself in.'

Rolt glanced up at once. 'Oh no. I have no key to the flat. I never have had.'

'Then you borrowed one,' Naylor said firmly. 'From Paul Hulme. He still had a key from his own time at Fairview.' He had no idea whether this was in fact so, and in any case it would probably have been only a front-door key that Hulme would have kept, he wouldn't have had a key to Mrs Rolt's flat. Or could he have? Might he have got temporary possession of her key, had a duplicate made, either during his stay at Fairview or afterwards? Was his the hand that had rummaged through her things – if indeed any such hand had existed outside Mrs Rolt's imagination?

Rolt shook his head emphatically. 'I most certainly never borrowed any key from Hulme. It would never have occurred to me that he might possess one.'

'Then how did you get into the flat?'

'Quite simply. The front door wasn't locked I rang the bell. There was no answer. I tried the door and it opened. I thought Alison was probably out, that she might be in before long. So I went inside. The door to her flat was standing wide open. I went in and sat down.' Quite feasible, Naylor thought. Why should she bother to lock the door of her flat when the rest of the house was empty? As to the front door, she could very well have gone out in a hurry, just pulled it to behind her, without thinking. He stood up.

'I won't keep you any longer,' he said. 'I can see you're a busy man.' Hulme might have reached home by now. If not, he could go on to Maynard's. But he would much prefer to talk to Hulme again before seeing Maynard. Immediately after the inquest he had put through a call to the main police station in Eldersleigh. Stephen Maynard had taught in Eldersleigh but had lived – together with his wife – in an old cottage in Peachfield, a village a few miles outside Eldersleigh, too small to rate a constable of its own. Naylor had received a return phone call some little time later; it had contained a great deal of interesting information.

'I had occasion to speak to Alison more than once about her carelessness in locking up properly,' Rolt said. 'When she was married to me.' He paused, let out a tiny sighing breath. 'When she was still living with me, I should say.'

He pressed a bell on his desk. 'Miss Webb will show you

136

out.' A short, alert-looking girl came into the room, glanced at Naylor with sharp curiosity.

Webb, he pondered as he hurried through the rain to his car. The name had surely arisen already in the course of the investigation. Ah yes – it came to him as he reached the vehicle. Webb was surely the name Miss Ratcliff had mentioned when he had questioned her about Mrs Rolt's visit to the hotel to deal with Wickham's paperwork. Mandy Webb, Miss Ratcliff had said, sometimes she used to go along to the Wheatsheaf if I was away ill or on holiday. That was during the time Wickham used the Tyler agency of course.

'Right,' he said to the driver. We'll pick up Sergeant Viner.' See if Bennett had turned up anything new, then on to Hulme's place. As he leaned back against the upholstery he remembered something else. Webb was the name of the girl Tessa Drake shared a flat with in Leofric Gardens, the flat where the birthday party had been held on Saturday night, the party Robin Ford had gone to.

He frowned, trying to work out some connection between the random-seeming pieces, but without success. He raised his shoulders, said aloud, 'Ah well, nothing for it but to press ceaselessly on.' He ran a hand across his mouth and felt a sudden acute stab of pain in his upper jaw. Oh Lord, he thought with dismal foreboding, I hope I'm not in for a bout of toothache. He uttered a low groan. The driver, being well used to the Chief's little ways, made no comment but concentrated on edging the car through the traffic.

CHAPTER XVI

THE RAIN had ceased by the time they reached the district where Hulme lived. He rented the top flat in a solidly built house in a quiet road on the outskirts of Barbourne. A yellow glow shone through the fanlight above the front door; in the two lower flats the curtains were not yet drawn across the windows. Looks as if he's got back, Naylor thought, glancing up at the top storey; thick drapes shut out the last of the day, a narrow band of light showed through a gap in the folds.

At the sound of the car sliding to a halt the gap widened suddenly, a hand clutched back the heavy fabric, a girl's face appeared in the aperture.

'Mandy Webb,' Viner said. 'Hulme's girl-friend. She works at CeeJay.' The face vanished, the curtains closed again.

'She keeps popping up,' Naylor said as they stepped out on to the pavement. 'It seems she did occasional work for Wickham.'

The front door yielded to a turn of the knob. At the top of the final flight of stairs Naylor put a forceful finger on the doorbell. For a full minute no one answered his ring. There was no sound of movement from behind the door; the flat had a silent, listening quality. He raised his hand again and jabbed his thumb at the bell, kept it there. 'Come along, Miss Mandy,' he said to the door panel. 'We're not going to oblige you by going away.' He ran a finger experimentally along his jaw. Miracle of miracles, the toothache appeared to have gone.

There was a crisp patter of footfalls at the other side of the panel and the door swung open.

'Yes?' Mandy said on a high, challenging note.

'We'd like a word with Mr Hulme,' Naylor said pleasantly.

She turned her eyes on Viner, a full, open stare. 'He's not here.'

'I imagine he'll be here before long,' Naylor said. 'We'll come in and wait.' He didn't waste time. At any moment Hulme might walk in and he very much wanted to be able to devote his entire attention to that young man from the very second he crossed the threshold. 'Sit down,' he said to Mandy without ceremony. She looked briefly surprised but dropped into a chair. He settled himself opposite her, got down to business at once.

'I understand you sometimes went out to the Wheatsheaf Hotel to do work for Gerald Wickham during the time he made use of the services of the Tyler agency.'

She gave a slow nod as if reluctant to let any superfluous information escape her. 'Yes. I went three or four times.' She sat up very straight, unsmiling. 'When Miss Ratcliff wasn't able to go.'

'Are you aware of any connection between Wickham and Brian Yardley?' Naylor asked suddenly.

She gave no indication of surprise. 'Yes,' she said without hesitation. 'I remember Mr Wickham phoning Mr Yardley once while I was at the Wheatsheaf.'

'What did Wickham say to Yardley?'

'I don't know. He just asked me to get the number. I didn't pay any attention to what he was talking about.'

'But you remembered the fact that this call took place. Why? Was it the only time Wickham ever asked you to get a number for him?'

'Oh no,' she said at once. 'I put through quite a few calls for him.'

'Such as?'

She frowned, held her head to one side. 'Other dealers,

making appointments, confirming prices and so on. The airport – tickets, seats, that sort of thing. Room service of course. Coffee, meals. And those flower people.'

'Flowers?' Naylor said sharply.

'Yes, you know, they deliver flowers and plants, you ring up and they'll send them to any part of the country.'

'Was Wickham in the habit of sending people flowers? Who did he send them to?'

She raised her eyebrows. 'You surely don't expect me to remember who he sent them to after all this time? It's quite a few months since I did any work for him.' She paused. 'I think he got me to phone about flowers two or three times, more than once, anyway. It was always women he sent them to.' She grinned. 'I suppose it always is.' She leaned back in her chair, looking more relaxed. 'I have the impression it would be wives of dealers he'd just done buiness with, or maybe he'd been given a meal or been put up for the night. Saying thank you, in other words.' She grinned again. 'Of course, for all I know, they might all have been his girl-friends.'

He flicked her a swift glance. 'Why do you say that? Did he strike you as being a ladies' man?'

'You mean there's some other kind?' she asked with an impudent air.

'Did he, for instance, ever make a pass at you?' Naylor persisted.

She shrugged. 'Not what you'd call a pass.'

'Can you give me the names of any of the women to whom he sent flowers?'

She shook her head. 'I don't know. That is, I knew at the time of course, but I don't remember now. No business of mine. I just do what I'm paid for.'

'But you remembered Yardley,' he said again. 'Why?'

She gestured with one hand. 'I don't know why. I just do.' She slid him a glance, alert, intelligent. 'There doesn't have to be a reason for everything.'

'Oh yes, there does,' Naylor said. 'We may not always know the reason, but it's there all the same.'

'But not necessarily a sinister or criminal reason.' She sighed, her face took on a bored look. 'I simply heard him say, 'Hello, Brian, it's Gerald Wickham.' Then I got on with my work.'

Naylor leaned forward. 'You never said anything about Christian names.'

Her look of boredom deepened. 'Didn't I?'

'Did Wickham sound as if he knew Yardley well?'

'Oh yes, as if they were friends.' She raised a hand and touched the collar of her blouse. 'Yardley wouldn't do anything to hurt anyone,' she said suddenly, fiercely. 'Not deliberately, anyway. He's been hurt too much himself.' She stopped, frowned, as if regretting her outburst.

In the little silence that followed Naylor heard a car halt outside the house, a door slam. Mandy's face assumed a guarded, stubborn expression. It was the best part of a minute before Hulme came running up the stairs, time enough for Naylor to reflect that her fierce rebuttal did not apparently include Wickham.

Hulme didn't at first seem to object to the presence of the two detectives in his flat. He'd have seen the car parked outside, Naylor pondered, he could easily have driven off somewhere else for the evening if he'd wanted to avoid a confrontation.

'We meet again,' Hulme called out in a lively, good-humoured voice the moment he threw open the door of the flat. Then his eye fell on Mandy. He halted, his face became closed and wary. He didn't speak to the girl, removed his glance from her, took care not to let his gaze rest on her again.

'Have you been up at CeeJay?' he asked suddenly, shooting at Naylor a look that was now far from friendly.

Naylor made no reply. 'Have you been on to Rolt again?' Hulme asked, offensively insistent. 'Why can't you leave him alone? Show him a bit of ordinary human decency? Rolt didn't murder anyone. He's had one hell of a shock, he's trying to get over it. What chance has he got with you pestering him every five minutes? You'll push him over the edge.'

Naylor slanted a thoughtful glance at Hulme, apparently a fervent adherent of the doctrine that prescribes attack as the best means of defence. 'Are you in the habit of rummaging through other people's flats?' Naylor asked in a tone of calm curiosity.

Hulme's flow dried up abruptly. He looked at the chief inspector with astonished ferocity.

'You kept your key to Fairview,' Naylor said, still with the same mild air. 'You used it from time to time. You lent it on occasions to Andrew Rolt.'

'Oh, for crying out loud,' Hulme said.

'How long did you occupy the Fairview flat?' Naylor asked. 'And precisely when did you leave?' That was a mistake, he registered at once with a thrust of irritation, observing the change of expression in Hulme's eyes. So you don't know, Hulme's look said, you've asked around and no one's sure.

'Can't quite recall,' Hulme said, his tone now pleasant again, friendly. 'You know how it is. One leads such a hectic life. Difficult to keep track of mundane details.' He waved a hand in an expansive gesture, smiled at Naylor with open mockery.

We mightn't be able to come up with the information about the flat, Naylor thought with annoyance. Viner didn't know, Yoxall wasn't at all certain, Mrs Lingard professed herself only vaguely able to distinguish one of the young male tenants of the middle flat from another. I suppose it doesn't really matter if we never find out, he added in his mind. But he would just like to know the answer, mainly for his own satisfaction.

Hulme struck him as a man of strongly obsessional tendencies. It was not yet clear whether he had had any kind of personal interest in Alison Rolt, though certain tenuous indications suggested that this might be so. And what the chief inspector would have dearly liked to know was whether such interest, if it existed at all, had been sparked off by the fact that she had taken up residence in the flat below his or whether the opposite was the case, that he had installed himself at Fairview because that was where she lived, and he already harboured compulsive notions about her.

'One thing you may be quite certain of,' Hulme said. 'I never set foot in Fairview on Saturday. I was never at any time anywhere near Mrs Rolt's flat.'

Naylor made no reply to that. 'Were you pleased that the Rolts had decided on divorce?' he asked, shifting abruptly to another tack.

Hulme kept his head perfectly still. 'That was none of my business,' he said flatly. His eyes left Naylor's face, wandered to Viner. 'Ah, the dashing sergeant,' he said mockingly as if until this moment he hadn't been aware of Viner's presence in the room. 'You were a – friend – of Mrs Rolt's, weren't you?' Naylor slid a glance at Viner. The sergeant remained in the same alert, controlled posture as before. He looked back at Hulme in silence, his expression calm and neutral.

'Let's cut out the funny stuff,' Hulme said suddenly. 'Let's get down to brass tacks.' The defensive posture seems to be totally alien to him, Naylor thought; he bounces back constantly to the attack.

Hulme dropped into a chair, stretched himself out with

an air of relaxation. 'You've come here because you've been in touch with the police in Peachfield,' he said. 'Or, more precisely, in Eldersleigh.' He looked across at Naylor. 'You've found out one or two little items about Stephen Maynard and his late if not altogether lamented wife.' Naylor remained silent.

'Of course you did,' Hulme said with certainty. 'You were on the phone the moment you left the court-room.' He raised a hand in an airy gesture. 'A bit of a ladies' man, our Mr Maynard. Did you realize that? La Ratcliff is rather smitten with him. Or was. Events may have changed her attitude by now.' He gave Naylor a brilliant smile. 'One can never be totally sure in such delicate matters.'

Was it conceivable, Naylor asked himself, that Hulme might actually go so far as to commit murder, and commit it in such a way as to direct suspicion convincingly at another person, not from the usual complex motives but in order to justify to himself at some deep, probably unconscious level, his own dark, compelling notions about that other person? Could such a theory be psychologically sound? Was it credible that Hulme nursed some fantasy about Maynard so deep and twisted that it could drive him to kill a woman merely in order to demonstrate to himself as well as to everyone else that Maynard was actually a murderer?

And if one accepted the idea at all, might one not also have to accept the further idea that in that case it was not beyond credibility that Hulme no longer knew what he had done, had dropped a shutter over part of his mind, might now believe absolutely that Maynard had in fact killed Mrs Rolt?

'Something I didn't get round to telling you this afternoon,' Hulme said in a clear incisive voice. 'When I found out about the death of Maynard's wife, I wrote him a number of anonymous letters on the subject.' He waved his hand in a gesture of mock deprecation. 'I was but a simple unsophisticated lad at the time, you understand, a schoolboy, dewy-eyed and innocent. But while I certainly didn't go so far as to sign the letters, I took not the slightest trouble to disguise my handwriting.' He grinned. 'Or my literary style. Maynard was perfectly familiar with both. But he never said one solitary syllable to me about the letters, never indicated by a look or any change in his manner that he knew what I was up to. And furthermore it was blindingly clear to me that he didn't go near the police with the letters. Because if he had, the very sketchiest sort of enquiry would have brought the coppers straight round to me. And no one ever came near me about it. You can go back and check your files but I'm ready to lay good money you won't find that Maynard ever went to the police with his little bundle of letters. One must ask oneself why, Chief Inspector, one must ask oneself why very long and very earnestly.'

'One must also ask oneself,' Naylor said, 'why you stopped sending the letters.' Hulme gave him a level, steady stare. 'One assumes, that is, that you did eventually stop sending them,' Naylor said. 'Otherwise, presumably, you'd be sending them still. And one notes that your artless tale refers to the entire matter in the past tense.' He sat waiting for Hulme to answer.

'No mystery about that,' Hulme said at last, still fixing Naylor with his eye. 'I told someone else the whole story, about Maynard and the letters. That person advised me pretty forcefully to stop sending them. So I stopped.'

'And that person was?' Naylor said. Again there was a pause, shorter this time.

'Brian Yardley.' Hulme leaned back in his chair. Under the overhead light his face looked pale and tired.

Yardley, Naylor thought. Again Yardley. Hulme must have been on pretty close terms with him for a long time. 'How did you come across Yardley in the first place?' he asked.

Hulme closed his eyes. 'It was during one of my school holidays, the Easter holidays, I remember there was still some snow on the ground. I was doing a job at one of old George Yoxall's houses. I often did holiday jobs for him, he owned a lot of property and most of it was pretty ancient, there was always plenty to be done in the way of decorating, gardening, general handyman stuff.

'This particular house, I remember it very well, a big Victorian place, just one woman living there, quite well-to-do, an elderly spinster, the sort of stupid woman who's never had to do a real day's work in her life and thinks that entitles her to forelock-touching and hat-doffing from common working folk.' He sat up, jerked his eyes open, looked savagely into his own recollections.

'Yardley was employed by George Yoxall at that time, rent-collecting. He called at the house when I happened to be working there. We got talking.' He paused. 'Stupid cow of a woman told me she was a bit scared of Yardley.' His voice mimicked her tone. 'Said she never felt comfortable with him on account of his burned face.' He shafted at Naylor a glance of fierce contempt. 'If it hadn't been for Yardley and men like him she might very well not have been alive at all to feel uncomfortable, or have a garden where she could grow her blasted weeds. I haven't much time for people like that – they think life's a pretty, Victorian, nursery picture-book version of existence, they like it deodorized, scented, washed and trimmed. They're not too keen on the real thing.'

'And at that time,' Naylor said casually, 'Yardley was working full-time for George Yoxall? He hadn't yet formed the intention of setting up in 'business on his own?'

Hulme examined the question, seemed unable to discover any masked pitfalls. 'Not as far as I knew,' he said warily. 'But it is quite conceivable that he didn't feel impelled to discuss all his plans with a schoolboy.' He gave Naylor a direct glance. 'I liked Yardley. The chips were stacked against him but he kept trying. More than that one cannot do. I saw him at the Fair. He was trying to help, clearing up the stalls. That genteel Medusa, Mrs Beryl Ford, kept waving him away as if he was a bad smell.'

Naylor turned his head and glanced at Mandy. She was sitting with her head tilted back, her eyes half closed. 'You were at the Fair,' he said abruptly. She jerked her eyes open. 'You and Tessa Drake. Did you help at any of the stalls?'

'I didn't,' she said at once. 'Tessa did for a short while. We went round all the stalls, bought a few things, had some tea and cakes, and then I went off into town by myself, I wanted to get Tessa's birthday present. Miss Ratcliff asked us if we'd help at the fancy goods stall, seeing that Mrs Rolt hadn't been able to come. I explained that I couldn't stay, but Tessa said she'd love to. I was away about an hour. I came back and collected Tessa and we both went home.'

'How long have you and Hulme been friendly?' Naylor said. At the sudden switch in his line of questioning she blinked, seemed for a moment at a loss.

'Oh, she's been friendly with me for a long, long time,' Hulme said in a tone laced with amusement. 'I've been around since who can remember when. Difficult to be exact.' His eyes never for an instant strayed in Mandy's direction. Stupid of me, Naylor thought, I should have asked her when she was by herself.

'That's right,' Mandy said. 'Difficult to be exact.'

Naylor stood up, glanced at his watch. Better see Maynard first and then Yardley. 'Allow me to show you out,'

Hulme said with mock civility. When they reached the door he threw it open, gave a little bow. 'In case you're still in any way uncertain about my attitude towards Mrs Rolt,' he said urbanely, 'it's really very straightforward. Quite simply, I didn't like the bitch.'

CHAPTER XVII

'MIGHT I ASK,' Naylor said to Maynard in a light, pleasant tone, 'why you didn't report the fact that you received a number of anonymous letters?' He'd got Viner to halt the car and phone the station just after they'd left Hulme's flat, on the offchance that someone might remember something, if in fact Hulme had been mistaken and Maynard had laid a complaint. But he'd had no luck. The episode had occurred some years back, no one had any recollection of such a matter; it would take time to consult the records.

Maynard continued to look down at the pen in his hand. His head was tilted at a courteous, listening angle. He had been in his sitting-room, working at a table neatly stacked with books and papers when Sergeant Viner had pressed a finger on the doorbell; Maynard had resumed his seat at the table as soon as the two men had settled themselves into easy chairs. His whole attitude strongly conveyed the impression that the moment the front door closed behind them again he would bend his head over his work, dismiss his visitors instantly and totally from his mind. Half-term holiday, Naylor thought, and apparently all Maynard could find to do by way of relaxation from teaching history at the grammar school was to read and write about history in his cottage. He had the air of a man who had been working for many hours and would continue to work till irresistible fatigue drove him to bed.

'I saw no reason to report the letters,' Maynard said in a detached, reflective way. 'I was quite certain I knew who had written them.' He glanced up briefly at the chief inspector; his look was calm and disciplined; it left Naylor with the sensation of having run up against the unyielding surface of a granite wall.

'Paul Hulme,' Maynard said. 'We had got across each other a little while earlier. I had detected him in a piece of cheating at an end-of-term exam. Nothing of major importance but I did mention the fact to the headmaster and he made rather a song and dance about it, sent for the boy's father, issued grave warnings and so forth. I hadn't been at the school very long, I wasn't all that familiar with the head's rather stringent views on such matters.

'I didn't repeat my mistake of course. After that I kept my knowledge of minor peccadilloes to myself. All of which must have led young Hulme to suppose that I'd chosen to single him out for especially harsh treatment. We were never on what you might call friendly terms during all the rest of his time at the school.' He gave Naylor another glance, longer this time, veiled, dispassionate, ironical. But there was nothing he could do about the iron quality in his look, Naylor thought; no trick of muscle or lid could diminish its powerful impact. Small wonder that the schoolboy Hulme had fought his adversary by devious means; it would have been a very exceptional lad that would have chosen to confront in open conflict the possessor of that inflexible regard.

'Given the basis of Hulme's temperament,' Maynard said, 'I didn't find it hard to understand how he might come to write such letters. I felt no urge to land him in what could turn out to be rather more serious trouble this time, so I decided to ignore the whole thing. I trusted to the passage of time to deal with the matter. And my decision was justi-

149

fied. The letters ceased.'

Naylor indicated neither by a nod or a word if he considered the explanation satisfactory. He said, 'Brian Yardley came up to your table in the lounge bar of the Unicorn three or four weeks back. He created a little disturbance. Why?'

Maynard raised his shoulders, let them drop again. 'Yardley doesn't have to have a sensible reason for everything he does. He'd had more than enough to drink. As usual.' His eyes dwelt for a long instant on Sergeant Viner. You knew Alison, the look said, it was very probably she who told you of that little episode. That – and how much more besides?

'Did Yardley know about the circumstances of your wife's death?' Naylor asked. This was not the moment to be unduly sensitive on Maynard's behalf. And it had all happened a long time ago. 'Was Yardley blackmailing you?' he persisted. 'Was Hulme blackmailing you? Or the two of them together, in collusion?'

Maynard's attitude remained composed. 'No,' he said, without apparent resentment. 'I have done nothing which could offer scope for blackmail to Yardley, Hulme or anyone else, acting singly or in unison.'

It took a strong effort of will on Naylor's part to resist the impulse to bombard Maynard with questions about the death of his wife. He would in any case very shortly know a good deal more about it; an inspector who had dealt with the matter at the time was coming over from Eldersleigh either this evening or tomorrow morning. If Maynard had had no hand in the death of either his wife or Mrs Rolt then the whole Eldersleigh business was irrelevant – but if he was not innocent then he was a highly dangerous man, intelligent, purposeful, with massive fissures in the structure of his personality, to be handled with extreme wariness and according to a well-thought-out plan, certainly not to be assailed with any chance query that happened to spring up in the course of routine interrogation.

But one small indulgence Naylor did permit himself. His eyes, roving about the room, had been able to light on no photograph of Maynard's wife. One would have expected some likeness, framed, standing on a table or desk. Not to display her picture seemed to Naylor to make a powerful statement about Maynard's attitude towards either his wife or the manner of her death but the precise nature of that statement he was unable to determine. So he said on a firm, courteous note, 'Would it be possible for me to see a photograph of your wife?' and left the words hanging there without qualification or explanation.

Maynard appeared to cease breathing for several seconds. He knows I can get hold of a photograph from the Eldersleigh files, Naylor thought, there's no point in his refusing to produce one now – unless he really doesn't possess one. And that would surely be a markedly significant state of affairs.

Maynard said nothing. He stood up with a slow controlled movement and walked over to the bookshelves on the right of the chimney breast. His back screened the action of his hands from Naylor's gaze; within a few seconds he turned round holding a framed photograph, face down. He didn't glance at it but held it out in silence towards Viner. Colin took it, reversing the frame as he did so, looking down at it with no more than mild curiosity. Naylor saw the shock freeze him in his chair. Then he drew a long breath and handed the photograph to the chief inspector.

Alison Rolt! Naylor stared down at the lovely smiling face, the edge of his surprise blunted by the sight of Viner's reaction. A moment later he saw the message slanting across the shoulder of the dress: To my darling Stephen,

With all my love, Ann.

He raised his head, flashed at Maynard a piercing glance. 'That was what made me notice Mrs Rolt in the first place,' Maynard said in a flat unemotional tone. 'The strong likeness to my wife.' I don't wonder it threw Viner for an instant, Naylor thought, it gave me a nasty shock. He looked down again at the delicate, perfect features. If a man had killed his wife in an access of tormented, half-insane jealousy and if the murdered woman had risen up before him in a single heart-stopping instant years later in the casual happenings of an autumn afternoon – might not the same overwhelming impulse spring to life a second time?

He laid the photograph face down on the table. He was seized by a feeling that he was picking his way through a minefield. He sent a swift mental glance over the filed statements, the details of Maynard's account of how he had spent last Saturday evening. He had helped at the Fair till just before eight o'clock, had gone home, taken a bath, phoned Mrs Rolt at about eight-thirty, made himself some supper and then settled down to work. He had gone to bed shortly after midnight. Not worth twopence as an alibi of course but exactly what he might have been expected to do – and certainly there had been no attempt to set up an intricate structure of times and movements such as a guilty man might very well create.

He'd have to put someone on the job of testing Maynard's alibi right away, questioning the neighbours, looking for any mention of lights – or darkness – in Maynard's cottage on Saturday evening, the sound of a car arriving or departing.

It occurred to him once again that if Maynard had lied about either the fact or the timing of his phone call to Mrs Rolt, then a great many suppositions based on the occurrence of that call would come crashing to the ground. But does that matter? Naylor asked himself in the same breath. For if Maynard had lied about the call there was the vast probability that it was because he had murdered Mrs Rolt and so for all practical purpose it was of little significance what effect the toppling of his story might have on the credibility of any other person connected with the case.

He stood up, glanced round the room. 'Did you buy a cushion at the Fair?' he asked in a conversational tone. There were three or four cushions on the sofa and chairs but none remotely like those offered for sale on the fancy goods stall.

'No.' Maynard was still standing by the chimney breast. He had his back now to the shelves, facing into the room; he had something of the air of an animal at bay.

He didn't accompany them into the hall but remained where he was, replying with a single brief nod to the chief inspector's routine remarks as the two detectives took their departure. Viner had barely laid his fingers on the handle of the front door when he heard from inside the sitting-room a little clatter and scrape, followed by the insinuating opening bars of the third Brandenburg concerto.

CHAPTER XVIII

ALREADY BY seven-thirty in the evening Yardley's voice was faintly slurred. 'Naturally I told Paul not to be such a damn fool, to cut out writing silly letters,' he said on a mildly challenging note. He was leaning against the frame of the sitting-room door in the living quarters behind his shop. He looked down with a glance edged with self-mockery at the chief inspector who was comfortably seated in an upholstered chair.

'A prominent citizen such as myself,' Yardley said.

'What else would you have expected me to say to the lad?'

What else indeed? Naylor thought. You'd have told him to lay off in any event. From ordinary commonsense if all you had at heart was the boy's welfare; from alert self-interest if you suddenly perceived an opportunity for lucrative blackmail and didn't wish to have your pitch queered by an unskilful amateur.

Yardley had opened his shop a few months after his first encounter with Hulme. According to his own account, the necessary money, by no means a large sum, had come to him on the death of his widowed mother. He had decided to set up in business of his own at that particular time because he had once again found himself out of a job a couple of weeks after he had got his hands on the legacy.

As to why he had been given the boot by old George Yoxall, he had made no bones about it. 'Drink,' he said to Naylor with a grin. 'As usual, the demon drink.'

Demon it may have been, Naylor had thought with a flick of insight, but I imagine it kept you from putting your head in the gas oven at more than one bleak and bitter moment in the past.

'That particular sacking was the best thing that ever happened to me,' Yardley said; 'it gave me the push I needed at exactly the right moment. *Plus ça change,*' he added, throwing back his head and laughing aloud, '*plus c'est* totally and permanently a different kettle of fish altogether.'

All quite credible, Naylor pondered, all quite feasible. But then again the money to start the business could quite conceivably have come not from the estate of his mother but out of Maynard's pocket, could have continued to dribble out from the same source over the ensuing years, helping Yardley at long last to a modest show of prosperity.

'Did you at any time blackmail Maynard?' Naylor suddenly asked Yardley.

Yardley gave him an unflinching look. 'Why do you ask?' he replied with an easy manner. 'Did Maynard ever complain that he was being blackmailed? By me or anyone else?'

'No,' Naylor answered after a brief pause.

Yardley raised his shoulders. 'Well then,' he said, and left it at that.

The interchange inexorably led back to Paul Hulme. 'Good lad, Hulme,' Yardley said with marked approval. 'Plenty of strong feeling in Hulme, even when he was a green schoolboy.' Something in his tone seemed to imply that he was defending Hulme against some unspoken accusation on the part of the chief inspector. 'The first time I met him,' Yardley said, 'he was doing odd jobs at one of old Yoxall's houses. I called to collect the rent and the old girl who lived there – decent enough sort in her limited way, you couldn't really blame her for living by the toffee-nosed principles she'd been reared in – she was making a cup of tea when I happened to press the bell. She kept me waiting at the door while she poured out tea for herself and Paul. It was a very cold day, I remember that well. She didn't give me any tea, she never gave me any tea.' He laughed, apparently with genuine amusement. 'Didn't want to encourage me, I fancy. Heaven knows what unspeakable liberties she imagined I'd take if she got out another cup and saucer.' He shrugged. 'It didn't bother me. I was used to that kind of reaction by then. The war hero stuff had worn thin a long time before.' He fell silent for a moment, looked down at the floor.

'Anyway, young Hulme didn't drink his tea. He left it on the table, told the woman he wouldn't be working for her any more, only he expressed himself rather more for-cibly than that – and then he followed me out of the gate. There was a café a little way up the road, we went in there, he bought me a cup of coffee and we talked. We talked for a hell of a long time. An intelligent lad, some interesting ideas, a strong natural sense of justice. I often saw him after that. He got another holiday job easily enough, a house a few doors along from the one he walked out on.

'It was with an old man who'd served in the first war, another of Yoxall's tenants. He'd have the kettle boiling before I arrived on rent day. Many a good chinwag the three of us had sitting round the kitchen table.' He gave Naylor a deprecating half-smile. 'Hulme had a bit of a thing about the Battle of Britain at that time. You know how it is, a young lad, a touch of hero worship.' He drew a long sighing breath, jerked himself suddenly upright, away from the door frame. 'I don't know about you two,' he said, 'but I'm bloody hungry.' He had been engaged in clearing up the shop when they'd arrived, hadn't yet got round to eating. 'I don't know how an offer of bread and cheese would strike you. I'm not much of a hand with the Cordon Bleu stuff.'

'No, thanks,' Naylor said automatically for himself and Viner, not bothering to glance across at the sergeant. Yardley went out into the passage and a few moments later they heard him clattering about in the kitchen. Viner sat in silence, looking about the room, small, packed with furniture, some of it old and probably valuable, but jammed against the walls without any care for effect, very probably simply stray pieces from the crowded shop.

Naylor leaned back and closed his eyes against the overhead light. Yardley didn't have much of an alibi for Saturday evening, in fact for all practical purposes he had no alibi at all. He had called in at a few pubs, was hazy about times and places. An alibi virtually impossible to check, for who among the thronged, smoky bars would have noted the exact moment at which Yardley's familiar unlovely visage no longer obtruded on his gaze?

And in every pub there was more than one bar; Yardley

could have vanished from one and into another a couple of yards away, or with equal ease he might have slipped into the car park, driven to Fairview, left his car in a dark side road, let himself into the ground-floor flat with the aid of keys obtained one way or another from Paul Hulme. He could have let himself out again with scarcely a breath of sound, surfaced a few minutes later in the same pub or another near at hand – and who would have been any the wiser?

Motive, Naylor said to himself with fierce thought. Some powerful, irresistible motive. He cast his mind about with concentrated energy but was unable to come up with anything new. The possible smell of blackmail, the shadowy suggestion of some kind of export racket. There should be something else, he thought, searching relentlessly on the perimeter of his mind for the wispy notion that continued to elude him but was surely there, phantom, eel-like, always a hair's breadth away from his snapping grasp.

Export . . . his thoughts came back yet again to the possibilities conjured up by the word. No mystery about my dealings with Wickham, Yardley had said lightly a few minutes ago when asked to explain the connection; I knew him in the Air Force, as a matter of fact he was my senior officer. I met him again after I started up in the book trade, he dropped quite a lot of business into my hands. One way and another, Yardley had added with a fleeting grin, after a fractional pause. It was that little pause Naylor hadn't altogether cared for, that and the transient grin, touched with deep secret amusement.

Certainly he had looked in at the Fair. He'd lent a hand briefly here and there, but he hadn't stayed long, an hour or two in the early part of the afternoon. Affairs of my own to attend to, as I'm sure you'll appreciate, he'd said to Naylor with a businesslike air undershot with self-mockery. No, he very definitely had not bought a cushion.

157

Nor had it occurred to him to take Mrs Rolt a conciliatory bunch of flowers. Natural enough in the circumstances, Naylor's manner had implied. Natural enough to others perhaps, Yardley's manner had answered, natural to handsome, whole, self-confident men, no longer in the slightest degree natural to me, not by thirty twisted years or more.

He came back into the sitting-room, still chewing, carrying a glass. His clothes gave off an odour of stale drink as he moved. His face was faintly flushed, his features had a slack, sleepy look. He's had a bibful in the kitchen, Naylor thought, he's sunk three or four in quick succession.

'Any other little question you wanted to ask?' Yardley grinned broadly at the chief inspector, raised a hand and rubbed it across his mouth, ran his tongue round his lips. The gone-to-seed, live-alone manners flung up suddenly in Naylor's brain a vision of that other Yardley long ago, and himself, a wartime schoolboy, hunched over the local newspaper, devouring the details, savouring the heroic exploits of that godlike young man.

'What was your reason for accosting Mrs Rolt outside the Kingfisher on the morning of her death?' he asked abruptly, closing his eyes for an instant on that treacherous memory.

'Accost?' Yardley said on a note of critical surprise. 'Rather a loaded word, wouldn't you say?'

'Your reason for speaking to her then.'

Yardley edged his way through the room, skirting the furniture. He twitched the curtains across the window, shutting out the dark blue sky. Naylor let out a small sigh. But there was no law to compel Yardley to sit down and keep still. Or come to that, to stay sober.

'A couple of papers turned up,' Yardley said, adjusting the heavy, none-too-clean curtains. 'Part of some book lists Kingfisher had duplicated for me. They'd disappeared, so the lists went out incomplete.' He turned from the window and gave Naylor an unsmiling glance. 'Lost me quite a bit of money.'

'I take it,' Naylor said, 'that you had blamed Kingfisher for the disappearance of the papers.'

Yardley gave a brisk nod. 'Yes. I just wanted to tell Mrs Rolt to forget about them. It wasn't the agency's fault at all, my own carelessness actually. They'd got in with some papers I'd put aside for Gerald Wickham. When I saw him on Saturday morning at the Wheatsheaf I gave him the papers. He looked through them and came across these two pages, nothing to do with him.'

'So your manner towards Mrs Rolt when you addressed her,' Naylor said, 'would not have been in any way aggressive or alarming?'

'Far from it.' Yardley passed a hand across his eyes. 'I just called out to her, walked towards her. She jumped back.' He drew a little shuddering breath. 'I must have frightened her, I can see that now. But it was certainly not intentional on my part.' He picked up his empty glass, looked into it. 'I imagine I frightened her just by existing, by being precisely what I am.'

He raised his head and looked at Naylor. 'I knew her father. I liked and respected him. I felt hopeful that morning. The sun was shining. As if I was getting a grip on things at last.' He closed his eyes. 'If she hadn't jumped back, if she hadn't hurt herself, hadn't been compelled to stay in the flat, she might very probably be alive now.' He remained silent for several seconds, then he opened his eyes and moved towards the door, clearly bound for another drink.

Naylor stood up. 'We won't keep you any longer. If anything else crops up, we'll be in touch.'

'I don't doubt it,' Yardley said. 'I won't be running away. Look for me here. Or in one of the Barbourne pubs. You'll find me. I can promise you that.'

CHAPTER XIX

VINER HAD JUST set the car in motion when he suddenly said, 'Hulme – I've just remembered, sir. Hulme said that Yardley was trying to help with the clearing up of the stalls at the Fair. That would have been about seven-fifteen or seven-thirty.'

'Pull in to the side of the road,' Naylor said at once. He frowned down at his clasped hands. 'Yardley's just told us he was at the Fair only for an hour or so, right at the beginning. And Hulme – what did Hulme tell us about the length of time he spent at the Fair himself?'

'I don't recollect that we asked him,' Viner said.

Naylor pressed his hands against his face. 'Just that one inadvertent reference on Hulme's part to seeing Yardley helping to clear up,' he said slowly.

'Inadvertent?' Viner said.

Naylor threw him a swift glance. 'Ye . . . es, I see what you mean. You may be right.' He drew a long breath. 'I wonder.' He sat in silence for several seconds, then he sighed loudly. 'I'm not too happy about Master Hulme. I think we'd better have another word with him.' He looked at his watch. A quarter to eight. Hulme might still be in his flat, with the Webb girl. Cooking supper perhaps. Or eating it. Or amusing himself in some other way.

But the flat, when they reached it five minutes later, was in darkness. 'It's just possible that they've gone over to Leofric Gardens,' Viner said. 'To the girls' place.'

'Mm,' Naylor said. Possible but not very likely. But the other girl might be there. Tessa Drake. She might have something to say on the subject of Hulme's presence at the

Fair. And what she had to say might be rather more accurate than what Master Hulme might be disposed to tell them. 'All right,' Naylor said. 'We'll try Leofric Gardens. We'll look in and have a word with Bennett on the way.'

Gerald Wickham was at the station when they called in. He had been engaged for several minutes in a finely-balanced struggle with Inspector Bennett, a duel conducted on both sides with civility and resolution. Wickham was determined to get his baggage released and himself freed from semi-captivity at the Wheatsheaf Hotel, and Bennett was equally insistent that both Wickham and his merchandise must remain where they were for the present. The combatants had just about reached the conclusion that neither was going to give way when Naylor and Sergeant Viner walked into the station. Bennett was manœuvring his opponent along the corridor into the reception area as Naylor came into the building.

'Ah!' Wickham said with pleasure, catching sight of higher and possibly more reasonable authority. But the chief inspector, halted in mid-stride and addressed with persuasive appeal by Wickham, came down firmly on Bennett's side.

'I'm sorry,' he said with finality. 'We'll let you know the moment your cases can be cleared.' Nothing obviously amiss with the stuff so far, the art expert had intimated in the course of the afternoon, but there had been time for only an incomplete and superficial examination. The expert would do his best, would press on as speedily as possible, but it would be several hours yet before he could make any more positive pronouncement.

'Ah well!' Wickham raised his shoulders in philosophic resignation.

'There is one little matter though,' Naylor said. He gestured Wickham into a quiet corner and brought up the question of his connection with Yardley. Five minutes later he said good night to Wickham, watched him go off towards the door. He had learned nothing new in the course of the conversation. Wickham had told him precisely the same tale as Yardley. He had been Yardley's superior officer in the Air Force, had come across him again in recent years, steered what business he could towards him.

Naylor yawned, rubbed his chin, walked over to where Bennett was standing in an attitude of weary righteousness.

'That complaint made a few weeks back by the two girls, Drake and Webb,' Naylor said.

'Made by one of the girls,' Bennett corrected him. 'By Tessa Drake. Mandy Webb simply came in to lend moral support. She wasn't present when the incident happened. If it ever did happen.'

'That's what I'm getting at,' Naylor said. 'Did it ever happen? If the girls got wind of the existence – or rumoured existence – of a prowler, from gossip or hearsay, then one or both of them may have picked up the story and decided to make use of it for strictly personal reasons. And in pursuance of those reasons, walked in here to lodge a complaint.'

'There never was a prowler,' Bennett said with an air of cheerful conviction. 'Young girls and old women, nothing they like better than scaring the wits out of each other with tales of mad attackers lying in wait in lonely places. Makes life seem exciting, attracts attention to them for a moment, helps them to feel less insignificant.' He levelled an amused, half-malicious glance in the direction of Sergeant Viner standing patiently nearby. 'As for Miss Tessa Drake,' Bennett said a shade more loudly, 'there's no mystery there, she just fancies Viner. She's been in here more than once to make sheep's eyes at him. I dare say she'll be in again when the fit takes her.'

Naylor yawned widely as the car moved out of the forecourt. A long strenuous day, and still not over. He'd be lucky if he got to bed before midnight the way things were going. He leaned back, closed his eyes and allowed his brain to slip into neutral. His thoughts had begun to swim and dissolve when he heard Viner's voice, echoing, dreamlike, telling him they had reached Leofric Gardens. He felt the car slide to a halt, and came instantly awake.

Number twenty-nine was a tall narrow house set in a once-fashionable terrace, now with a far from prosperous air, its dwellings chopped into portions dignified with the title of flats.

Tessa Drake answered their ring at the bell. 'Oh – it's you,' she said, looking at Viner, giving him a hesitant smile. 'I've been wondering if you'd want to see me.' She held the door back for them to step inside, slanting at Naylor only a brief incurious look.

A decidedly pretty girl, Naylor thought. Languid, fluid type. He'd had one or two interesting encounters in his time – and his time was by no means over – with females cast in a similar mould.

She led the way into a room on the left, opening off the hall. She uttered a little series of apologetic remarks about the state of the room – actually reasonably clean and tidy, certainly a far cry from a great many apartments the chief inspector's feet had taken him into during more than a quarter of a century in the force.

The two men remained standing, in spite of her gestures towards chairs. There was no sign of Hulme or Mandy Webb, and it wouldn't take more than a minute or two to deal with the query about the Fair.

'They've gone to the pictures,' Tessa said. 'They won't

be back till about half past ten.' She looked mildly disappointed when she realized she was not the object of their visit.

'A couple of minor details you might be able to help us with,' Naylor said casually. Her face immediately took on a livelier, pleased expression. 'I understand you went to the Charities Fair last Saturday, that you helped at one of the stalls.' She nodded. 'Was Paul Hulme there at the same time as yourself?'

'He didn't help at any of the stalls,' she said at once.

'No, I didn't mean that. I simply want to know how long he was there, when he arrived and when he left.'

She gave him a glance that surprised him by its acuteness. 'Why? What's he done?' she asked.

Naylor smiled. 'I don't know that he's done anything. We ask these questions about a very large number of people. We certainly don't imagine they've all been up to something. It's part of the routine, helps to establish a picture of what happened.'

She didn't return his smile. 'Paul wasn't at the Fair while I was there,' she said slowly. 'I'm quite sure of that. I don't know anything about the time he got there or when he left.'

'Brian Yardley, then,' Naylor said in a bantering tone. 'Do you recollect anything about his presence at the Fair, or his time of arrival or departure?'

She looked down at the floor for several seconds, then raised her eyes again. 'No, I can't remember seeing him there at all. But I was only there for a couple of hours.' She glanced at Viner, looked away again. Bennett was right, Naylor registered, she does fancy Viner, she definitely and strongly fancies him.

A thought bobbed up in his mind : I wonder what she made of his acquaintance with her employer, Mrs Alison Rolt? Did she imagine it was something other than it was?

And behind that thought, another, bright and sharp: Did we ever take Miss Tessa Drake's fingerprints? The answer flashed back at him almost in the same instant: No, we did not, her name was never on anyone's list of suspects, however fancifully composed. He had a vivid picture of that set of prints, unidentified, almost complete, the palm of the left hand, the thumb, the middle three fingers, beautifully clear on the jamb of the sitting-room door.

'Did you ever have occasion to visit Mrs Rolt's flat?' he asked suddenly. 'In the way of business perhaps?'

'Not in the way of business,' she said immediately. 'And I can't say I ever actually visited the flat. I was only ever inside the house once.' She looked at him with wide eyes, her look eager, gentle. 'That was last Saturday.' In the stillness which followed her words Naylor put out a hand and rested it against the back of a chair.

'The day of her death?' he said gently. 'You should have told us. We like to know every little thing.'

'Nobody asked me,' she said on a surprised, defensive note. 'I didn't know anyone would think it important. It was in the afternoon, quite a few hours before she died.'

Naylor gave her a long look. 'I think we'd all better sit down.'

She told her tale fluently, without hesitation. She had been helping Hazel Ratcliff at the Fair, Hazel had sent her over to Fairview – only a short distance from the hall – to fetch a few things from her flat. A cardigan, a notebook, a small bottle of aspirin tablets. On her way upstairs Tessa saw that the door to Mrs Rolt's flat was ajar. She knocked, put her head into the sitting-room and asked Mrs Rolt – who was lying back in a chair with her feet up, dealing with a sheaf of typewritten papers – if she could be of any assistance. Mrs Rolt thanked her, said she was quite all right and not just then in need of anything. Tessa then went up to Miss Ratcliff's flat, collected what she had been sent to fetch and returned to the Fair.

Ye . . . es, Naylor thought, that's how she'd have stood, on the threshold, her right hand on the knob, her left hand pressed against the doorpost, looking into the room.

'We'd like your prints,' he said easily. 'Nothing to be alarmed about. Routine matter, anyone who was anywhere near the place, enables us to eliminate innocent people. You'd better call in at the station.'

They were on their way out, a few paces from the front door, when some impulse turned Naylor's head towards the room on the opposite side of the hall. He paused. 'That's part of your flat, I take it?'

She nodded. 'Do you want to see it? It's a bit bigger than the room we've just been in.' She threw open the door, made a small ritual grimace. 'It's in a terrible mess.'

The room was pleasantly furnished, brighter, gayer-looking than the other. A couple of vivid posters on the wall, a large mirror over the fireplace. Near the window a small table with a pottery urn standing on its polished surface.

And in the urn a number of very fine chrysanthemums of an unusual shade of rosy orange, the petals of each large incurved bloom tipped with sulphur yellow.

Naylor's eyes met Viner's. There was a long moment during which their glances remained locked. Then Naylor smiled at Tessa, nodded over at the flowers. 'Magnificent specimens,' he said lightly.

She looked pleased. 'Yes, they're very pretty. But they're really rather delicate. You mightn't think so, they look so big and strong. But they're actually quite easy to damage.'

'Is that so?' Naylor said with manifest interest.

She nodded. 'One head was broken off already when he brought them. A shame, they must have been very expensive.'

Naylor felt a prickle move along his spine. 'They were

166

a present then? A very handsome one.'

'Yes.' She smiled. 'Robin brought them. For my birth-day.'

'Robin?' Naylor said lightly.

She nodded. 'Robin Ford. He works at CeeJay. That's where Mandy works now.'

'And he's your boy-friend?' Naylor asked with a fatherly smile.

She laughed. 'Well, hardly.' She slid a look at Viner. 'I scarcely know him. He's only been here once before. Mandy felt sorry for him, his parents grind him down a bit, so she suggested asking him along.' She raised her shoulders. 'He's all right really. A bit of a drip.' She grinned. 'Not my cup of tea. Or Mandy's.'

'And what time did Robin Ford get to your party?' Naylor asked casually.

She frowned. 'I couldn't really say. I know it wasn't early because his parents had people in for supper and he had to wait till after they'd gone.' She broke off suddenly, put up a hand to her mouth. 'I remember now. One of the people they asked to supper was Mr Rolt. Mr Rolt,' she said again, on a deeply thoughtful note. She looked from Naylor to Viner, back again at Naylor. 'Are the flowers something to do with Mrs Rolt's death? Yes, of course they are,' she answered herself a moment later when neither of the men said anything. 'You wouldn't be standing here talking about them if they weren't.' She smiled faintly. 'I imagined you were just making conversation.'

'And the time Robin got to your party?' Naylor persisted. 'Try to be a little more exact.'

She bit her lip, looked down at the floor. 'There were a lot of people here already when Robin came, I remember that. And I was eating a hot dog, and talking to one of the girls from Kingfisher. We didn't start making the hot dogs till after ten o'clock, so I expect it would be about half past ten when he got here. It could have been later but I don't see that it could have been earlier.'

'You are quite certain it was young Ford who brought you the flowers?' Naylor said.

She looked back at Saturday evening. 'Well, I couldn't exactly take my Bible oath on it,' she said at last. 'There was quite a crowd, you know how it is, everyone jostling and dancing and pushing, and this beautiful bunch of flowers was shoved into my face and someone said, "Happy birthday." I looked round and saw Robin smiling at me.' She screwed up her eyes, was silent for a few seconds. 'I didn't turn round right away, of course,' she said slowly. 'I couldn't, there was too much of a crush. The flowers were pushed at me, more or less over people's heads. I took them, looked at them, it was a minute or two before I struggled round to see where the voice had come from. I saw Robin's face, he smiled at me, I naturally assumed it was him.'

'Think about it again, very carefully,' Naylor said. 'I want you to be quite sure. I'll see you later, I'll ask you about it again. In the meantime, don't discuss it with anyone else. Anyone at all.'

She nodded, she looked very serious. Naylor didn't bother to inform her that the next time he saw her was going to be in an hour or two, when Mandy Webb and Hulme might be expected to return from the cinema.

He walked out into the hall. 'You're on your own then for the rest of the evening,' he said casually. 'You don't mind being alone?'

'The other two won't be all that late,' she said. 'They'll be back as soon as the film's over. Mandy wants to wash her hair. I'm going to make some coffee and sandwiches for them.' She opened the front door, looked out at the dark chill evening. 'It's not much of a night to be out in, anyway.'

'A good film, is it?' Naylor said lightly. 'The one they've gone to see.'

She made a little face. 'It's that Hitchcock film at the Roxy. Paul's very keen on Hitchcock. Not my cup of tea.'

'Better get back inside and keep warm,' Naylor said with an affable, fatherly air. 'It's a raw cold evening.' But she remained by the open door, watching till the car was out of sight.

As they rounded the corner Naylor said to Viner, 'We'll look in at the Youth Club, see if young Ford's there. I'd rather catch him when he's away from Mum and Dad.' He was silent for a little while, then he said, 'Of course there could have been two separate bunches of flowers. Young Ford could have bought his bunch quite properly, from the same place where the murderer also bought his flowers.' None of their enquiries at florists' shops and flower stalls had so far provided any kind of clue to the origin of the blooms.

'There was one head missing from the bunch that was given to Tessa Drake,' Viner said. 'It's hardly likely that two separate bunches would each lose one bloom.'

Naylor sighed. 'No, probably not.' There was a brief pause and then he said, 'Suppose young Ford had a crush on Mrs Rolt. He would undoubtedly hear that she had injured her foot – he'd hear about it at the Fair if nowhere else. Then suppose he decides to take her some flowers. He calls at Fairview, is admitted to the sitting-room. He offers his flowers, Mrs Rolt smiles and says, "Very sweet of you, but I'd better not take them. You find a nice girl of your own age to give them to," and she shows him gently out. On the way to the door the head drops off one flower. Robin decides to take the bunch along to Tessa's party and give them to her as a birthday gift. Could all be perfectly innocent.'

'Except,' Viner said, 'for one thing. When is this visit

to Fairview supposed to have taken place? Robin was in his parents' house helping to entertain Rolt until after ten. If he called into Fairview with his flowers on his way to Leofric Gardens, that would be, say, twenty past, twenty-five past ten, and we're pretty certain that Mrs Rolt was already dead by then, well before then, probably.'

'Could he have called in earlier?' Naylor said. 'Before he went home to help entertain Rolt. He was certainly in his parents' house when the guests arrived, so he must have got home at the latest by seven-thirty.'

'Andrew Rolt was at Fairview from seven-fifteen till seven-thirty,' Viner said. 'He made no mention of seeing young Ford anywhere near the flat.'

'Surely Robin could have called and offered his flowers before seven-fifteen,' Naylor said. 'Could have left well before Rolt came on the scene. Seems straightforward enough.'

'He helped at the Fair,' Viner said. 'He could have come by the flowers at some point during the afternoon. If he heard that Mrs Rolt had injured her foot, if he hit upon the notion of taking her some flowers, then he could have slipped away from the hall, bought the flowers in some shop – though heaven knows which shop – and then returned to the Fair. He could have called in at Fairview on the way home from the Fair, had his flowers refused, dropped the flowerhead on his way out of the flat, taken the bunch home, secreted it in his room – as any lad would who had parents like his – and then taken them with him to the party to give to Tessa. All still perfectly innocent.'

'Yes,' Naylor said. 'That would mean of course that the flowerhead was lying on the carpet while Rolt was talking to his wife. And he most specifically told us that he saw no sign of any chrysanthemums in the flat.'

'I can't see that that matters,' Viner said. 'The head wasn't in full view. Rolt wouldn't be gazing round the room, he'd have been absorbed in talking to his wife. And the head might have been even less in view at that time. It might have been kicked into greater prominence later on, by Mrs Rolt herself, awkwardly moving about with her stick, or during the little struggle when she was killed.'

'Just suppose,' Naylor said in a light easy tone, 'merely for the sake of argument, that young Ford is not completely innocent.'

'You mean,' Viner said, 'that he killed her. It would be rather difficult to think up a motive for him.'

'Just for argument's sake,' Naylor said. 'Then he wouldn't have taken his flowers to Fairview at six forty-five or seven, because Rolt and others saw her alive after that, so he must have taken them later, at the time when she was killed.'

'But she was killed no later than nine-thirty,' Viner said. 'We've pretty well established that. And at nine-thirty and for a couple of hours before that, Robin Ford was at home, constantly in the presence of other people.'

'Yes,' Naylor said decisively. 'You're absolutely right. So he's very probably totally innocent and we can forget all about him.' The car drew to a halt outside the youth club. 'Just a matter of seeing him and confirming our suppositions,' Naylor said. 'And of course,' he added as he opened the car door, 'finding out – for the sake of my sanity if for no other reason – precisely where he bought his precious bunch of flowers.'

Robin was playing table tennis with another lad. 'No need to interrupt the game,' Naylor told the club leader. 'We'd just like an opportunity to have a quiet word with the boy. You might drift in to watch the game, bring him along as soon as it's finished. The other boy doesn't have to know anything about our being here.'

'You can talk to him in my office,' the leader said. 'You can be private in there.'

When Robin came into the office a few minutes later he

appeared calm and self-possessed.

'One small matter you might be able to help us with,' Naylor said pleasantly. 'The bunch of chrysanthemums you took Tessa Drake on Saturday evening – '

'I didn't take Tessa Drake a bunch of chrysanthemums,' Robin said firmly and courteously.

Naylor frowned. 'She says you did.'

Robin looked at him with unshaken assurance. 'Then she's mistaken.'

'Did you see anyone else give her a bunch of chrysanthemums?' Naylor asked.

Robin looked away for a moment. 'I do seem to remember some flowers,' he said. 'But I didn't particularly notice, I didn't have any reason to.' He smiled slightly. 'It was a bit of a crush, I wasn't exactly in my element.'

'Is there anyone here in the club,' Naylor asked, 'who saw you arrive at the party?'

Robin shook his head. 'No, none of them were at the party. I went by myself. The two girls don't mix with this crowd.'

There was a brief pause. Then Naylor said casually, 'So if I were to suggest to you that you bought a bunch of flowers at some time during Saturday afternoon and took them along to Fairview to present to Mrs Rolt – '

'To Mrs Rolt?' Robin echoed in a voice of astonishment. 'Why on earth should I do a thing like that?'

'She'd injured her foot,' Naylor said. 'You might have thought she'd like some flowers.'

'I hardly knew her,' Robin said with protest. A trace of amusement crept into his tone. 'And in any case, buying bunches of flowers – it's not exactly my style.'

Naylor sighed. 'Have you any idea where the flowers might have been purchased?'

'I don't know anything about them at all,' Robin said with finality.

A thought flashed into Viner's brain. 'Perhaps you called on Mrs Rolt for some reason connected with the Fair?' he suggested. Bringing her an account of the takings of the art stall, perhaps. There could have been half a dozen reasons for calling; or someone might simply have asked him to give her a message.

'No,' Robin said at once. 'Hazel Ratcliff lives at Fairview. She would have done anything like that if it was necessary.' Mm, probably so, Naylor thought.

'Then you made no contact with Mrs Rolt at all on Saturday evening?' he asked.

Robin's eyes met Naylor's in a steady gaze. 'I neither saw her nor spoke to her at any time on Saturday,' he said.

'He seems pretty firm in his denials,' Naylor said to Viner as they left the club.

'It could easily have been some other person who thrust the flowers at Tessa Drake,' Viner said. 'Robin Ford might just have chanced to be standing nearby when she turned round. Easy enough mistake to make.'

'Yes, I suppose so,' Naylor said. He ran the tip of his tongue delicately along his gums. Mercifully the pain still seemed to be quiescent. He glanced at his watch. 'Come on,' he said on a cheerful note. 'We've time for a cup of coffee before we need go back to Leofric Gardens.'

CHAPTER XX

THE HITCHCOCK film ended at ten-fifteen. At five minutes past ten Naylor and Sergeant Viner left the car discreetly parked in a side street and walked briskly towards the girls' flat.

Tessa answered the door. She appeared neither surprised nor disconcerted to see them so soon, concluding, it seemed, that they had decided after all that it was necessary to speak to Hulme about his activities at the Fair.

'I've had a good long think about those flowers,' she said when they were all in the sitting-room. 'It definitely was Robin Ford who brought them for me. I'm quite certain about it.'

Naylor merely nodded. He could see no point now in questioning her about it again. It was evident that there had been a good deal of confused movement at the time the flowers were thrust at her. It wasn't likely that further questioning would clarify her memory of the incident. In fact it would most probably simply serve to harden her original recollection – a process which seemed to have already happened to some extent. Instead he passed the next five minutes in trying without success to discover if Miss Drake had any more little surprises up her sleeve.

Just after ten-thirty there was the sound of a car drawing up outside, the slam of a door. 'Here they are.' Tessa said. She jumped up. 'I'll get the sandwiches and coffee.' The street door opened. Mandy's voice sounded, calling something back to Hulme who was apparently still outside; the words were indistinct, the tone lighthearted. A moment later she came crashing into the room, crying out, 'I'm absolutely starving!' She halted on the threshold, and her mouth dropped open at the sight of the two detectives.

Tessa was still standing in the middle of the room. 'Do you remember,' she said to Mandy without preamble, 'who it was that gave me those flowers at the party? I say it was Robin Ford. It was, wasn't it?' Naylor let out a long irritated breath.

Mandy flicked a glance at Tessa. Her eyes came back to Naylor, her look was level now, controlled.

'Oh no,' she said with force. 'It wasn't Robin.' She gave

174

a short laugh. 'Hardly likely.'

'All right then,' Tessa said. 'Who did bring the flowers?'

The tip of Mandy's tongue showed for an instant between her teeth. 'I don't know.' She raised her shoulders. 'But I know it wasn't Robin.' She grinned at Naylor. 'And how do I know? Because I saw him when he came in and he definitely wasn't carrying any bunch of flowers.' She gave another brief snort of laughter. 'As if he would.'

The street door banged shut. Hulme appeared behind Mandy, not saying anything this time by way of greeting, taking in their presence and adjusting to it all in the same moment, giving Naylor one penetrating glance and then immediately assuming a lively, good-humoured air.

Naylor was now totally resigned to the certainty that one of the girls would instantly put to Hulme the same question about the origin of the flowers, but instead Mandy looked at Tessa and said, 'Come on, let's get some food. I'll drop dead if I don't eat.' She turned and pushed past Hulme without looking at him. Tessa followed her out of the room.

Hulme stood looking down at Naylor, faintly smiling. 'This is getting to be a habit,' he said, 'What's it about this time?'

'One or two details,' Naylor said. 'Among them the bunch of chrysanthemums in the next room.' Hulme stopped smiling, he looked thrown out of his stride, puzzled. 'I'd like to know who brought them here,' Naylor said. 'Simple enough question.'

'Very simple.' Hulme's manner was assured again. He gave the chief inspector a long assessing glance. 'Nothing in fact could be simpler.' His voice was easy, almost friendly. 'I brought the flowers, I gave them to Tessa.'

There was a short silence. 'And may one enquire how you came by them?' Naylor said at last in a tone that neither accepted nor rejected the statement.

'One may indeed,' Hulme said. 'I am happy to supply the information.' He looked at Naylor with an expression of keen enjoyment. 'I found the flowers in a litter bin. In Church Street, near the Town Hall.' He grinned, jerked his head in the direction of the kitchen. 'I hope you don't find it necessary to advertise the fact to the girls. I'd rather leave them with the impression that I paid hard cash for them.'

Naylor said nothing. He gave Hulme a steady stare. 'I don't normally go looking in litter bins for birthday presents,' Hulme said with a high laugh. 'But I'd forgotten to get something for Tessa. I was driving along on my way to the party – it was about half past ten or a quarter to eleven on Saturday night – and I suddenly remembered I hadn't bought her anything.' His manner was relaxed now, co-operative. 'I had to stop for the traffic lights. I turned my head and saw these gorgeous flowers sticking up out of the bin. I couldn't believe my luck. They were done up in stout blue wrapping paper, open at the top so you could see the flowerheads. They were just shoved a few inches into the bin, half keeling over as if they'd been dropped in in a hurry.

'I didn't waste any time. Manna from heaven, I said to myself. I leapt out and grabbed them, back into the car and away, in case the fellow who'd dumped them changed his mind and came back. He might have been boozed or had a row with his girl, pushed them into the bin in a mad fit, could have wanted them out again five minutes later.'

He laughed again, a short brittle note. 'But I don't understand why you couldn't have asked Tessa. She'd have told you I brought the flowers. No secret about it. I shoved them at her the moment I arrived. I said, "Happy birthday." There was one hell of a crush. She turned round and took them. She buried her face in them and said, "Oh, marvellous!" She looked mightily pleased, looked up at me and said, "How absolutely lovely," as if she thought me a most generous fellow.'

The sky was bright with stars when they came down the steps into the cold night air. As they walked away up the road Naylor said heavily, 'If anyone of them changes their tale about the flowers, Hulme, young Ford or either of the girls, I will refuse to believe a man jack of them without some totally disinterested person to back up the story.' Half-a-dozen totally disinterested persons if at all possible. Preferably the Archangel Gabriel and five fully paid-up and highly distinguished members of the heavenly host.

'It's easy to understand a certain amount of confusion in the stories,' Viner said. 'A party like that, crowded, jostling, the flowers are thrust out, someone speaks, someone smiles, a conclusion is drawn, mistaken perhaps, but then the moment is gone, the mistake isn't corrected, it becomes hard fact in the mind. The flowers are put in a vase, comments may be made about them later, admiring them and so on, but it would probably never come about that anyone needed to refer to the fact that they had been presented by a particular individual. Everyone would be under the impression that the origin of the flowers was known to all of them.'

Naylor gave a grunt. 'A mistake wouldn't become hard fact in everyone's mind,' he said. 'Not in the minds of Hulme or Robin Ford. Each of them knows whether or not he brought the flowers.'

'I can see why young Ford would lie about it now, even if he did bring flowers,' Viner said. 'He could be totally innocent of any hand in Mrs Rolt's death and yet lie about the flowers. From fear of being suspected of the murder, from fear of ridicule from his mates – or parents – if indeed he did have a crush on Mrs Rolt.' He found it easier now if, even in his own mind, he always referred to her as Mrs

Rolt. He looked back for a moment across the gulf of ten years that separated him from Robin Ford. 'Ridicule is possibly the thing one would fear most of all at that age.'

'Possibly so,' Naylor said. 'But as far as Hulme is concerned, the very opposite could be true. I wouldn't put it past that young man to have invented the entire tale about the flowers out of one of half-a-dozen devious motives. Seeking at bit of importance, wanting to gum up the works out of general dislike of the police, a wish to obscure the truth in any particular that comes his way, either because he's involved in the murder or he's trying to protect someone he has reason to suppose is involved in it. And then again he might invent a tale out of nothing more complicated than sheer devilment.'

He let out a long groan. 'He might have had nothing whatever to do with the flowers. Or he might have acquired them in some totally different way from the one he chose to tell us about.' They reached the car, and Viner opened the door. Naylor settled himself into his seat, leaned back and closed his eyes.

'Both of those young men could be lying for quite different reasons,' he said. 'The flowers could very easily have been given to Tessa by someone else altogether.'

In the wide spaces of the reception area the sounds of voices and footsteps had acquired the muted, echoing quality they took on late at night. Naylor stood by the desk, frowning down at the polished surface. I do believe, he said to himself with growing certainty, there's a piece of root left in my jaw.

He pushed the tip of his tongue round the rear section of his top gum. One hell of a time to be plagued with toothache. He let out a long noisy sigh. Perhaps it was just a touch of neuralgia, might be gone when he woke up in the morning. And then again, perhaps not.

Inspector Bennett came up to him with a quick, lively tread. 'I'm off then,' he said with irritating energy. 'If no one requires my services any further tonight.'

Naylor closed his eyes for a moment. 'I'll be here for another half-hour or so,' he said without enthusiasm.

'Waste of time, ninety per cent of all this activity,' Bennett said cheerfully. 'Andrew Rolt did it. Not a shadow of doubt. Always the husband. Mark my words. Don't go telling me afterwards I never told you. Like to bet a fiver on it? Tenner if you prefer.'

Naylor closed his eyes again. 'I would not,' he said in a low intense voice. 'Thank you very much.'

Bennett fastened his coat, adjusted its set about his shoulders. 'Ah well,' he said. 'You had your chance.' He patted his pockets. 'No substitute for wool,' he said breezily. 'That's what the ads used to say. And they're damn well right.'

Naylor kept his eyes fiercely shut. And no substitute either for judgement, intelligence, compassion or wisdom, he thought sourly. Or come to that, for tolerance, tact, and common-or-garden good horse sense.

Barely two hours after he had dropped poleaxed into sleep, Naylor came sharply awake with a single clear thought needling his brain: I never did get it straight about precisely when Hulme and Yardley were at the Fair.

I'm quite certain about it, Hulme had told him stubbornly a few hours ago, Yardley was trying to help with the clearing up of the stalls, that must have been – oh, about half past seven. When Hulme was asked how he had come to be at the Fair himself at that hour, he had grinned and raised his eyebrows. I was lending a helping hand, he said with a challenging note. Looked in to see if there was anything I could do, just happened to be passing. Stayed about an hour and a half, humping stuff about, seven o'clock till half past eight, more or less. Then I went back to my flat, had a kip till about ten o'clock, to put me in good shape for the party. You ask around, someone'll remember seeing me at the Fair.

Someone probably will, Naylor thought with bleak cynicism, some pal or other Hulme would have suitably briefed by the time they got to him. Perhaps it wasn't important to discover exactly when either of the two men was at the Fair – but one could never be sure which small detail might not be the one to unlock the puzzle. He gave a fragmentary groan.

The question is, he said to himself once again, is Hulme telling an out-and-out lie about the flowers, is he telling the complete, unadorned truth, or is he steering a course some way between the two? He linked his hands behind his head. How much simpler his job would be if people would only make up their minds to adopt one unified set of characteristics and attitudes, and obligingly stick to them in every conceivable kind of vicissitude.

There really could be no doubt about it, the bunch of flowers which ended up in Tessa Drake's vase was the same bunch which had originally been taken to Mrs Rolt's flat. Now – how had the flowers got from Fairview to Leofric Gardens?

Mrs Rolt might have refused the flowers, either because she didn't much care for the giver or didn't think it wise to encourage the giver to make her presents. She could have said, 'I'm sorry, I can't accept your flowers,' and the person would then have taken them away with him.

Or Mrs Rolt might have been dead at the time the flowers were taken away, dead by the same hand that had presented them to her; self-preservation would have dictated the removal of the flowers which could otherwise point an unmistakable finger at the murderer.

It was also conceivable that the flowers had been taken

to the flat by one person and later removed by someone else.

Naylor sat up in bed and pulled at the light switch. Suppose an entirely innocent person had taken Mrs Rolt a bunch of flowers from sheer goodwill, and she had accepted the flowers; then some time later Hulme might have entered the flat – by one means or another – and killed Mrs Rolt, picking up the flowers on a macabre impulse to take to Tessa Drake as a birthday present? Such wantonly gruesome touches were by no means unknown in the history of violent crime.

By the same token of course, Robin Ford could have done the same thing, entered the flat – saying he had a message about the Fair, for instance – killed Mrs Rolt and taken the flowers.

But if the flowers had been thrust at Tessa by some third person, neither Hulme nor young Ford, then there must have been among the guests at her party someone with a connection with the dead woman, someone they hadn't as yet cottoned on to. He sighed. They'd have to get a complete list of the guests from the two girls. Or, more correctly, attempt to get a complete list of guests. He had a very good notion of how it would be, friends who had brought friends, strangers who had gate-crashed, assertions, doubts, denials. But it would have to be gone through all the same. One simply never knew at which point the blinding flash might occur. If it ever occurred at all.

He saw all at once that Mrs Rolt might have accepted the flowers from one person quite happily, and then made a present of them to someone else who admired them. That person could have been Hulme or Robin Ford. Either of them might have said to her as he looked at the flowers, 'That reminds me, I'm going to a party later this evening, I realize now I haven't bought a present,' and Mrs Rolt could have said amiably, 'Take these, you're welcome to

them.' She might have felt an impulse to be generous towards the party-going young man, he might have just
given her some cause to be grateful to him, performed a
service, brought her news she was pleased to hear. Or he
might have been a young man she knew and liked, felt a
wave of affectionate sympathy for. According to Sergeant
Viner she hadn't been over-fond of Hulme. As for Robin
Ford – she knew him, she had worked with his father;
Robin was a pleasant, well-mannered lad, she might very
well have liked him, might have given him the flowers to
take to the party.

And the lad might very well lie about it now, Naylor
thought, sliding back against the pillows, from a very real
fear of being suspected of having had a hand in her death.

What about Hulme's story of finding the flowers in the
litter bin? If he was telling the truth, how had the flowers
come to be dumped there? If the murderer had presented
Mrs Rolt with the flowers and then decided to remove
them, he could have thrust them into the bin as being a
swift and anonymous method of disposing of them. The
Church Street litter bin was about three-quarters of a mile
from Fairview. That figures, Naylor thought; the murderer
couldn't go dropping the bunch into a bin immediately
outside the flat. Nor presumably would he deposit them in
a bin close to where he lived. So it was possible that the bin
was roughly half-way between Fairview and the place where
the murderer lived or was bound for immediately after
leaving the flat. And a fat lot of use that highly conjectural
conclusion will probably turn out to be, Naylor thought
bleakly.

If on the other hand Mrs Rolt had refused the flowers
from the giver, he could then have left the flat – with Mrs
Rolt alive and well – and thrust the flowers into the first
bin he noticed, in a fit of anger or petulance. And Hulme
could have come along some time later, spotted the

flowers and rescued them. In which case the flowers had
nothing whatever to do with the murder, Hulme could be
telling the truth all along the line and so could Robin Ford.
And the person who had taken the flowers to Fairview and
received a snub for his pains could very well be simply
holding his tongue about it out of fear. Or that person
might be someone we haven't thought of yet, Naylor
realized without pleasure. He might not have lied to us
about the flowers for the very good reason that we have
never asked him about the flowers, having at present not
the slightest cause to connect him with the dead woman.

According to both Hulme and Tessa Drake there had
been no florist's name on the wrapping paper. But that
proved nothing. For a variety of reasons, innocent or guilty,
Hulme would be unlikely now to disclose the florist's name
if it had in fact appeared on the paper. And by the time
they had got around to questioning Tessa about it she had
realized that the flowers had assumed importance, she
would scarcely be likely to wish to land Hulme in trouble;
if she had seen a name on the paper she would keep her
mouth shut about it now from a general feeling that the
less she said about anything connected with the case, the
better.

Naylor passed a hand across his eyes. At that moment
the ache began again in his jaw. He didn't waste time. He
got out of bed at once and went moodily along to the
bathroom, found the bottle of aspirin in the wall cabinet.
Sleep, he thought, I've got to get some sleep, otherwise I'll
be fit for nothing tomorrow.

CHAPTER XXI

It was after eleven on Tuesday morning when the meeting broke up. An exhaustive review of the case so far, a consideration of fresh lines of enquiry. Sergeant Viner made his way out of the crowded room; his head ached slightly from the stuffy atmosphere. With luck he might have time to snatch a cup of coffee and a sandwich before the hand of duty landed once more on his shoulder.

Over on his left Chief Inspector Naylor gazed fixedly down at the floor as he gave a small part of his attention to Bennett who walked beside him, chatting in great good humour.

'I thought all along it was a waste of time trying to round up the cushion-buyers,' Bennett said with irritating complacency. 'Even if we managed to get an accurate list it wouldn't get us anywhere that mattered. And accurate is about the last word you could apply to the list we've been putting together.'

Naylor ran his tongue round his gum. I hope to God it isn't an abscess, he thought with deep gloom. He had spent a restless night, had filled himself up again with aspirin the moment he dragged himself from bed at the ring of the alarm, was already beginning to regret it, for although the pain in his jaw had diminished to a dull ache, he was conscious now of vast sleepiness and grinding indigestion. Black coffee, nothing else for it. And a couple of digestive mints. He jerked his mind back with difficulty to what Bennett was rambling on about.

'Yes, yes,' he said impatiently when he'd got the gist of it. 'You're quite right.' They weren't very likely to come up with anything valuable by fretting about who did or did not have anything to do with the cushions. Much too wide a field, too much left with a question mark beside it. Far better to concentrate effort where it seemed capable of producing results. An elementary principle, often overlooked, one he had always devoutly upheld.

He reached the corridor, stood mustering his wits. First the coffee, then he'd better go along to the Kingfisher, see Miss Ratcliff, clear up a couple of points with her.

'I knew you'd be coming to see me.' Miss Ratcliff gave the chief inspector a complacent glance. 'And I knew what it would be you'd want to know.' Oh, you did, did you? Naylor said in his mind with weary patience. How extraordinarily helpful and perceptive of you. He had in fact opened the conversation two minutes earlier by asking her about Gerald Wickham's visit to Fairview on Saturday afternoon but she hadn't uttered a syllable in response to that query but had instantly launched into her own spiel.

'It's about the cushions Mother made,' she said with massive certainty. 'I realized how important that would be.' She leaned forward and pulled towards her across the desk a bulging suède handbag. 'So I made a list of all the people I could remember that Mother gave a cushion to.' She fished about inside the bag and took out a folded sheet of paper. She opened it out and began to recite a string of names.

Naylor inclined his head, listening with keen attention in spite of the perspiration starting to trickle down under his collar. The windows in Miss Ratcliff's tiny office were tightly closed, the heating switched full on. I wonder she doesn't melt into a pool of lard, he thought, attempting to place the names as she read them out in a clear voice. Most of them meant nothing to him, most probably friends, neighbours and relatives of old Mrs Ratcliff. Nothing at all to do with the case; they would never have set eyes on

Mrs Rolt in their lives.

And then right at the end she couldn't refrain from raising her head fractionally, shooting him one swift triumphant glance before dropping her eyes again, uttering the final name. Here it comes, he thought, registering the pleased malice in that glance, here's the cherry on the bun.

'Two cushions to Mr Stephen Maynard,' she said. 'One round, one square, both in gros point, Jacobean designs.'

Well, well, Naylor thought, quite a sizeable cherry at that, rather an unexpected cherry. 'That's the end of the list?' he said with an air of faint boredom.

'It is,' she replied, not in the least taken in by his studied casualness. Her eyes, large, really rather pretty, had a brilliant, liquid look.

'Your mother was a friend of Maynard's?' Naylor asked with the same almost indifferent manner.

She didn't answer the question directly. 'I've done quite a bit of work for him over the last few years. He's a Kingfisher client now of course.' She pursed her lips. 'We don't have a private arrangement.' No? Naylor said to himself. But I bet you'd have liked one. Rather smitten with Maynard, Hulme had said; could be he was pretty accurate in his assessment. 'Mr Maynard ran me home more than once.' Hazel made a gesture of dismissal. 'Simply in the way of business, you understand. When my mother was ill he sometimes stayed for a while to talk to her.' She looked down at the desk, her fingers toyed with the strap of her handbag. 'She did a lot of embroidery, it helped her to pass the time. She liked giving presents to people. And people like getting them. Her work was first class.' The sharp edge had vanished from her voice, she spoke now in a tone of simple affection and sorrow.

'On Saturday afternoon,' Naylor said, returning abruptly to his reason for calling in at the Kingfisher, 'you were just about to go along to the hall to help with the Fair – '

He questioned her closely about Gerald Wickham's visit to Fairview and she answered readily. Yes, she had met Wickham on the doorstep; yes, she had admitted him to the house – knowing that Mrs Rolt wouldn't wish to be called unnecessarily to the door with her injured foot. No, she most certainly had not admitted him to the house a second time, much later in the evening. She looked fiercely agitated at the suggestion.

'Just a routine question,' Naylor said, vaguely soothing. 'When you encountered Wickham on the doorstep, did you happen to notice if he was carrying a bunch of flowers?'

'No,' she said at once. 'He was carrying his leather brief-case. He didn't have any flowers. I'm positive about that.'

Naylor pushed back his chair and got to his feet. 'You know about Maynard's wife of course?' Hazel said. She appeared now unwilling to let the interview end. Oh yes, we know about Maynard's wife, Naylor said inwardly. The Eldersleigh inspector had come over to Barbourne first thing that morning, had brought with him files and photographs, all the available data. But I don't propose to discuss any of it with you, Naylor thought, observing the faint flush rise in Miss Ratcliff's cheeks. I imagine all you'd be able to add to the official version would be a strong spice of malice.

'I mustn't keep you any longer,' he said courteously. 'It was good of you to spare me your time.'

'Yes, certainly, Mrs Ratcliff gave me a cushion,' Maynard said at once in reply to Naylor's question. He had been working on his notes at the table in his sitting-room when the chief inspector pressed the doorbell. Naylor could almost have credited that he had worked non-stop since their last conversation. Certainly he looked haggard enough to warrant the notion.

'A gros point cushion,' Maynard said in a flat voice.

'Would you like to see it?' Naylor gave a nod and Maynard stooped to open the lowest drawer of a small walnut chest standing near the window. 'There you are.' He took out a circular cushion worked in a Jacobean design. 'I didn't much care to sit looking at it,' he said. 'Not after last Saturday. But I thought I'd better not destroy it. I fancied I'd have to produce it to the police sooner or later.' The skin beneath his eyes was pale and puffy, there were deep lines round his mouth. 'I knew I'd have mud thrown at me again,' he said in a detached tone. 'I know the smell of that mud.' He passed a hand across his face. 'So I kept the cushion. Are you satisfied now? Can I get back to work?'

'There is one point,' Naylor said. 'Hazel Ratcliff was quite certain that her mother gave you two cushions.' Maynard became very still. 'According to her description,' Naylor said, 'the other cushion was very similar to this one except that it was square.'

'I was given only one cushion,' Maynard said as if repeating a lesson learnt by heart. 'This cushion. I never had another.' He closed his eyes for a moment. 'Miss Ratcliff may have made a simple mistake. But I can offer you an explanation as to why she might feel impelled to lie about me.' He gave Naylor a sudden piercing glance. 'You've seen her. Not the most attractive of women. She had a crush on me. I did nothing to encourage it but that seems to be irrelevant in such matters. I don't imagine any woman likes to have her overtures disregarded. Now she simply can't resist the opportunity to take a jab at me in retaliation.'

Naylor gave a non-committal grunt. His eyes came to rest on the radiogram housed in its polished wooden cabinet against the wall. The type that took a dozen records at once, played them through automatically. He took a step towards the door, observed the way Maynard's shoulders immediately relaxed their tension.

'I'll be on my way then,' Naylor said amiably. With some difficulty he managed to restrain himself from asking any of the questions that leapt to his mind when he glanced at the notion of how Maynard had spent – or said he spent – last Saturday evening; he had the strongest feeling that it would be immeasurably unwise at this moment to broach the subject in even the most casual fashion.

As he walked away down the path he looked over to his left. A wooden garage, a substantial structure, stood at some distance from the cottage; an electric light bulb enclosed in a glass shade was fixed above the double doors. A detective-constable had spent an appreciable stretch of time yesterday evening calling at every dwelling in the vicinity, doing his best to check Maynard's alibi. Only at one house had he come up with anything worth mentioning. Maynard's cottage stood by itself at the end of a short lane on the southern tip of Barbourne. A neighbour, an elderly man by the name of Fleming, had been out walking his dog on Saturday evening. The animal, a recently-acquired Irish setter with puppyhood only just left behind, had suddenly darted away from its owner, had raced up the lane and rushed excitedly all over Maynard's garden.

In the course of his chase Fleming had caused almost as much damage to the beds and borders as the setter. When the dog was once more safely in his grasp he had rung Maynard's bell to express his apologies. But he had got no reply. Lights showed in the cottage, he could hear music playing. He pressed the bell several times and then gave up and took himself off, concluding that Maynard was at work on his writing, protected behind a barrier of music, out of reach of mundane sounds.

As he walked towards the gate Fleming noticed that the garage doors were open and the outside light was switched on. He thought nothing of it, merely registering the fact that Maynard must have forgotten to switch off and lock up. It all squared with his impression of Maynard as a scholarly type with a mind above such details. He had not actually glanced into the garage, had not observed whether or not Maynard's car was inside at the time.

When pressed about the time that this episode occurred, Fleming had been rather vague. It was some time after his supper, which he ate at about seven, and he was certainly back in his own house before ten because his wife – who had spent the evening visiting a woman friend nearby – had returned at ten minutes past ten and by that time Fleming had been snoozing in his armchair. His recollection was that he had been out with the dog for about an hour and that this hour had probably been somewhere between eight-fifteen and a quarter to ten.

Naylor reached his car and stood for a moment looking back at the cottage. Easy enough for Maynard to set the radiogram going, leave the lights on in the house, slip away for a brief interval. And the return drive from Fairview would take him through the centre of town, past the Church Street litter bin.

'I think we can get back and have a bite to eat,' he said to the driver. He stepped into the car, leaned back and closed his eyes. If Maynard had absented himself from the cottage in that way, gained admission to Fairview and killed Mrs Rolt, then it would seem that the murder was not the result of a sudden overwhelming impulse but had been planned with some care. Actually, a combination, now he looked at it a little more closely, of calculation and opportunism. First the totally adventitious happening, the minor accident which left Mrs Rolt vulnerable, restricted in movement, confined to her flat. Then the swift recognition of the opportunity offered by this chance. And finally the plan, rapidly worked out to suit the needs of the moment.

Naylor jerked his eyes open. The sequence had the very same flavour as the hotchpotch of circumstances that surrounded the death of Maynard's wife. The earth wire that had finally parted company with the ancient metal rod plunged into the flowerbed by the back door of the Maynards' Peachfield cottage, thus setting up the first essential requirement in the chain of events. The flaw in the insulation of Mrs Maynard's hairdryer, possibly there since the day it was manufactured, but also possibly the result of time and wear. Ann Maynard's habit – attested by more than one witness – of engaging in several household activities more or less concurrently. Her whim on this particular occasion to combine the drying of her hair with reading the newspaper and putting a batch of laundry to soak in the large old-fashioned stone sink in the cottage kitchen. The sequence of actions in which she first turned on the tap, then switched on the hairdryer and held it to her head, seated herself at the table and began to read the paper, then, when she judged the sink to be sufficiently full of water, merely extended a hand and touched the tap in order to turn it off, thereby providing the final link in the long chain of events, allowing the electric current to pass through her body from the fingers of the left hand across to the fingers of the right, holding her rigidly immobile until she was dead.

All these happenings, considered either as a whole or singly, were capable of perfectly innocent explanation. Maynard had returned home from school as usual at the end of the afternoon, had found his wife slumped forward over the kitchen table, her left hand clutching the hairdryer which was still plugged in, still emitting a stream of warm air. And behind her the water ran steadily into the sink, overflowing into the waste pipe. No question about it, Maynard had most certainly been in school all day, but then his physical presence in the cottage would not have been in the slightest degree essential to the success of the scheme if he had in fact engineered the whole thing.

The Eldersleigh police would not have been inclined to harbour any suspicion had it not been for a neighbour of the Maynards, a middle-aged divorced woman living alone. Two days after the death of Ann Maynard the woman had gone to the police with a story of having paid a visit to the cottage on the day before Mrs Maynard died. According to her, she had been regaled with a story of a violent quarrel between husband and wife and a long rigmarole in which Ann Maynard had described the jealous and possessive nature of her husband.

The purpose of the woman's visit – or so she had told the police – had been in order to borrow Mrs Maynard's hairdryer. She claimed she had borrowed it before, had never found it in any way faulty. But on this day, according to the neighbour and only according to the neighbour, Mrs Maynard had refused to lend her the hairdryer, saying that the last time she had used it herself she had received a slight shock, that she had asked her husband to look at it and wouldn't be using it or lending it to anyone until he had checked it.

The police had not been very impressed by the neighbour. An unhappy, resentful, malicious woman, not widely regarded in the village as a pillar of either truthfulness or kindliness. And it had apparently taken her two whole days to realize the sinister implications of Mrs Maynard's complainings – if the complainings had ever had any existence in actual fact.

In his statement to the Eldersleigh police Maynard had denied absolutely that his wife had ever made any complaint to him about the hairdryer. There had never been a violent quarrel between his wife and himself, either on the day before her death or any previous occasion. As far as he knew, his wife had never lent the hairdryer to anyone. She was not the kind of woman to sit tittle-tattling to a

192

neighbour about the real or fancied shortcomings of her husband; he was not a jealous or possessive man; his wife had never to his knowledge been on friendly terms with the neighbour and he strongly believed that the woman's visit to the cottage on the day before his wife's death was merely a figment of her own disordered imagination.

The police had believed him. A good deal of sympathy had been felt for him in the locality. No charge of any kind had been brought against him.

And yet, Naylor thought, it could have been murder. The neighbour might have been speaking no more than the truth. Maynard could have told his wife he had checked and repaired the hairdryer, could have pressed his foot against the rotten earth wire in the garden, deliberately severing the last frail strand. There was no mains water in the cottage, so the earthing at its best would have been far from satisfactory. With the earth wire gone, every electrical appliance became a potential hazard. And the hairdryer – normally held in the hand – was a particularly lethal weapon. There was no special reason why her death need take place on that day. Sooner or later all the essentials would slot into place at the right time. He could afford to wait.

I wonder, Naylor said to himself, staring out at the cold autumn sunlight. He became aware that the car was slowing down, and that he was very hungry.

CHAPTER XXII

IN A CORNER of the canteen Naylor sat hunched over the table, stirring spoonfuls of sugar into a mug of very strong black coffee. He lifted the mug to his lips and took a long fiery gulp. No one had ventured to keep him company over his coffee, his manner hadn't invited matiness. He raised a hand and stroked his cheek, circling the treacherous spot. Tomorow morning at the latest he'd have to give in, absent himself, get it seen to.

A constable approached the table, levelling at Naylor a wary glance. Can't get five minutes' peace, Naylor thought with irrational irritation. He inclined his head, listened to the constable with an air of savage resignation. Someone at the desk, someone with a piece of information that seemed to warrant attention, might be best if the Chief could spare a moment. Naylor gave a single fierce nod in reply, drained the rest of his coffee in a gulp that nearly took the top of his head off, and got slowly to his feet.

The man was waiting in the hall. A nervous-looking, ferrety-faced customer with a manner that contrived at one and the same time to be self-congratulatory, sly, insinuating, over-familiar and circumspect. Naylor listened to his tale without enthusiasm.

The man – Jauncey by name – was employed at CeeJay as a driver and a vehicle handler in the yard. There had been a good deal of gossip and speculation among the men since the death of Mrs Rolt. Various items of information had filtered out to them one way and another. Among the morsels of gossip, Jauncey had learned of the supper party given on Saturday evening by the Fords. And among the snippets of fact relating to the party were one or two that caused him disquiet. Or so he would have Naylor believe.

'It's like this,' Jauncey said, slanting at the chief inspector a look compounded of frankness and cunning. 'I happen to know that Miss High and Mighty Celia Brettell told the coppers she was tucking herself up in bed not long after ten o'clock on Saturday night.' His eyes gleamed with righteous fervour. 'Then can you explain to me how my sister's husband, who works as a waiter at the Old Barn, which as you know is a good five miles out of Barbourne, came to be taking an order for late supper from Miss Brettell at ten minutes past ten on that very same Saturday night?'

Naylor said nothing, gave him a look of concentrated attention. 'And if you should ask me,' Jauncey said with evident pleasure, 'how come my brother-in-law was so certain of the time, then I'll tell you.' He pursed his lips, gave an emphatic nod. 'They have instructions at the Old Barn not to take orders for grills after ten o'clock. And Miss Brettell fancied a grill, fancied it enough to make a fuss about it. Likes to get what she fancies, does our Miss Brettell. And my brother-in-law had to tell her – and tell her more than once – that she was ten minutes too late to order a grill.' He smiled with satisfaction. 'She didn't like that. Nor did the fellow she was with.'

'Of course I can explain,' Celia Brettell said. 'I was with a business colleague.' Her manner implied professional reticence, the accepted need for discretion in matters of trade.

But Naylor wasn't interested in playing that particular game. 'I'd like the name of this business colleague,' he said crisply. 'And his address.'

'Well now,' Celia said in an altered tone, a good deal more honest and forthright. 'This is really rather tricky.'

I've no doubt it is, Naylor said to himself, observing that Miss Brettell was giving herself a nice little space in which to think. He had found her at her flat, putting a few things into a suitcase, just about to set off on one of her regular buying trips.

'Tricky or not,' Naylor said uncompromisingly, 'we need that name and address. And we also need a highly credible explanation of why you told me you were putting yourself to bed here in this flat when in actual fact you were arguing with a waiter at the Old Barn about grilled steaks.'

She gave him a brief appreciative nod in acknowledgement of his jousting skills. 'Correction,' she said lightly. 'I didn't tell you I was putting myself to bed shortly after ten o'clock. You actually told me that I was going to bed at that time. I did possibly encourage you to adhere to that belief, I may even have added a credible detail or two in the way of hot milk and so forth, but I most definitely did not initiate the idea.' She grinned at him suddenly, a confident challenging grin. 'Who am I to contradict a gentleman? Never argue with them, my old granny used to say, or if she didn't she ought to have done, you'll get a lot more out of them that way.' She's a good deal more attractive than I thought the first time, Naylor registered with mild surprise.

'Come now,' he said in an amiable tone. 'Let's get down to brass tacks. If you're compelled to tell me something you don't want known in your line of business, you needn't worry, I'll see it doesn't get out.'

'Alastair Murray of Murdoch Factors,' Celia said abruptly, taking Naylor by surprise. 'That's the name of my colleague. He was staying at the Old Barn, I'd had lunch with him there a couple of days earlier. I was able to get away from the Fords earlier than I'd thought possible, so I stopped the car at a kiosk and phoned Murray. He told me to come over to the Old Barn, he'd give me a bite to eat, we could have a chat.'

She gave Naylor a level look. 'There's a strong possibility that Murdoch Factors will make a bid to take over my firm – Sugdens.' Ah, Naylor said to himself, that's it. You're making sure you're not going to be made redundant. You're buying your way into a good position with Murdoch's if the takeover comes off, and the coin you're using for the purchase is the supply of confidential information about your own firm.

Celia interpreted the quality of his glance. 'I believe you

get the picture,' she said lightly. 'Murray isn't at the Old Barn now of course. You can contact him at his home.' She wrote down the address and gave it to Naylor. 'I really would be most deeply obliged if you could refrain from contacting him at Murdoch's.'

She grinned again. 'I'm banking on you not to go shooting your mouth off about all this. Most particularly I wouldn't like a hint of it to get out at CeeJay.' Her eyes, shrewd, amused, met Naylor's. 'Arthur Ford would only have to get a sniff of it and he'd have it all round the trade.'

She laughed. 'Not one of my most ardent fans, Arthur Ford. But then, to be scrupulously fair, I'm not crazy about him.'

'And the precise time at which you left Ford's house on Saturday evening?' Naylor said. 'I would prefer the truth this time.'

She raised her shoulders. 'I'm afraid I can't be very precise. If the waiter at the Old Barn likes to be so definite about my being at his table at ten past ten, all right then, I'll go along with that.' Her voice was unconcerned. 'Other than that, work it out for yourself. The time it takes to drive from Ford's house to the Old Barn, allowing for the stop for the phone call to Alastair Murray. Oh – and I did call in at a garage for petrol. That must have taken a few minutes.'

She paused, slid a glance at Naylor. 'I suppose you know,' she said casually, 'about the phone calls.'

'Phone calls?' Naylor said sharply. 'What phone calls?'

'The calls Mrs Rolt was getting.' She raised her eyebrows. 'I was sure you'd know about them. Or I'd have mentioned them earlier.'

'Mention them now,' Naylor said crisply.

'Alison told me someone was phoning her,' Celia said. 'Not saying anything. Just ringing her number, waiting a minute or two and then ringing off.'

Naylor frowned. 'When did she tell you this?'

'On Saturday afternoon. I rang her myself – to ask her something about the Fair. She mentioned it then,' she added with a frank look. 'Andrew had told me –' She stopped.

'Yes?' Naylor said. 'What had he told you?'

The tip of her tongue showed for an instant between her lips. 'He told me Alison had asked him if he was the person who had been making the mysterious phone calls.'

'And of course he denied it,' Naylor said flatly. What had she been about to say a few moments back when she broke off? He had a strong feeling that it would have been quite different from what she eventually uttered.

She smiled slightly. 'Naturally Andrew denied it.'

'And in actual fact,' Naylor asked with a bantering air, 'was it Rolt who'd been making the phone calls?'

Her smile vanished. 'No, of course not,' she said sharply.

He put the tips of his fingers together. 'How do you know?'

She was silent, looking down at the floor, and then she said, 'Well, of course I don't actually know. Not in any police sense of the word know. I simply feel he wouldn't have done such a thing. And that's evidence enough for me.' She glanced at her watch. 'I'll have to be pushing off. I hope I've been of some assistance. Sorry I wasn't able to be more exact.'

He sighed as he came out down the steps. He'd have to talk to the Fords – and Rolt – again, do his best to square the timings. He shook his head. A hopeless, frustrating task, like trying to grasp a fistful of jelly.

Among the phone messages waiting for him when he got back to the station was one from the art expert who was vetting Wickham's luggage. Naylor rang back at once.

'I still haven't finished the examination,' the expert began cautiously, but Naylor caught the note of satisfaction. He leapt at it like a terrier at a cat.

'You've found something, haven't you?'

'Well, yes, I have. It'll be tomorrow before I get through everything, you must understand – '

'Yes, yes,' Naylor said impatiently. 'I know all that. Just let me know what you've got so far.' I knew Wickham had a racket going, he thought triumphantly. Too smooth an operator by half for honesty.

'A watercolour,' said the expert's voice. 'Rather a good one. A Cotman. Stolen from the Aynscough Gallery six months ago. Removed from its frame, rolled up in a pile of prints. Very neatly done. I should think Wickham's an old hand at this game.'

'Oh yes!' Naylor said with deep pleasure. 'Oh yes!'

'I'm not promising anything,' the voice went on, 'but there are one or two pieces among the porcelain – but I'd better not say too much yet. I'll phone you again tomorrow.'

'That's all right,' Naylor said expansively. If a hundred further bits of the racket came to light it wouldn't materially alter the situation as far as Wickham was concerned. One piece was enough and that piece he had. The Cotman.

He pressed the bell on his desk and gave brisk orders for the rapid locating and snatching up of Wickham, and for depositing him at the other side of that desk in less than no time at all.

CHAPTER XXIII

'EVERYTHING I told you about my visit to Fairview was the truth,' Wickham said. He couldn't refrain from smiling. 'Except of course for my motive in going there at all.'

'You believed Mrs Rolt had discovered something while she was at the Wheatsheaf,' Naylor said.

'I thought she'd spotted the Cotman,' Wickham said with an air of great frankness. No point in playing the innocent as far as the watercolour was concerned. There was no conceivable way he could wriggle out of that one. He was well aware an even more thorough examination would now be made of every item in his baggage. He was resigned to the fact. But he hadn't the slightest intention of doing the work of the police for them. Let them ferret out what they could for themselves.

'She'd been nosing about while I was out of the room,' he said. 'She actually had the package of prints in her hand when I came back in.' He raised his shoulders. 'I wasn't worried. I had no reason to suppose she was any more knowledgeable in that respect than Hazel Ratcliff or the Webb girl. They wouldn't have known a Cotman if it had jumped out at them from a filing-cabinet.

'But just after she left, Brian Yardley called in at the Wheatsheaf. He'd seen Mrs Rolt, he began to talk about her, mentioned her father.' Wickham pulled down the corners of his mouth. 'I realized then that Mrs Rolt knew quite a bit about art. Her father was actually Lloyd the watercolour painter. I was in a bit of a sweat, I can tell you.'

'So you went round to see her,' Naylor prompted.

'Yes. I phoned first to make sure she'd be in. I concocted the tale about offering her a job to give me an excuse for calling. If she'd shown any sign of taking me up on that I'd have shoved in some awkward conditions that would have made it impossible for her to accept. All I wanted was a chance to talk to her. I knew I could tell from her manner if she was on to anything.'

'And was she?'

Wickham shook his head. 'No. I must have gone back into the room more or less as she began to pull out the prints. It was quite clear to me that she hadn't the faintest idea of the real purpose of my visit. After fifteen minutes I took myself off.'

Mm, Naylor thought. Could be. And then again, it might not have been that way at all. Wickham's original account of his movements on Saturday evening had been cursorily checked with no very conclusive result.

He said that he'd been making various calls of a business nature in the area. It was hardly ever possible in circumstances of that kind to arrive at a very exact list of times and places. It would have been easy for Wickham to go back to Fairview on Saturday evening without anyone being the wiser.

'Are you sure Mrs Rolt's manner didn't tell you she'd spotted something?' Naylor said. 'Perhaps you discovered that she had stumbled on the Cotman. Perhaps she made no bones about it, bluntly named a price for her silence. Or then again she could have revealed herself as a responsible citizen, indicated that she had every intention of going to the police. Perhaps you called back again later in the evening, bought some flowers to give her, to take her off her guard. Perhaps you found the door unlocked, walked into the flat and murdered her.'

'Come now!' Wickham said with protest. 'That'd be rather a lot of trouble to take over one painting.'

Naylor looked at him. He didn't bother to say, 'But it might not have been too much trouble to take over a nice broadly-based, many-sided and highly profitable racket.' The words said themselves in the silence.

'I didn't kill her,' Wickham said. 'She didn't know anything.'

'Is Yardley in the racket with you?' Naylor asked suddenly.

'Good God, no,' Wickham said with a surprised laugh that sounded genuine. 'Do you seriously believe anyone could operate anything successfully with Yardley sloshed half the time?' He shook his head. 'You can forget Yardley. I told you, I just pushed a bit of business his way. Old times' sake and all that. He had a lousy deal in the war. It could just as easily have been me, walking about with a face like that. Doesn't bear thinking about.'

'Mandy Webb?' Naylor said abruptly.

Wickham frowned. 'What about her?'

'Was she in on it?'

Wickham laughed. He looked at Naylor's face with an air of curiosity. 'You have some rum ideas about useful henchmen,' he said. 'The Webb girl doesn't know a thing. Or Hazel Ratcliff.' He spread his hands. 'Or for that matter, anyone else in your little net.'

'You don't know everyone in my net,' Naylor said calmly.

'No, maybe not. But I do know this. I'm in the Cotman thing on my own.'

'And the other things?' Naylor said. 'Are you in those on your own as well?'

'What other things?' Wickham said, widening his eyes in innocence. 'There aren't any other things. Just straight-forward merchandise. The Cotman was my one little venture from the straight and narrow, my first little flight.' He put a hand on his heart. 'And, I do assure you, my last.'

Oh yes, Naylor's look said. We'll see about that. All in good time. Much good your play-acting will do you then. He glanced at his watch. He must get a move on, must get off and talk to the Fords.

'I take it,' Wickham said pleasantly, 'that you've finished with me for the present.' He got to his feet.

Naylor gave him a sour glance. 'You're not going any place,' he said. He pressed the bell on his desk. 'As you very well know.'

'Worth a try,' Wickham said amiably. He smiled, raised his shoulders. 'Never anything lost by trying.'

*

In the reception area Sergeant Viner stood waiting for Naylor. Four-fifteen. Twenty-five past by the time they got to Ford's if they left right away. Beryl Ford'll probably be at home at this time of day, the Chief had said, by herself most likely. More polite to see the Fords separately, Naylor had added, pick them off one by one.

Then, after Beryl had been dealt with, on to CeeJay. Tackle Arthur Ford and Robin, then Andrew Rolt. It would probably be well on the way to half past five before they were through.

Viner sighed and glanced round the hall. A mild buzz of activity. A clergyman, smiling and deferential, making some request at the desk. Old James Ottaway sitting upright in his seat against the wall, staring ahead with an air of stern resolution, his arms folded over a bulging blue plastic sack that rested on his knees.

Ah – at last! The sound of Naylor's forceful footsteps along the corridor. Viner drew himself up into a more military stance. The Chief gave him an abrupt nod and went up to the desk. Over by the entrance there was a slight commotion, a raised female voice. Viner turned his head and saw the heavy figure of Mrs Cope, dressed in her nurse's uniform, her cheeks bright pink from the cold air, her manner at once coaxing and determined.

'Come along,' she said commandingly to a young girl following a couple of paces behind, half-minded, judging from her alarmed expression, to turn and make a bolt for it. 'There's Chief Inspector Naylor,' Mrs Cope said, seizing the girl's arm in a relentless grasp. 'You can tell him about it. There's no need to be upset.' With these loudly encouraging words she half dragged her shrinking companion across the hall to where Naylor stood watching their approach with a markedly unwelcoming eye.

'Glad I caught you,' Mrs Cope said briskly, delivering her victim at his feet.

Naylor looked down at his watch. 'Another couple of minutes and you wouldn't have done,' he said repressively. 'I'm on my way out.' He glanced at the desk sergeant. 'Someone else will attend to you.'

'What I've come about can wait,' Mrs Cope said to Naylor's surprise. 'I wanted to lodge a strong complaint about the hill path. The lighting. Or I should say, the absence of lighting.' Naylor closed his eyes briefly, emitted a discreet sigh. 'And those cars,' Mrs Cope said. 'They've got no business up there. I had to jump off my bicycle the other night, coming back from a case. I could have been killed.' She paused, glanced about to register the impact of these arresting statements on her audience. 'However, that can wait.'

She turned to the girl, gave her a push forward. 'It's this child I want to see you about. Rachel Wheatley. The family's known to me. Very respectable people.' As if the last two statements were linked together by a powerful natural law.

Naylor levelled at the girl a look of barely-controlled impatience. Thin, nervous-looking, on the tall side for her age which was probably thirteen or fourteen. Clean, neatly and conventionally dressed. 'I met her outside here, on the steps,' Mrs Cope said with an air of immeasurable significance. 'Couldn't bring herself to walk inside.' She gave her head an important jerk. 'I had a word with her, got her to tell me what the trouble was – or part of it at least. I persuaded her to come inside.' She fixed Naylor with an inflexible gaze. 'It comes to something when decent children can't go about their lawful occasions without being molested.'

'Molested?' Naylor said sharply.

'Yes,' Mrs Cope said. 'A couple of nights ago.'

'Let the girl speak for herself,' Naylor said. He looked at Rachel who gave him a jerky nod. With a question or two from the chief inspector and a number of promptings from Mrs Cope, she came out with her story.

She'd been coming back from the cinema, had been running up one of the hill paths alone. Someone – a man – had sprung out at her. There'd been a struggle lasting only a minute or two, she'd got hold of his coat, wrenched at it, heard it tear. A plastic macintosh, vinyl or some such material, she thought, black or some very dark colour. She had half-glimpsed his face, was doubtful that she could recognize him again. He'd caught his foot against a root or stone, had stumbled, slackened his grasp. She'd managed to run off, he hadn't pursued her.

'I presume,' Naylor said on a cold note, 'that you informed your parents of this occurrence as soon as you reached home?' She shook her head, avoiding his eye. 'And why not?' he asked. 'Could it be that the incident never took place? That you heard a few rumours, decided it was your turn for a little notice?'

'I wasn't supposed to be at the cinema,' Rachel said. Her manner grew even more uncertain. 'I was with a girl I'm not supposed to go about with. My father says she's a bad influence.'

'Indeed?'

'I was supposed to be at school,' she added. 'We have netball practice in the gym two evenings a week.' She turned her gaze away, stared at the wall. She began to talk more rapidly, as if anxious now simply to get the whole thing over and done with. 'I should have been home by nine o'clock, my father's very strict. It was turned half past, that's why I was running. If I'd told my parents about being on the hill, they'd have asked me why I came home that way. I'd have had to tell them where I'd been, they'd know I wouldn't have to go that way from school. My father'd have had a fit, he's always going on about not staying out late.'

From his seat by the wall old Ottaway rose suddenly to his feet, swung his bag over his shoulder and walked briskly up to the desk. Naylor flung him a glance of deep irritation and turned back to the girl. 'Why did you decide to come here today after all? Has your father suddenly turned into a mild-mannered man?'

She shook her head, shifted her weight from one foot to the other. 'I told my friend about it, the girl I went to the pictures with, and she kept on at me that I ought to go to the police. She said someone else might get attacked and it might turn out to be serious.' She drew a deep breath. 'So I thought perhaps I'd better.' She looked at Naylor with appeal. 'I thought perhaps you wouldn't tell my parents. I wasn't injured in any way. There isn't any need for them to know.'

'Just as long as you and your school pals know.' Naylor gave her a long unsmiling glance. 'That's about the size of it, isn't it?'

She shook her head violently. 'No, it isn't. It did happen. Why should I make it up?'

'Why indeed?' Naylor said heavily. From a few feet away Ottaway's voice reached his ears.

'Only doing my duty,' the old man said to the desk sergeant. 'If everyone did as much the country wouldn't be in the state it's in now.' The sergeant made indeterminate soothing noises. Suddenly, with a single powerful movement, Ottaway swung the plastic bag into the air, tipped it over, pulled its mouth wide open. A cascade of garbage descended, spilling out over the counter, landed on the floor.

'Good God!' Naylor said. He clapped his hand to his jaw. A fiery stab of pain instantly pierced his cheek.

Ottaway turned to him with a gratified smile. 'I thought you'd appreciate my efforts,' he said with vast benevolence. 'I spent quite a bit of time clearing up on the hills.' He

thrust a hand into his breast pocket. 'Something else you
might like.' He drew out an envelope, pressed it into Naylor's fingers.

Naylor gave the desk sergeant a look chiefly character-
ized by massive restraint. 'I'll leave you to get rid of this
customer,' he said in a low fierce voice. He flung a glance
at Viner. 'Come on. We'll be on our way before the next
wave of lunatics arrives.'

As they strode off towards the exit, Viner realized that
both Rachel and Mrs Cope had taken advantage of the
little uproar to remove themselves from the hall.

CHAPTER XXIV

DURING THE NEXT few minutes the chief inspector said not
a word, being afflicted by toothache and ill temper in equal
proportions. They had almost reached Ford's house when
the pain in his jaw miraculously began to subside, bringing
about a sudden marked improvement in his manner. He
glanced out of the car window at the neat rows of suburban
houses, at a municipal refuse wagon crawling between its
stops. The sight instantly brought to his mind a vision of
old Ottaway smiling proudly over his offering of garbage.
A vague sense of compunction awoke in Naylor's breast.
It was stupid to allow trifling annoyances to destroy one's
composure. Ottaway meant well; he was harmless enough.

Naylor drew a long breath. He had possibly also been
a trifle rough with the Wheatley girl. He looked back at
her story, contemplated it for several seconds. No doubt
about it, he'd been a bit hasty there. He ought to have
gone into her tale properly. But no real harm had been
done. Mrs Cope would know where the girl lived, she
could be contacted again if he decided it was after all

necessary. By the time the car drew up outside Ford's house he was in a reasonably good mood once more. He felt sharp, energetic, ready to spring on anyone anywhere at a moment's notice.

Beryl Ford answered the ring at the door almost before Viner's finger had left the bell. She was dressed for the street, looked put out at the appearance of the two detectives on her doorstep.

'I'm just going out,' she said with a frown. 'I've a bus to catch. There isn't another for an hour.' She burst into an irritated explanation. She always spent Tuesday evening with an old friend; the woman lived in a village several miles away, would be expecting her, would be upset if she was late.

'We won't keep you a moment,' Naylor said. He stepped inside, compelling her to retreat into the hall. 'If you do miss the bus we can give you a lift. We can overtake the bus, set you down at another stop, you'll be on the bus when your friend meets it.'

'What is it then?' she asked impatiently. 'What do you want to see me about? If it's Arthur you want he's still at CeeJay, he won't be back for a while yet.'

'I simply want to check your recollection of one or two details,' Naylor said. He took her rapidly over the events of Saturday evening but she showed no disposition to alter the account she had already given. When he questioned her for the third time about the accuracy of her statement concerning the time the party broke up, she suddenly shifted her ground and said, 'Well, yes, I could have been mistaken. You don't really notice things as much as you think you do. You've no particular reason to notice them at the time. Afterwards, when people ask you, you could quite easily fancy it happened one way when it actually happened another.' She just wants to get off to her bus, Naylor thought, she's saying now what she thinks will get rid of me in the shortest possible time.

'And Miss Brettell?' he said. 'I'm not altogether clear about her movements.' He had thought at first that Miss Brettell had left at the same time as Rolt, then it seemed there had been some question of her having to search for a brooch.

'Oh, that,' Beryl said when he had indicated his difficulty. 'I could perhaps have exaggerated about that.' She looked down at her wrist-watch. 'I was a bit fed up with Madame Celia just then. She did come back to look for her brooch but I dare say it didn't take more than a minute or two.'

'One other tiny point,' Naylor said. 'Do you by any chance remember if you saw either Brian Yardley or Paul Hulme at the Fair? Again it's simply a matter of establishing times, trying to eliminate people,' he added with vague reassurance.

'I remember Yardley,' she replied without hesitation. Something very like malice showed in her tone. 'He was being rather a nuisance. Just because he'd supplied a few things free for the art stall, he seemed to think it gave him the right to get under everybody's feet.'

'And the time that you noticed him?'

'Oh, somewhere in the middle of the afternoon.' She frowned. 'Say, between half past three and five o'clock.'

Naylor drew a little breath of resignation. It looked as if he was never going to be any more certain on that particular point.

'And Paul Hulme?' he asked. 'Did you see him?'

She shook her head. 'No. I don't remember seeing him at all.' She made a restless movement with her shoulders. 'Is that all?'

I suppose it is, Naylor said to himself, I don't think you're going to be very helpful. He turned his head, his gaze came to rest on the hall stand just behind her. All at once something stirred in his brain. The hall stand. Coats and jackets.

He'd been standing over there, that first day he'd questioned her. She'd been patting her hair in front of the mirror, he'd been watching her face in the glass. Ah – he put up a hand and touched his cheek.

'Who in this house,' he asked on a cheerful, rallying note, 'wears a black plastic macintosh?' She stared at him, taken aback. 'Your husband?' he said. 'Or your son?' He smiled. 'Or even yourself?'

'A black plastic mac?' she repeated slowly. 'Arthur and Robin sometimes buy plastic macs when we're on holiday. They bring them back home, but of course they don't last long, they get thrown away in no time at all.' Her tone grew firmer. 'There's certainly no plastic mac in the house now.'

'You're quite sure of that?' He had a clear picture now of her face reflected in the mirror and to one side of the glass the collar and sleeve of a black plastic raincoat protruding from amongst the other garments on the stand. 'Couldn't there still be one left over from your last holiday?' he asked.

She shook her head. 'No, there isn't. I'm quite sure. Oh – ' She broke off. 'There was one here, hanging up there.' She jerked her head at the stand. 'A few weeks back. But it didn't belong to any of us. It belonged to one of Robin's friends. Or someone Arthur brought home from CeeJay. Whoever it was that left it there, I do believe the mac was made of black plastic.' She looked at the stand. 'It's not there now, you can see for yourself. Whoever it was must have asked to have it given back, or called in for it. I can't recollect that, but it certainly isn't there now. Why did you want to know? Is it important?'

He didn't answer, raised his shoulders, let them drop. 'I won't keep you any longer,' he said on a note of finality. 'Are you going to be able to catch the bus?'

She looked at her watch. 'Yes, just about.' She followed

the two men outside, secured the door, began to walk swiftly off down the path, then halted as she realized they weren't keeping up with her, glanced back at them.

'You go on,' Naylor said with an encouraging wave. 'Don't wait for us.' She threw him another look, hesitated for an instant longer, then resumed her quick passage to the gate. They walked slowly after her, out on to the road, got into the car.

At the end of the road a bus went by. As Viner edged the car round the corner he saw the bus drawn up by the stop, Beryl Ford stepping into it.

'Don't drive off just yet,' Naylor said. 'Pull over there for a minute.' When the car was stationary he sat in frowning silence for several seconds. Then he said, 'She didn't seem all that anxious to leave us hanging round the house.'

'Something's just occurred to me,' Viner said. Naylor gave him an abstracted look. 'When Mrs Cope came into the station just now with the girl,' Viner went on, 'she said "A couple of nights ago." She said Rachel Wheatley told her she was molested a couple of nights ago.'

'I take leave to doubt that the Wheatley girl was molested a couple of nights ago or any other night,' Naylor said brusquely.

'But a couple of nights ago would make it Saturday night,' Colin persisted. 'The night Mrs Rolt was murdered.'

'Yes, I dare say,' Naylor said, his mind still on Beryl Ford and her uneasy manner.

'There could have been a prowler,' Colin said. 'And that prowler could be the person who murdered Mrs Rolt.'

Naylor expelled a long weary breath. 'I fear things don't resolved themselves as neatly as all that in this business.' He raised his shoulders. 'Still, we can have another word with the Wheatley girl.' His mind circled back to Mrs. Ford. 'How would you get rid of a plastic mac,' he asked, without any very clear idea of his own line of thought, 'if you had no open fires? And in any case, attempting to burn plastic would make a hell of a mess. Something you couldn't very well conceal from the rest of the household.'

'Bury it in the garden?' Viner suggested without strong interest. 'Rachel Wheatley didn't strike me as a liar,' he said on a deliberately non-argumentative note.

'Oh, for goodness' sake – ' Naylor made an impatient gesture, pushing aside the Wheatley girl and her adolescent imaginings. 'You might be spotted burying the mac in the garden.'

'Put it in the dustbin then,' Viner said at random.

Naylor puffed out his cheeks. 'Mm, might do that. Bit obvious, but still. Come on, we'll go back to the house. Won't do any harm to take a look-see.'

He had a sudden memory of Robin's eyes meeting his at the youth club, the precise manner of his reply. He told me he didn't call at Fairview, Naylor thought, and then I said to him: So you made no contact at all with Mrs Rolt on Saturday evening, and he didn't simply say no, as he might have been expected to. He said: I neither saw her nor spoke to her at any time on Saturday. But he could have phoned her, Naylor thought, he could have rung her number and then said nothing, could have listened in silence to her baffled protests. He never said he didn't phone her.

Viner put the car in motion. 'I rather fancy it was young Ford who was the mysterious phone caller,' Naylor said.

Viner studied the idea. 'Could be,' he said. It seemed to fit in with his idea of the boy's psyche.

'Probably a bit sweet on Mrs Rolt,' Naylor said. And all at once Viner's brain flung up at him a memory of Alison all those years ago at the Chaddesley Grammar School. He saw again with piercing clarity the group of girls in the cloakroom – a sizeable group, fifteen or sixteen of them. Giggling, nudging each other. Himself standing unobserved by one of the cloakroom entrances, listening, taking it in. Alison perched on a chair, reading out with mocking gestures and satirical exaggeration a poem sent to her by a lad in Viner's form. A love poem, awkward and amateurish, but every callow word written from the heart.

Viner had walked rapidly away from the cloakroom, full of anger, Alison's laughter echoing in his ears. He'd never mentioned the episode to anyone, neither to Alison nor the boy – least of all to the boy.

Mrs Rolt led young Ford on out of mischief, Yoxall said. Had she for once bitten off more than she could chew? Started something she couldn't control? Had Robin been phoning her? Dogging her for weeks? Had he called at Fairview, on the excuse of some business connected with the Fair? Made some kind of approach to her? She was capable of cruel and cutting remarks, Yoxall said. Had she said something unforgivably wounding to Robin? Laughed at him? Taken his adolescent self-esteem and ruthlessly shredded it?

The car rounded the corner. Naylor said suddenly, 'I think we'd better get a move on.' He jerked a finger at the refuse lorry which was now drawn up by the Fords' gate.

Viner pulled into the kerb, jumped out and ran up the path, round to the back of the house. A brawny young man in overalls was standing by the dustbin. He had one hand on the lid, he looked round at the sound of Viner's approach.

'Hold on a moment,' Viner called. He seized the lid and set it down on the ground with a bang.

'What's up, mate?' the young man asked. Naylor came lumbering into view round the side of the house. 'Oh, coppers,' the young man answered himself, instantly placing the chief inspector's face. He withdrew a couple of discreet paces and watched with lively interest as Viner tipped out the contents of the bin and began to sort through them.

Right at the bottom of the heap was a square parcel made up of several thicknesses of newspaper. Viner crouched on the ground and unfolded the sheets. Inside was an orderly pile of black plastic, cut up into little pieces.

'Mm,' Naylor said. 'We'll take that little lot.' He glanced at his watch, turned and looked consideringly at Viner. 'What time do they knock off work at Ford's place?' he asked. 'Is it five or half past?'

Cars and bicycles were coming out through the gates when they reached CeeJay. 'You're too late to catch Mr Ford,' one of the homegoing female clerks told Naylor. 'He left twenty minutes early today. His mother's not been well. Mr Ford and Robin were going to call in to see her on their way home.' She tried to be more helpful. 'I don't know if there's anyone else you'd like to see instead. I'm afraid Mr Rolt's not here either, I think he's gone off on one of his business trips. He was here this morning but he left again about eleven o'clock. I shouldn't think he'll come back into CeeJay again today.'

'There isn't anyone else I want to see,' Naylor said. 'Thanks all the same.' He turned to go, feeling a faint sense of relaxation. No need to break their necks. They could take their time now, look in at Ford's house later in the evening – Ford and his son would very probably spend some little time with the old lady.

At that moment a sharp stab of pain pierced his cheek. He couldn't repress a groan, he raised a hand to his face.

'Are you all right, sir?' Viner asked.

Naylor gave an irritated nod, began to walk quickly back towards the car. Half-way there it occurred to him that there was really no reason now why he couldn't sneak half an hour and nip along to the dentist's. His spirits rose sharply at the prospect of relief.

'I think I'll call in on Plimmer,' he said to Viner in a

cheerful tone. 'I rather fancy I've got a bit of trouble with
a tooth,' he added with massive understatement. 'I'll see
if I can persuade Plimmer to do something about it right
away.'

As the car moved off Viner turned his head and saw
Paul Hulme standing by the front entrance. The woman
who had spoken to them was standing beside him, talking,
gesturing, and Hulme was listening with his head tilted to
one side, his eyes following the progress of the car out
through the gates.

CHAPTER XXV

'YOU'D BETTER have the jaw X-rayed,' Plimmer said.
'You'll have to come into the other room.'

Naylor stood up, thrust a hand into his pocket in search
of a handkerchief and encountered the stiff edges of an
envelope. He drew it out, frowned down at it. Ah yes –
the envelope old Ottaway had shoved into his fingers at
the station.

He followed Plimmer out of the room and across the
corridor, ripping open the envelope as he went, taking out
the sheets of paper, unfolding them, glancing rapidly at the
topmost page with scarcely a flicker of interest, leafing
through the manifestations of Ottaway's obsessional im-
pulses.

'If you'd sit there,' Plimmer said, indicating a chair
facing a machine. Naylor nodded, turned the final page,
cast over it a perfunctory eye, his fingers already tensed to
crush the rubbishy sheets together and drop them into the
waste basket.

DETAILS OF VEHICLES PARKED FOR UNLAWFUL PUR-
POSES, Ottaway had written in bold capitals.

And underneath, in orderly columns, registration numbers, dates, times and places.

I'll take a stroll, Viner decided, I'll get a breath of air while the Chief's at the dentist's. He felt tired, flat. I'd like to get right away, he thought as he made his way along the early-evening pavements. Or failing that, I'd like a really good long sleep.

He looked into shop windows, glanced at the faces of passers-by. Once, in the distance, he saw a girl he thought was Tessa. She was standing by a bus stop reading a newspaper. He began to walk more quickly in her direction. But when he was still several yards away she lowered the paper, folded it, put it under her arm. Now he could see her face. It wasn't Tessa, he realized with a surge of disappointment that took him by surprise. It was just a girl of the same height, with the same slim supple figure.

He paused for a moment. I like Tessa, he thought, halted by the realization. She's honest and warm and vulnerable. I'll see her when all this is over, when I have time again, when my mind's free.

He moved on. He felt suddenly quite cheerful. He turned a corner where the traders sold their wares at the permitted times.

Today was market day; most of the stalls had already been taken down. A couple of men were busy dismantling a textile stand, piling bolts of cloth into the back of a van. Over on the right stood a small booth, deserted, still with its ranks of china teasets, stainless steel dishes, bowls and vases made in a local pottery. As Viner glanced idly about, the stallholder came grumbling up behind him; an elderly woman, walking slowly and with some difficulty.

'He's gone and let me down again,' she said with resigned irritation. 'You wouldn't think it would be much to ask, would you?' She addressed Viner – who had never clapped

216

eyes on her before – as if they had been conducting a conversation from which she had absented herself for a moment. 'All I ask is that he should fetch me here and pick me up again, help me to set up and help me to take down. And for that I pay him good money.' She shook her head, struck her hands together. 'But can he be relied on to turn up? He cannot. I can't hump heavy stuff about. Not at my age. And with my bad hip.'

'I'll give you a hand,' Viner said. 'I've got a few moments to spare.'

Her weatherbeaten face broke into a smile. 'Oh, would you? I'd be ever so grateful.'

He walked rapidly towards the stall. 'Come on then. Let's get cracking.' He gestured at the teasets. 'I suppose you pack those into boxes? Where do you keep them?'

'Under the stall. In there.' She jerked a finger at the opening that allowed the stallholder to walk into a central space from which customers could be served on all sides of the four-square structure.

Viner edged his way in and stooped under the stall. He began to pull out cardboard boxes and pass them up to her.

'I shall need something stronger for this lot,' she said. 'Look under the other counter, that's where I keep the heavier stuff.' He turned and half knelt down, then remained where he was, poleaxed. To one side of the boxes was a plastic bucket half full of chrysanthemums, pink, white, cream, apricot. And among them, not very large, rather battered, but still unmistakably members of a noble breed, two well-shaped blooms, incurved, a curious shade of rosy orange, tipped with sulphur yellow.

'Have you found the boxes?' the woman asked with impatience. 'They're in there, staring you right in the face. They must be.'

'Yes, I've found them,' Viner said. He seemed all at once

217

short of breath. He reached in and drew out the bucket, straightened himself, set it down on the counter.

'Not that,' the woman said with exasperation. 'The boxes.'

He stooped again, pulled out the boxes, passed them across to her. 'I didn't know you sold flowers,' he said in a casual voice.

'No more I do,' she answered briskly. She glanced at the bucket. 'My daughter brought me those on Friday night.' She began to pack the boxes with china, quickly, expertly. 'My daughter's the cook over at the Grange,' she said with pride. 'I don't know if you know the Grange, it's that big place fifteen miles the other side of Chaddesley. She's been there a couple of years now, she likes it very well. She comes over to spend the weekend with me once a month at the very least. She's a good daughter to me.'

'I'm sure she is,' Viner said. 'And they're beautiful flowers,' he added admiringly.

'Oh yes.' The woman nodded her head importantly. 'They come from the greenhouses at the Grange. My daughter's boy-friend's one of the gardeners there.' She pursed her lips, gave him a weighty look. 'If you think those are beautiful, you ought to see the really top-quality stuff they've got there. They put them in for shows and exhibitions. They win prizes too with them, quite often.'

'And you get hold of them from time to time,' Viner said. 'To sell here on the stall.'

'Well, no, not exactly. There always used to be a flower stall here. There were two or three at one time; they did a good trade too. The last one went a few weeks back. The council won't let anyone else start up. But folk still stop by, they still expect to be able to buy a nice fresh bunch of flowers here. They come up to my stall, seeing it's the first one as you come into the square, they say "Where's the flower stall then?" I get tired of explaining.

'So when my daughter fetched me this lot on Friday, I thought, Right, I'll take those along to my stall, someone's sure to come asking for flowers, I'll make a bob or two on those.' She jerked her head with satisfaction. 'And I was quite right. They did come asking. More than one.'

She paused in her packing of the china, gave the chrysanthemums an assessing look. 'Throwouts, my daughter called them. They may be throwouts to fancy gardeners, I told her, but they look good enough to sell, to my way of thinking. Of course what you see there is only the leavings of what she brought me. I've sold the best, naturally. I sold them on Saturday, and a few more today. I had two big bucketfuls from my daughter. Her boy-friend brought her over in his car, so they carried them in the boot.'

'Your customers must have been pleased to find such good-quality blooms,' Viner said.

She nodded. 'Indeed they were. I sold four bunches on Saturday. One of them just as I was going to clear up for the night. It must have been about half past seven. You don't get many customers at that time. Particularly not ones that'll demand top-quality stuff.' She gave a sudden cry, midway between relief and exasperation. 'There he is! And about time too!' She gestured towards the entrance to the square, at an ancient van turning in.

'I'll be all right now,' she said to Viner. 'Thanks for helping.' She nodded at the bucket of flowers. 'Help yourself to some of those, seeing you like them so much. I shan't sell any more this evening and we don't open the stalls again till Friday. They won't be much good by then.'

'Thanks,' Viner said. 'I'd like to take a few.' He lifted out the pair of rosy-orange blooms, added three or four others to make a bunch.

'Here, have a bit of paper,' she said. 'Otherwise they'll drip all over you.' She picked up a sheet of stout blue wrapping paper from a pile on the counter. 'Lovely shade, those two flowers, aren't they?' she said with pride. 'Most unusual. That's what the customer remarked, the one that bought the bunch just as I was clearing up on Saturday evening.'

'Yes, very distinctive,' Viner said. 'He must have been pleased to find them at the last moment like that. I am right, I suppose, it was a man that bought them?'

The Chief was standing by the car, looking impatiently up the road, when Viner came rapidly round the corner. Under the street lights Naylor's look was animated, almost exuberant. As soon as the sergeant was within earshot the Chief called out, 'Where the hell have you been?' His eyes focused on the blue-wrapped sheaf of flowers in Viner's hand. 'What have you got there?' he asked sharply.

'Sorry I kept you waiting,' Viner said. 'I found something out.' He couldn't keep the triumph from his voice.

'So did I!' Naylor grinned, and waved a piece of paper under Viner's nose. 'Look at that!' He stabbed a finger down at Ottaway's heavy capitals. 'Do you know whose car that is?' The number leapt out at Viner. An easy one to remember, the digits arranged in sequence. 'You see the time?' Naylor said with fierce pleasure, jabbing at the next column. 'And where the car was parked. Add all that up and see what it makes. It wouldn't take four minutes to get to Fairview on foot from that part of the hill.'

The house was in darkness when they arrived. Naylor didn't press the bell but tried the front door, without success. The side entrance also remained closed against them. They went round to the back and found a french window that yielded. Viner ran a hand along the inside wall, clicked on the light.

Rolt was sitting a few feet away, slumped forward over a table, his head resting on his arms, his face turned away from them.

Naylor went silently round the table, glanced at the whisky bottle, three-quarters full, at the glass lying on its side. He put out a hand and shook Rolt by the shoulder. Rolt stirred and made a sound of protest. Naylor set his jaw and gave another rougher shake. Rolt came awake, sat up and shook his head, blinking at the light. His eyes focused on Naylor.

'You took a hell of a time getting here,' he said. His voice sounded petulant, blurred. He began to cry, a whimpering noise like an animal in distress.

There was the whir of a car in the drive, slowing down, coming to a halt. A door slammed. Footsteps sounded, quick and purposeful, coming round to the back of the house.

Rolt was on his feet, supporting himself against the table when the door banged open and Hulme came in. His eyes ranged over the scene, his look was wild, almost defeated, full of pain.

'It'll be all right,' he said to Rolt. 'Don't worry.'

'It won't be all right,' Rolt said with immense weariness. 'I killed her. You'd better get my solicitor.' He began to cry again, more loudly now, in a more abandoned manner.

'I must ask you to accompany us,' Naylor said to Rolt in a formal voice. He must have bought the flowers after leaving Fairview, on his way to spend the evening at Fords. Bought them on an impulse, stowed them away in his car, intending to call on his wife again at the end of the evening, hoping perhaps to find her in a better mood.

'I'll come with you,' Hulme said to Rolt. He went up to the table and tried to get a hand under Rolt's elbow. Rolt edged himself free, shook his head. 'No, you're not coming,' he said. 'I don't want it. Do what I tell you, get the solicitor.'

Viner could barely catch the rest of his words. 'Hold the fort,' Rolt said to Hulme, and again, 'Hold the fort. Do as I say. Get the solicitor.'

His whole body seemed suddenly slack and defenceless. 'I didn't mean to kill her,' he said, half crying, half mumbling. He looked at Naylor like a sick dog. 'It's like a terrible dream.'

'Come along,' Naylor said. His voice was firm, expressionless. The supper party at Ford's must have ended before half past nine. Arthur Ford had left the house by then, it would have suited the others to ride along with the timings Rolt gave for the evening. Celia Brettell, with her dubious loyalties: Robin Ford, wandering at night over the hills: his mother, half suspecting at last the truth about her son, appalled by the shadowy notion that if it came to light at this moment the police might conclude that his nocturnal activities hadn't stopped at throwing scares into females but might have included a random, murderous visit to Fairview: she'd be ready to snatch at any convenient distortion of the truth, wherever and however offered.

They came out of the house into the evening air. A little milder now, breezy, with a threat of rain.

'She didn't give a damn about me,' Rolt said. 'Or for a single living soul. Just for herself. That's all she cared about. Herself.'

He fell silent. A slow trembling started along his jaw. He began to shake from head to foot, great silent tremors that shivered right through his frame. Viner put a hand under his arm to help him into the rear seat. He felt the smooth cloth of his sleeve, and the arm beneath it, warm flesh and steely muscle.

'I'll ride with him in the back,' Naylor said. His voice was flat now, exhausted. He got in beside Rolt, he looked out to where Hulme stood in the doorway, watching them go, his stance rigid and defiant, not yet stripped of challenge.

Naylor put up a hand to his face, conscious all at once

of harsh ache in his jaw. Rolt lay back in his seat, still
shaken by shudders, breathing loud and deep.

As they approached the main road Viner slowed down.
A little knot of youngsters, boys scarcely in their teens,
lounged and jostled on the pavement, glanced at the car,
placing it with ease. They stared inside with lively interest.

'Coppers!' one of them said on a loud, jeering note as
the car pulled away. 'Pigs!'

'I didn't plan to do it,' Rolt said suddenly in a voice
that sounded almost normal, tinged with surprise. 'It was
the last thing in the world I intended. There was a job
coming up, exactly the sort of thing I wanted. I couldn't
let it pass, I had to apply for it. So I went round to see
her, to ask her what she'd decided.'

He clenched his hands into fists, banged them together.
'I was tied hand and foot, I couldn't move a step till she
made up her mind.' So the divorce hadn't been settled after
all, Viner thought, she was still playing cat and mouse.

'She said she'd think it over.' Rolt's tone now was
eminently reasonable. 'I said, I've got to know pretty well
right away. She said, Don't worry, I'll let you know. But
I couldn't wait any longer. I'd been waiting long enough
already. I had to know. So I called round again later on in
the evening. I got away from the Fords' earlier than I'd
expected. She didn't seem to mind me coming back. She
looked pleased, relieved. She said, 'I thought you were
Brian Yardley coming back again, making a nuisance of
himself.' She told me he'd called at the flat about nine. He'd
been drinking. He brought her a gift, a cushion he'd picked
up while he was helping at the Fair. He thought she'd like
it. He wanted to apologize for causing the accident. She
didn't let him into the flat. She kept him at the door,
managed to persuade him to go. She asked me to come in.
She seemed in a good mood. She liked the flowers.

'And then she told me she'd made up her mind. She

223

was going to strike a bargain with me.' He closed his eyes. 'I could have the divorce, and in exchange she wanted –' he paused, jerked his eyes open – 'damn near everything I've got.

'I was absolutely staggered. Gosling said she might do that but I wouldn't believe him. I never dreamt she'd do that to me. I couldn't say anything. I was too knocked back. She said, "What do you say, Andrew? I'm selling. Are you buying?" And she laughed.

'I stood up. I didn't want her to see how much I minded. I said, "It's my turn now to say I'll think it over. Can I get myself a drink?" She said, "Certainly, help yourself, fix me one as well".' His tone was detached, explanatory.

'She leaned back in her chair. She said, "Get me a cushion before you fix the drinks – a cushion to put behind my head." She was smiling, she looked pleased. I looked round and picked up the cushion. I went over to her chair.'

He began to sob again, the words came through thick and distorted. 'I leaned forward to slip the cushion behind her head. She looked up at me and said, "You can always wait another three years, Andrew, you could have the divorce for nothing then." And she laughed again. She knew I couldn't wait that long. It would destroy me. I put the cushion down over her face.' He stopped and looked about him in a baffled way.

And now that the car was at a safe distance, one of the pavement loungers raised his hand and aimed a stone. Viner heard it strike the window behind Rolt's head and fall away again into the road.